MARC W. SHAKO

This is a work of fiction. Names, characters, businesses, places, events and incidents are either the products of the author's imagination or used in a fictitious manner. Any resemblance to actual persons, living, dead, or undead, or actual events is purely coincidental.

No part of this book may be reproduced, or stored in a retrieval system, or transmitted in any form or by any means, electronic, mechanical, photocopying, recording, or otherwise, without express written permission of the publisher.

Copyright © 2020 Marc Wobschall All rights reserved

To Rod
Happy Birthday!
Marc W Sparks

"All truth passes through three stages. First, it is ridiculed. Second, it is violently opposed. Third, it is accepted as being self-evident."

-Arthur Schopenhauer

How these diaries have been placed in sequence will be made clear in the reading of them. All needless matters have been eliminated. On occasion, the events depicted within the diaries have been dramatized. Where this has happened, nothing outside of the events described within the diaries has been changed. Dialogue consistent with the character or nature of the person speaking may have been supplemented.

All persons within are actual individuals; there are no composite characters. These recollections were recorded on, or close to, the dates as described in the coming pages and given from the standpoints of those who made them.

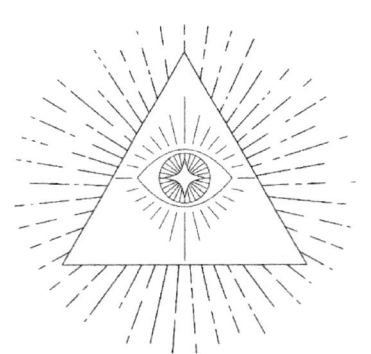

THE BOX

10th October 2015

If I had my time again, knowing then what I know now, would I do the same? The unusual email that had graced my inbox the night previous was the first I'd heard from Seth in months. There again, the only gift Seth Haywood had that exceeded his talent for writing and flair for the dramatic was his ability to keep secrets. A little more than a year had passed since he'd bought the house, and while we were never the type to stay in constant contact, that strange message was the first time I'd received an invitation. Over 12 months. It was nothing personal, in fact, to receive the invite at all was an honour. I was quite sure that this invitation placed me in a very select group. We went back a long way, studying journalism together, but after uni Seth Haywood and I parted ways, Seth liked his privacy, and I respected that. It would be fiction to say Seth was close with anyone, including his own sister. That said, I was the closest thing he had to a best friend.

After uni, Seth got a job at Music Maker Magazine,

quickly building a reputation first as a respected reviewer and later as an interviewer. No cheap shots, no false praise. You knew if you were reading a Seth Haywood column, you were getting the truth, his truth at least, and I'd like to think that in this day and age of Fake News and false headlines, that meant something. From interviews he progressed to biographies, using the list of contacts he'd built up over the years to develop an impressive back catalogue of music non-fiction. That he was an awesome musician himself made it all the more likely the talent he spoke to would open up. Reveal their wounds. To them, Seth was a kindred spirit. To see his name on the bestsellers list, on both sides of the pond, was commonplace.

And me? Well, after being overlooked for a promotion at the magazine where I worked straight out of university, I decided it was time for a change of location. I got myself a job at the local paper, working my way up to the position of editor. Not as glamorous as my good friend, I'll grant you, but it pays the bills. Just. To supplement my income, in my spare time, I became a self-published horror novelist. Actually, I wasn't "overlooked" for promotion. I was sabotaged. Stabbed in the back. But that's another story entirely...

I always felt embarrassed around Seth. He said he loved what I wrote, but I imagine it's the same way I love Die Hard. Fucking great popcorn movie, but not the kind of thing the Academy fawns over at their annual love-in. Whatever. So what did Seth want?

THE WILDE DIARIES

Seth's house was previously owned by a rock star, though he never told me which one (he said it was a surprise), and the last I'd heard from him, said rock star was the focus of his latest work. That was nine months ago. Out of our little uni gang, he said I was the only one he'd told about the new project, I'm guessing because of my penchant for classic rock, but since that minor revelation, I'd heard not a peep. He was too cool for social media, and absent minded enough to check emails only once every blue moon.

Then, last night, he emailed me out of the blue. In the email was his address, and a message saying I should come at once, it's urgent. That's it. Nothing else.

I don't mind, it's one of those relationships. We don't see each other for months, then when we do get together, it's like we spoke yesterday. I tried to drag more info from him, to no avail. After trying all morning and afternoon to contact him on his landline (Seth isn't one for mobile phones), I finished work early and set off on the hundred-mile trip, heading for the remote house I'd spied online, praying this wasn't some pointless goose chase.

I needn't have worried.

The sun was sinking towards the horizon and I flipped the visor down to block it. The stereo was all I had for company and I cranked it up. Mick Jagger was singing about killing Kennedys as the setting sun cast an orange glow over the ploughed fields flanking my beat-up Nissan. From somewhere distant, the stench of pig shit drifted in in thick invisible clouds. I rolled the windows up, but the damage was done. I was approaching a quiet village and, according to the satnav, I was just under an hour away from wherever it was Seth was living now. I sped up.

***

Seth wrote fast. He was a much faster writer than me, and his third draft was always going to be better than my eighth, so I imagined that the big story was that his new book was done, and that he wanted to celebrate. That was my first thought. But even someone as absent minded as Seth wouldn't have me drop whatever I was doing and drive the better part of three hours for that. He was an artist, not an arsehole. No, there was something more, but as I eased around the latest tight curve in the road that put the deep orange ball of setting sun on my right, I was damned if I knew what that reason was.

I knew what *I* wanted the reason to be.

Deep down, I wanted him to be struggling with the book. Not through jealousy. I wasn't selling much myself. In fact, it had been months since I'd come up with a new idea. A real one, big enough to squeeze a novel out of. Some short stories, sure, but nothing like enough for a hundred-and twenty-thousand-word novel. Christ, I'd settle for 80k. I wanted him to need my help. Maybe do some donkey work. An interview here, some research there. Anything. The reason I wanted Seth to need my help was simple: whatever Seth wrote, sold. Whatever the book sold; I'd get a cut of. Then maybe I

THE WILDE DIARIES

wouldn't have to drive a twelve-year-old Nissan.

Who was I kidding? The Seth Haywoods of this world didn't ask for help from the likes of Joel Brewer. Seth was fine. And so was the book. I was a fan of the subject and he wanted someone to celebrate with, and maybe my opinion.

The distance between properties in the Northern English countryside was growing. I was getting further from civilisation and closer to Seth's. A lonely white building with a red roof had appeared on the horizon a few miles back, a magnetic place that online pictures could never do justice. That had to be it. I can't say why but as I looked, I didn't want it to be the place, and yet... Your eyes gravitated helplessly towards it and it was easy to imagine what compelled Seth (or old rock stars) to part with their money.

The house was enveloped by overgrown garden and set back off the road. Not a long way. Nothing grandiose. Just far enough for a short gravel driveway that stopped alongside the two-storey structure. The run-down dwelling drew my sympathy for it was easy to imagine a simple coat of paint restoring it to its former glory. What with the glowing orange sun setting behind and bright red skies forming a backdrop, the house looked almost melancholic.

Gravel crunched underfoot as I approached the front door. The blackness bleeding from the windows had me convinced the old place was deserted. The last town was almost half an hour away, and had an inn, but whether the inn had a room was another matter entirely. The thought of sleeping in the car did not appeal. I'd have sooner broken in and paid for the window to be replaced than sleep surrounded by the empty, black fields.

'Joel Brewer, breaker and enterer. Yeah right,' I said, mocking myself.

A shiver ran through me as I entered the shadow of the building and climbed the two, worn stone steps that led to the front door. I stared at the peeling paint, wondering when the last coat had been applied. It could have been painted by Mr Rock Legend himself. The cold metal of the brass doorknocker drew the warmth from my hand, and I shivered again, before rapping hard. The clack fell away along the foyer inside. I waited, hoping to see Seth's smiling face opening that faded red door.

I knocked again, harder this time. I was tired after my journey, but curiosity was the overriding emotion. The compulsion to discover why Seth had chosen now to reach out was driving me onward. I moved to one of the dark windows and cupped out what little light there was. Nothing stirred inside. The first star of the evening had appeared, twinkling gently alone in one of the few gaps in cloud in the darkening sky. The scrape of a sliding chain lock turned my attention back to the door. When it swung open, I saw not the athletic figure of my old university mate, but a gaunt, stooping skeleton of a man. Even though the hour was relatively early, this man was decked in thin blue pyjamas and a heavy burgundy dressing gown. It was only after a moment

THE WILDE DIARIES

staring at his face, I realised I knew this poor soul.

'Seth?'

'Joel.' He smiled, but it was clear it was an effort. The worry lines never left his forehead, and the smile never made it to his dark, deep-set eyes. I grabbed his outstretched hand and shook it. The grip was surprisingly strong, if only for a moment. He stepped aside to let me into the dim hallway of the house. At that moment, I wanted to turn and leave. I went in anyway. One of those moments we look back on and ask, what if? Or if only.

***

Seth's house was as dark on the inside as the outside suggested. A mustiness hung in the air, as if the house was unoccupied, and judging by the lack of belongings here, that was a real possibility. An unsettling silence pervaded the dark, unwelcoming hallway and as Seth closed the door, he appeared to be checking the surroundings outside. His landline phone stood atop a small table in one corner. When the door swung shut it revealed unopened mail piled behind, with many of the envelopes marked in red. Had the phone company finally grown weary of asking for money and disconnected the phone? Was that why I couldn't get hold of him?

Without a word, he shuffled along the hallway and as I followed, the growing crackle of a fire emanated from the room at the end. It was this door that my friend pushed open, stopping to let me in. Truth be told, while I was dying to know why I was here, I didn't want to enter. The house was silent but for the crackle of that fire, but I felt like there was someone behind me, scrutinising my every move.

From where I stood I could see that the room was large, lit only by the real fire crackling in the ornate fireplace and a thin shaft of light from the setting sun speckled with dust. The floor was dark wooden floorboards covered over with a rug, patches worn threadbare by years of service. The walls were lined with bookshelves, but there were no books. It was as if my friend never lived here at all. I could see in those eyes of his, a pleading desperation urging me into the room.

'Please, Joel.'

I nodded and entered. More empty bookshelves greeted me as I stepped inside and saw the heavy curtains parted ever so slightly, allowing the slice of fading daylight into the room. A few feet from the fire were two wing-backed armchairs facing one another, separated by a small coffee table. Atop the table sat a box; the tattered cardboard worn, tape reinforcing the corner. The leaves on the top were folded inward but offered a tantalising glimpse inside. I was struck at once by the box's allure. If the house had some force drawing you toward it, this small box emanated the same tenfold, almost as if the energy had an epicentre. As I tried to make out the contents, Seth stepped in front of me and hoisted the box up and off, lowering it to the floor beside the table.

'Please. Sit.'

THE WILDE DIARIES

I didn't much feel like sitting after four hours stuck in the miserable driver's seat of the Nissan, but I lowered myself into the armchair facing the window and the back curved around me as if the chair were tailor made; the seat like some memory foam dream beneath me compared to the lumpy misery parked outside. Seth sat too, the glow of the fire leaving an unflattering impression of his worrying appearance, emphasising the lines and unhealthy pallor of his waxy skin. I tried to hide my revulsion but judging by Seth's lack of eye contact, he was as unsettled by his looks as I was.

'I know. I look different.'

'What's going on, Seth? Are you...' I paused, unsure of how to finish such a grim sentence. I needn't have worried, Seth did it for me.

'Dying? No.'

It came as a relief, however small. He might not have been dying, but to a betting man like me, he may as well have been. It would be a generous bookie that gave ten-to-one for him to see out the year.

'I've not been in good health, that much is true. And I've been having trouble sleeping.'

'Trouble?' It looked like he hadn't slept for days. That would account for the appearance of premature ageing. A good night's rest works wonders.

'I haven't slept for more than a few hours for the past few weeks.'

'Jesus, Seth. Are you in trouble?'

I could see from his eyes that he'd choked back an involuntary "yes", and the slight hesitation confirmed as much.

'No. No. Not really.'

I knew it was a lie, but for someone who embraced privacy as much as Seth did, I knew that pushing him was the easiest way to clam him up for good.

'What then?'

'The last time we spoke, I told you I'd bought this place...'

It wasn't a conversation. It was an email exchange. But for him it could have been as up close and personal as pillow talk. I didn't interrupt.

'I told you it belonged to someone famous, but I didn't tell you who. I'd been doing quite well off the last couple of books and I was up here for a little bit of rest and relaxation, trying to work out what I was going to work on next. I knew that the owner of this place was from around here, but that wasn't why I was here. Just a coincidence. I heard that he had this place. I'd seen a picture of it while researching the Bowie book.

'Anyway, I was walking down the high street in the town and I spotted the photograph in an estate agent's window. At first, I thought I must have been mistaken, but the house is quite distinctive... And the price was incredible, so I went in.'

Seth was a method writer. Very old-school. He never used Google to research, and always visited the locations in his books first hand, if time and money allowed. If they

THE WILDE DIARIES

didn't, he'd read volumes at libraries. All the more impressive when you considered his prolificacy.

'I asked if the picture in the window was what I thought it was. The woman smiled and said that yes, this was once the house of Lucas Wilde.'

***

The setting sun peaked above the horizon as the car cut through the countryside. Edith glanced down at the GPS display on her phone before turning her gaze to the speedometer.

'Can't you go any faster?'

David glanced at the speedo himself, before looking back to the road, doing nothing to adjust his speed.

'Do you want to get there in one piece?' David replied. 'I'm already doing over the limit. On these roads...' he tailed off.

'Just go.' Edith sighed.

'What did he say to you?'

She didn't want to answer. That would lead to goading and the goading to a row.

'Well?' he pressed. 'Can you at least tell me why we're nearly killing ourselves? Has there been an accident? Because if there has, we should be calling the police, not—'

'It's not what he said... It's *how* he said it.'

'Jesus wept.'

'I fucking knew it.' Edith snapped.

MARC W SHAKO

David took advantage of the stretch of straight road ahead to turn to Edith, turning quickly back, spooked by the sight of bare hawthorn hedgerow whizzing by outside.

'It's just that I'd prefer not to die in a fiery inferno of twisted metal based on a hunch that you've got about your brother.'

David's confidence had attracted her to him in the first place. That had been the driving force for his meteoric rise up the ladder at the magazine. Well, that and that ruthless streak of his. His confidence and good looks she'd fallen for, and his progress at the magazine had led to her saying 'yes' to his marriage proposal. But mum was right. Mum always was. That confidence - always teetering on the line between cockiness - was now grating on her.

'It's not a hunch, David. If you'd heard him—'

'As long as it's not twin telepathy.'

She whipped her head around, 'When have I ever mentioned that? It would really help now if you could avoid being such a twat.'

'I'm a twat? You're the one who's got us racing through the countryside because you think your brother's got the blues.'

She said nothing. Honestly, looking from David's point of view, she could see how it might appear that way. That was the reason she didn't want to mention it in the first place. Only it was more than the blues. She'd never heard him sound that way. So empty. So despondent. It scared her. The

THE WILDE DIARIES

last thing on her mind right now was to reveal to David that actually, for the first time ever, she did feel that connection, that telepathy to her brother.

'I think he might hurt himself.'

An abrupt laugh escaped from David, so sharp it was more like a cough. He looked across again, raising an eyebrow. 'Seth? Seth Haywood is going to hurt himself. Edie...'

'You didn't hear him, David.'

'Honey, if there is one person on this earth that will not do anything to himself, it's your brother.'

Seth was as level-headed and balanced as anyone she'd ever met. Not prone to emotional outbursts. She'd seen him cry once, when Coco was hit by a car, but they were just kids then. Back then the Scottish Terrier was the closest thing Seth had to a best friend. She'd never seen him angry and he was always cautious in his expressions of happiness. Even when his Bowie biography made the NYT bestsellers list, all he did was shrug and smile. "It's a good book" was all he said. Conversations with him were always enjoyable though. He always took great care to ask about her. And he actually listened to the answers. He was engaging. Interesting...

Then he bought the house.

The frequency of his phone calls tailed off. He was distracted. That was sort of normal when he was in the middle of a first draft. But he wasn't writing a first draft. He was researching. While he was researching he'd always share some interesting titbits he'd picked up. Now he was guarded.

Closed. This had gone on for nine months, culminating in the phone call she'd received a little over an hour ago. It was hard to pinpoint what was different about this call, God knows she'd love to be able to tell David something to get him to drive faster.

When Seth put the phone down, a voice in the back of her head told her to go. Go to her brother, or never see him again.

The stench of pigshit drifting through the car jarred her back to reality.

David glanced across. 'You're serious, aren't you?'

She nodded, a tear spilling down her cheek.

David reached across and squeezed her leg, 'Don't worry. We'll get there,' he said, easing his foot down on the accelerator.

***

The very mention of Lucas Wilde hit with an instant smack of awe. The Lennons and the Dylans of this world impressed me, as did the Claptons and Hendrixes. But for me, there was one guy who stood out above the rest. A mixture of the poetry of Leonard Cohen, the presence of Mick Jagger, and the cool of Jim Morrison. That man was Lucas Wilde. To find out I was in the room where he would have sat, strumming away at that battered acoustic of his, was mind blowing. Mind blowing enough for me to forget, if only for a second, that my old friend looked out on his feet and as close to death's door as

THE WILDE DIARIES

I've ever seen anyone.

Seth's haunted face stared at me for a second, as if he'd registered my level of amazement and was waiting for it to subside before he continued. My noticing this was enough to do it. He went on.

'I'd done well off the previous books and was looking for a new project and this fell into my lap. Almost like a gift.' He let out a chuckle that had not an ounce of humour and gazed momentarily at the waving flames in the fireplace before continuing. 'I had to ask why it was so cheap. I mean, it was ridiculous how low the price was. If I told you, you wouldn't believe me. I remember the estate agent blushing before she told me.'

His face washed over with something like regret. It was an expression which didn't suit Seth for a minute, even in this dishevelled state. He paused, and I thought then it might have been for dramatic effect.

'She couldn't even look at me as she said it. "It's supposed to be haunted". She looked at her colleague and giggled. And you know me, I don't believe in all that...'

He let his voice tail off and right there and then I realised why Seth had chosen me, the horror writer, out of our small group of friends. I didn't have time to be offended.

'At least,' he said, 'I didn't...'

'What do you mean, *didn't?*'

Seth looked away, glancing at the tattered box before staring into the hypnotic dance of the fire. Maybe it surprised him that a horror writer didn't believe in ghosts.

He hushed his voice as if the house could hear him. 'This place, Joel. Things happen.'

'Things?' I tried not to offend my friend, but looking at him now, how tired – how worn out – he looked, I was sure that he'd been mistaken. Seth was absent-minded enough to imagine hauntings before he lived here.

'Stay here. You'll see.' His eyes darted at me, before stopping again at the box on the way to the fire. He seemed to be shrinking into his chair with each passing moment. The idea that someone so rational could be so rattled scared me, ghosts or no ghosts.

'Stay here? Why would I do that?'

The thin orange slip of light had turned red and the room had darkened further as the day slipped into memory, giving way to twilight. Seth stood and turned on the lights, though the low watt bulbs did little to lift the gloom of the strange and barren parlour.

He sighed as he returned to his seat, the whole journey taking him twice as long as it would have taken a healthy man. 'This project I'm working on, my Lucas Wilde project, it's bigger than I thought. I need your help.'

I was shocked again. The Seth Haywoods do need help from the Joel Brewers, from time to time. Even if it is because spooky is their stock-in-trade. He reached down to the box sitting by the table, that tattered, plain brown cardboard box. He placed it onto the table. The tape holding the side together

THE WILDE DIARIES

had given way and left a thin gap, though in the dim light I couldn't see a thing inside. I reached to lift it and Seth moved with a swiftness I hadn't seen all evening to turn it away from me.

'When I moved in here,' he said, drawing my mind away from the jolt I'd just felt, 'the place was in a bit of a mess. The previous tenant had been a musician too, and keeping the place clean was low on his list of priorities. The place was furnished, but the furniture was thrown around, almost like the place had been ransacked. I didn't mind, I'd got the house for a song anyway. The things I didn't like I could sell to recoup some of my outgoings. I set about tidying up. Straightening the things I did want to keep and removing the things I didn't. I took a couple of chairs up to the attic. The attic is huge. The whole size of the house, split into two rooms, including the boarded-up room I told you about...'

I vaguely recalled his talking about a boarded up attic room, but that thought passed quickly as my mind turned swiftly back to the box.

'It was in the other room that I found this. This old box,' he pointed at the thing sitting between us, the thing with an energy and life of its own. 'Just sitting in the middle of the floor it was. The things inside here...' he broke off again.

It was clear from Seth's voice he held genuine reverence for that plain looking box and its contents, and I couldn't help but wonder if that's what had my friend looking like the Picture of Dorian Gray.

MARC W SHAKO

'When I found this, it took my plans for my book in a whole new direction. A new book almost. Different from anything I've written before. It's that book I want you to help me finish.'

***

Working on any book is a huge undertaking. I know, I know, poor little writer, has to put words in order. It's not fighting wars. It's not saving lives. But it's no overnight success either. There's research. Plotting, if you're into that kind of thing (many aren't). Then there's the writing itself. One word in front of another for weeks, months, sometimes years on end. And that's the easy part. After that you have to edit the thing. Second, third, twelfth drafts. And yet, knowing all of this, I was still interested.

There was so much this project had to offer. Working with Seth alone would be a boon. Not to help him out; that would be a happy by-product of my helping him finish this new project of his. It was purely selfish. Getting to work side by side with someone you respect every day, to see how his processes work, how his *mind* works, that would be a huge learning curve for me. It would improve me as a writer no end. Not only that, but getting my name on a front cover with him, even as second billing? That's publicity you can't put a price on. On top of that, helping him finish this book just so he could put the whole thing behind him and get back to his normal self, that was as good a reason as any to agree. I'd

THE WILDE DIARIES

spent long enough in the trenches. I'd done my time on the front lines. I'd got this chance because I'd earned it. Because Seth thought enough of me as a writer to invite me in on this project. I could finally get rid of the Nissan that sat out front. Upgrade. Nothing flashy. I'd always wanted a Beemer. And no more renting. I'd have enough to get a deposit on a house.

Those were all good reasons. Rational reasons. But they were secondary. The main reason was curiosity, pure and simple. That box, with the gap where the tape had lost its stickiness, seducing me to peer inside, like a gap in the hot neighbour's curtains. In that box were things that had belonged to one of my musical heroes. Seth was holding it tantalisingly out of my reach. A guitar that can't be played. A ball that can't be kicked. And all I wanted to do was play. I wanted it so badly. It was a Golden Ticket to the hottest party in town, and more than anything I wanted to get my grubby little hands on it.

So if you want to boil it down to nuts and bolts, it was greed. Selfish greed, and curiosity. That's why I said yes.

'Joel, this is dangerous.'

A flashing neon sign popped into my mind's eye:

NO RISK = NO REWARD!

I said nothing.

'You should take more time to think on this.'

He was right. It was a huge undertaking, and if Seth's

appearance was anything to go by, a dangerous one. I didn't know exactly how writing a book could be dangerous but looking at Seth it was clearly an issue of life or death.

But my own life had reached a crossroads. I was forty-two years old. Single. No house. No kids. No career to speak of. Sure there was the local paper, but I was stuck there. The paper was too small for me to make huge money, but it was just enough of a salary to keep me from moving on. This was a foot in the door of success. Truth be told, I was scared that if I took my time, fate would snatch my chance away and slam that door in my face.

Seth observed me, waiting for me to speak. I said nothing, acting on the old Chinese proverb that if you let a man talk for long enough, he'll tell you more than he thinks he knows. I wanted in, but I also wanted more information.

'If you are happy to join me, there's no going back. Once you're in, you're in...'

That dark space on the edge of the box where the folds didn't quite meet was staring at me in the dim light of that parlour. Inviting. Enticing. Happily sitting in my peripheral vision, knowing the longer it stared at me, the harder I'd find it to refuse his offer.

'One question.'

'Only one?'

'Why me?'

He turned back to me and just for a second, something washed over his eyes. At the time, it barely registered. Slipped

THE WILDE DIARIES

into my subconscious like an uninvited guest. I think back to that moment now and I shiver every time. It was as if time around us stood still and his face changed. A malice in the eyes. A sinister curl in the corners of his mouth. A loud *POP!* burst from the fireplace and the moment was gone. Seth was staring into the fire, like I'd imagined the whole thing. Maybe I had. I spoke again.

'Why not ask Edie? ... Or David?'

His sister and her husband were both better writers than me. Both more successful. Either one could do a better job.

He kept staring into the fire. He shook his head. 'No.'

For a moment, I thought that was all he was going to say.

'They don't know the subject matter like you do. Your passion will show through. You'll write a better book. It has to be you.'

'Seth, look at me.'

His eyes shifted from the fire and came into focus.

'One more question.'

'Of course.'

'When do we start?'

He nodded, choking back tears. I didn't speak. I was sure that I didn't have the right words.

'Please, give me a moment.'

'Of course.' I said.

Seth nodded again, more to himself than to me, rose and left the room. I turned my attention to the box. I didn't open it. I wanted to be invited. We just stared at one another. Me and that dark space on the corner of that box.

In the background, a door closed, one of the other two in the hallway outside, and after a few moments, I heard the faint sound of music. Too faint for me to recognise. I didn't move. I just stared at that dark gap in the box for God knows how long. After a minute the sound of footsteps came from above. Heavy. The clump of a boot on bare wood. As soon as I heard the steps, they were gone, until I couldn't be sure I'd heard them at all. My attention turned back to the box. That empty space was where I stared until the music coming from the next room stopped.

I might have stared all night, had I not heard the gunshot.

***

I jumped to my feet and turned in the direction of the gunfire.

'Seth?'

I'd never heard a gun being fired before, outside of a Hollywood production. It wasn't like the gunfire you hear in the films, more of a loud pop, yet I knew exactly what it was.

For a second there was total silence. There was no crackle or pop from the fire. No creaking sounds of the house settling. Just the rising thud of my own heart beating in my ears. I'd never known a silence so complete. So threatening. So sinister.

I wanted to run. Run to see what was going on. To see if

THE WILDE DIARIES

my friend was okay. Or to escape. Burst out of the front door and just keep going. If I started, I wasn't sure I'd even pause to get in the car. Just run. I wanted to be anywhere but here. But I looked past the gap in the door and into the endless black of the hallway and my legs were frozen.

'Seth?'

The cracking of my voice served only to add to my own fear. I drew deep breaths as the fire seemed to come back to life, crackling gently beside me. I managed to get one leg free from the magnetic hold the floor had upon it. I took a small faltering step. Then another. Towards the door that Seth had left ajar. The blackness beyond daring me to step within. I placed a hand on the painted stone wall to steady myself and recoiled from the cold. I reached the doorway and stopped. Air rushed into my lungs and I realised I'd been holding my breath. I leaned forward, out into the darkness.

'Are you there, Seth?'

I stood long enough for my eyes to adjust to the dim light in the hallway and it was then that I noticed that of the doors there, one was closed. Gentle light spilled from beneath into the hallway. I staggered out, leaving the crackling fire behind. The silence was unbearable as I made my way along the uneven floor to that one closed door. The hallway extended out before me, lengthening, stretching. The door getting further away with each step like some nightmare. I moved onwards, stopping only when my feet were bathed in the light spilling from under that solitary closed door.

MARC W SHAKO

I stared at the door in the silence. An old four-panelled door, crudely painted white with heavy gloss, a thin line of light spilling from beneath and washing up the toes of my shoes. I stared at the brass handle as if it were a leper; the thought of touching the cold metal repulsive. I reached out a hand, and knocked.

'Seth? Are you in there, Seth?'

I waited a few seconds, hoping that he would answer. Hoping that he would call back, "Come in!"

But he didn't.

I just stood in that cool, dark hallway, my own heartbeat for company.

I knew that he was scared of something, his ragged appearance was testament to that, but had no idea that he'd been scared enough to buy a gun. My hope was, that he had fired off an accidental shot. A less attractive idea was that maybe he'd caught an intruder, firing off a warning shot. *The footsteps.* Or worse. But deep down, in my heart, where the oldest and best guarded secrets reside, I knew that none of those speculations were true. I drew a deep breath and grabbed the handle.

I half expected the door to be locked, but I pushed, and it opened. Slowly it swung, without a sound, into the bright lights of the room, revealing one item at a time, the contents within. Another old armchair that had survived the cull of furniture deigned too ugly to avoid the attic, sat upon another faded, worn, old rug. The door swung out more to reveal an

THE WILDE DIARIES

old chest of drawers, then the old reel to reel tape player sitting on top. And on that player, tape spooled to no doubt play the song I'd heard. It dripped with thick red blood. Behind the reel to reel, the floral wallpaper dripped with droplets of a wet grey substance, and when the door finally stopped, I saw a slipper. A slipper and a leg and a hand – palm facing upward, fingers curled like the legs of a dead spider. Next to the hand sat a gun. A small black pistol. I didn't see the face, but I didn't need to. I recognised the burgundy house coat, shoulder wet as more blood and wet grey gore dribbled out. My friend Seth was dead.

***

My legs buckled beneath me. I recoiled from the horror and retreated to the hallway, grabbing the door handle and pulling it to as I did so. I staggered back towards the room I'd left what seemed like a lifetime ago, the dark hallway stretching out like a nightmare, the crackling fire drawing me instinctively closer to its welcoming warmth.

I collapsed into the chair, my mind racing to form a plan. Calling an ambulance would be pointless. Seth was as dead as Lucas Wilde and all the ambulances in the world couldn't change that. The police. I'd have to call the police to report... it. They would call coroners and everyone else. There would be funeral arrangements. And the next of kin would need to be notified.

Edie.

MARC W SHAKO

I hadn't seen her in years. I'd been invited to her wedding. That was a laugh. Invited to the wedding where she was to be joined with David Thorne: the man who she'd left me for. The man who had sabotaged my promotion for his own gain. That smug bastard.

Joel!

The police.

Call them.

I stood, reached into my pocket with a trembling hand, and pulled out my mobile. A red 'X' showing on the screen where the signal should be. No service. Not that something like that would have bothered Seth. To him, it would have been a selling point. Great views. Spacious bathroom. No mobile signal. I paced staring at the screen hoping that a bar would appear. Then I saw the message. 'Emergency calls only'.

I tapped three nines into the keypad and hit dial. It rang. As I turned mid-pace, my eyes fell immediately on the box. The battered box Seth had shown me stared back at me, into me, from that black gap down its side. From that seemingly insignificant slip of darkness it beckoned, drawing me in to its clandestine embrace.

If the police come they'll surely take evidence from the scene. It's not in the same room but what if? They take that, I may never see it again. Never know its secrets.

They'll take it and I'll be back behind the office desk. Writing stories about ring-roads and shop closures. Back to the humdrum. No

THE WILDE DIARIES

rock and roll secrets for me.

I ended the call and rushed to the box. When I picked it up, something felt wrong. The box was at once too light to have anything of significance inside, but heavy enough to surprise me. There was no way the police should have this. It's nothing to do with them anyway. Seth left it for *me*. He wanted me to have it.

The idea that the police had to be called and that someone would have to tell Edith about Seth's suicide were squeezed into the back of my mind, still there, but secondary. I thought about lifting the lid of the box to see what was inside, but I was grabbed by an urgency the likes of which I'd never known. Hide the box, or lose it forever. This was more than just a box. It was a peek behind the curtain, into a glamorous and dangerous world. And it was mine.

When the police did finally arrive, they might remove anything from the house as evidence, so I had to take it outside. If I put it in my car, it looks like I've brought it with me. I ran to the front door, cradling the box as if it were a newborn. As I passed the room holding Seth's body, the crack of light from the door revealed his leg in my peripheral vision and I was struck with the horror that the door would wrench open and Seth would reach out, brain and gore still pouring onto his shoulder as he reached to grab the box.

I put the box down beside the car and frisked myself for the keys. I had to act quickly. The keys trembled in my hand and stabbed at the lock. Finally the door was open and I reached inside and around to the lock for the rear door. The box fit snugly into the foot well behind the driver's seat, but even in the twilight, it stood out. I took off my jacket and threw it over the box before locking the doors.

I turned and stood in the darkness, facing the open front door, light spilling into the dark hallway from the room where Seth had taken his life. Sickness hit me in the gut, rising into the back of my throat. I drew a deep breath, and stepped forward to the house, and that's when I heard a gentle crunching sound coming from over my shoulder.

***

I turned in time to see a black Mercedes crawling up the drive. It curved around to the entrance and drew to a halt. Edith and David got out.

'Where is he?' Edith shouted, running towards me.

But she wasn't coming for me. She was going for the door. I sidestepped to block her path, but she kept coming. In the end I had to grab her shoulders. David rushed towards us and stopped behind her.

She struggled against me, trying to force her way past. 'Get out of the way, Joel. Where's Seth?'

'Stop. Edie. You can't go inside.'

David eyed me with a frown as he strode around the two of us.

I shouted. 'David! Stop!' and the crunch of gravel behind me halted. Edith stopped her struggle and I let go, keeping her behind me as I turned to face David. He had one foot planted on the bottom step and the light from the study where Seth lay dead pooled in the hallway.

'What's going on, Joel? What are you doing here?'

'There's been... an accident.'

Edith screamed and ran past me. I managed to grab her. She kicked and screamed as David entered the house.

It took everything I had to hold her back. 'Please, Edie, wait. You can't go in.'

David got to the half open door and stopped, giving it a gentle shove and stepping back, not knowing the horror that awaited.

He turned away covering his mouth with the back of a hand, 'Oh Christ!'

Edie stopped struggling. She turned into a dead weight and sagged into my arms, in a flood of tears. As she did, the moment, the suicide, the box, it was all forgotten, replaced by the comforting warmth of nostalgia, just as the warmth of her body caressed mine. It evaporated as, inside the house, David collapsed against the wall and stared into the study at Seth's lifeless body.

Edith stood and turned screaming. 'What have you done? What have you done to him?' beating my chest.

I grabbed her hands and David appeared behind her, turning her to face him. 'It wasn't him. It wasn't him.'

David held Edie as she sobbed into his chest and he did all he could to soothe her. But while his words comforted her, his eyes burned into me.

***

It was half an hour before the police arrived. I sat on the cold stone steps in front of the house, hands shaking uncontrollably. Edith and David sat on the small wall that ran alongside the driveway, him soothing her, none of us wanting to set foot inside the house. Every now and then I'd feel the burn of his stare. I was glad to feel it. If he was looking at me, it meant he wasn't looking at my car. At the box. My eyes were drawn naturally to it, and it took all I had to avert my gaze. The constables that had arrived called for a forensics team and another hour passed before they filed in. The constables asked me if I wanted to wait inside, but I couldn't go near that place. I moved to my car.

I sat in the front seat and watched as forensics and photographers and detectives filed in and out, taking the things I'd seen in that glimpse of the room where he died. I would cast the occasional glance at Edie. She was crushed. She pressed herself against David and even in the poor light, I could see her shoulders shudder with sobs. He would alternate between comforting her and throwing accusatory glances in my direction. He'd protested my innocence to Edie, but his stares said otherwise. I just prayed that after her grief had passed, Edie would think differently.

Every now and then, amongst the commotion and confusion, it would occur afresh to me that Seth was dead. My

THE WILDE DIARIES

mind knew it was true, but hadn't accepted it, couldn't accept it, as reality. Anything I had from Seth now was memory. No new ones to be made.

A rap came at my window. I jumped in my seat and turned to see one of the detectives, one half of his body lit by alternating blue and red lights. He was clearly the victim of friendliness with alcohol and a sedentary lifestyle, and his face looked at me blank, like he wasn't sure how to read me. Innocent bystander or accessory. I rolled the window down.

'Mr Brewer?' He started like there was a question coming, but said nothing more.

'Yes?' I replied, my voice as shaky as my hands.

He frowned as he peered into the car, clearly sizing me up. 'Mr Brewer, would you mind stepping out of the vehicle?'

I did as I was asked, petrified that he would ask whoever to search my car, and that that person would find the box. *My* box.

I was about to close the door when the detective spoke again, and my heart skipped when I realised he was pointing at my car.

'What?'

He pointed at the gap at the top of the door, 'Your window's open.'

I rolled it up and closed the door.

'Mr Brewer, if I could ask you to lock the door. I'd like you to come with me to the station. We need to ask you some questions.'

'Am I under arrest?'

The detective shook his head. 'Not now. Just some routine questioning.'

'Not now? So I could be?'

'Please Mr Brewer. The car.'

My hand still trembled as I reached into my pocket and took the keys. More people trooped in and out of the house, ferrying plastic bags of evidence. I saw a forensics officer carrying the gun. The reel to reel tape player. But they didn't have the box. I turned to my car and locked the door, as I did I glanced at the bulge on the floor behind the passenger door. A bulge covered with my jacket. They wouldn't be taking that. That was mine.

'What's that?'

He was pointing in the car again. Ice crawled up the back of my skull. The back seat.

Jesus. He'll want to know why I've removed evidence from a crime scene.

Stall him.

'Sorry?'

'The bag. Does it have a change of clothes?'

'Oh, that. Yes. Just for one night.'

'Best bring it with you.'

I opened the back door and reached in for the bag, blocking the view of the box as best I could. All I could do was hope he hadn't seen it.

***

THE WILDE DIARIES

I'd paid no attention to the surroundings as we travelled back into town, to the police station. I stared at my hands, still trembling from the night's events. The detective was silent. I wasn't under arrest. Not in handcuffs. But I got the distinct impression that my answers to the detective's questions could change all of that, and very quickly.

Being put under arrest didn't worry me. And it shames me to say it, but even Seth's death was lower on my list of priorities. All I could think of as the car wound through the countryside was the box. My biggest worry being that the police investigating at the house would discover the secret hiding behind the seat in my car.

We stopped at the police station and the detective got out, strode around the front of the car and opened my door. I followed him into the station, paying little attention as to where I was going. The detective asked something about interview rooms to the desk sergeant, and then we were walking again, for what seemed to be too long for such a small police station. Next thing I know I'm sitting in the cold grey walls of an interview room, in a bright circle of light in the darkness, steaming cup of tea beside me (I don't remember asking for it, but it was just how I like it – strong with one sugar) and the detective is asking me if I'm ready. That's when the reality hit me of how serious this was. Not under arrest, but answering questions. Get them right. Or your under-arrest status could change.

'My name is Detective Paul Ellison, this is just an

informal Q and A, but to save me taking notes, I'd like to record it, and if you'd like legal representation, we can arrange that for you. All I want to do is to find out what happened, and why you think it happened. Okay?'

His voice sounded far away, like it had been manipulated in a studio. I snapped back to the best focus I could muster. 'Yes.'

'Okay,' he said, reaching for the record button on the tape player. 'So let's start at the beginning. How do you know the deceased?'

The deceased, Christ. He's really dead. Focus. 'We went to university together. In Winchester.'

'What did you study?'

'Journalism.'

'And how often did you contact each other? Whether that be phone calls, in person, emails...'

'Honestly? Not that often. The last time I spoke to him, before tonight I mean, was a few months ago.'

'A few?'

'Maybe six.'

He reacted to that comment. Just a gentle flick of his bushy eyebrows, but it was there all the same. 'So you weren't close?'

I paused, trying to collect my thoughts. I didn't want to come across as disrespectful to the dead. Especially when the guy sitting across from me thought I had something to do with it.

THE WILDE DIARIES

'Seth... didn't really have close friends. He wasn't a people person. He moved up here from the smoke after he got mugged. It affected him really badly.'

The detective frowned. 'So he had no friends?'

'There was a group of us, from uni. Me, Edie, his sister. And David. They're married now. We stayed in touch, Seth and me. Met for birthdays, the big ones. Me and David never really got along... In the end, it was just me and Seth, but he was always distant.'

'Would you say you had a good relationship?'

'Seth is... was, a writer. A very good one. He's an artist. It's very easy for him to get lost in his work. We all knew that, and none of us minded. We, Seth and I, had the sort of relationship where we didn't need to talk every few days. We could go weeks, months without seeing each other, but when we did, it was never awkward. It was like we'd never been apart, so, yes. I would say it was good.'

He scribbled a quick note in the small pad he had in front of him. I'd been so lost I hadn't really noticed that he even had one. Or the sheet of paper in the plastic sleeve beside it. It was blank but I could see that the other side had been written on.

'And did you notice anything unusual in him when you met tonight?'

My mind's eye flashed back to the red front door of Seth's house slowly opening to reveal the gaunt, haunted figure of Seth, only now, one side of his face was a bloody ragged mess where his temple should be. Blood and grey matter dripping onto his shoulder.

'He looked terrible. That wasn't the Seth I knew who answered the door to me tonight. He'd lost about three stone. And he looked like he hadn't slept for weeks. In fact, he said as much.'

'So he was having problems?'

'I would say so. Yes.'

'What do you think the nature of these problems was?'

I knew the questions were designed to trip me up somehow. Maybe get me to reveal some dislike for my friend or some evil plan I had.

'I don't know.'

'So you weren't that close?'

'Yes, we were. But what I'm trying to say is that Seth is a very private person.'

'So apart from the way he looked, what else makes you think he had problems?'

'Apart from the fact he's just blown his fucking brains out?'

The detective straightened up in his seat. 'We'll come to that in a moment, Mr Brewer.'

His eyes glanced to the notepad and the bullet points he'd written out. He covered them like a school kid hiding test answers before making another note.

He spoke again without looking up. 'Where did he get the gun?'

THE WILDE DIARIES

'I don't know. I didn't know he had one until...'

I was suddenly back in the parlour staring back at the black gap in the top of the box.

'...Until I heard it go off.'

'Okay, that's fine. Can you tell me, in your own words, what happened this evening?'

'I drove up this aft—'

'From where?'

'I drove up from Wisbech this afternoon. Let me go back a bit. Yesterday...' the detective looked at me, wanting me to address my vagary. 'Yesterday evening, around 9, I got an email from Seth. Out of the blue. He sounded nervous. His emails were always short and to the point, but this one didn't have a "hi" or "bye" on it. After months of no contact. It was something like, "Come up to the house. It's important". And the address. I emailed back and got no reply. He didn't have a mobile phone, so I couldn't text him and I think he just unplugs his landline whenever he can't be bothered dealing with it. I went to bed and first thing, I tried to contact him again. After not getting any replies all day, I set off this afternoon from Wisbech.

'I got here about half seven. When Seth came to the door,' again the images came, 'he looked haggard. He was an artist but he wasn't the messy type. He was always clean shaven. Always. Now there was growth and his face, well, Seth wasn't chubby, but, his face was never thin. He'd lost a lot of weight. As I said, two, maybe three stone. Enough to scare me.

'We went into the house. The house used to belong to Lucas Wilde,' the detective nodded, 'and that's when I realised that's what the new book must be about. Seth wrote biographies.'

Ellison nodded again, 'Read the one he did on Bowie. Good stuff.'

'Right. So he led me to the room at the end of the hallway, on the left, and asked me to help him finish the book.'

'Just like that?'

'I'm a writer too.'

'Oh?'

'I write horror novels.'

'Oh.'

'He asked me to help him finish the book. I said I'd help him, and then he excused himself and went into the room where he... where I found him.'

'So you agreed to help him, then he shot himself?'

'Not straight away.' The image came back of the reel to reel dripping in Seth's blood. 'I heard music.'

'Then?'

'Then the music stopped. And I heard the gunshot.'

'I see. And what were you doing while Mr Haywood was out of the room?'

Shit. Stall him.

'Sorry?'

'You said he left you in the room, last room on the left.

THE WILDE DIARIES

What were you doing in there?'

Don't mention the box. Don't mention the box. Don't mention...

'I was, just, waiting, I suppose.'

Ellison reached for the plastic sleeve and turned it over, before sliding it in front of me. 'Have you seen this before?'

It was a typed document, spattered with dark red patches of blood. Seth's flamboyant signature stood out at the bottom.

'No. Never.'

'Read it.'

A was already skimming the document as he said it. It was past one in the morning and I'd had little sleep the night before, worrying about Seth. I knew all of the words on the document. But I still didn't understand.

Ellison cleared his throat. 'Can you explain, Mr Brewer, why somebody you hadn't spoken to for months, somebody who, by your own admission, is not a close friend, would take his own life and leave you his house?'

I stared, looking up from the blood-spattered page in slow-motion. I did not have an answer. Ellison just stared.

'Are you going to arrest me?

He settled into his seat a little. His eyebrows flickered, 'No. But we're doing analysis on Mr Haywood's clothes. If it was suicide, then there'll be substantiating evidence. We'd like to analyse the clothes you're wearing. If I could ask you to change into the ones you brought with you, drop them into this.'

He produced a plastic bag. They were looking for cordite

on the sleeve; I'd written enough murder scenes to know that much.

'Do you have somewhere to go?'

I didn't.

'Well, the house, but I'd rather...'

'Of course. There's a settee in the other interview room. We'll put you in there. Get changed. I'll come back in five minutes and take you through.'

***

As Joel sat in an interview room, Edith Thorne sat puffy eyed in the room adjacent. A steaming cup of tea and box of tissues on the table in front of her, and a detective sitting across. He'd already introduced himself and she'd already forgotten his name, in fact, she'd been in the room a matter of minutes and she couldn't say what he looked like. Not that she hadn't glanced up, but most of her time had been spent staring into the steam rising from the too-strong tea in front of her. A damp tissue was balled into her hand but the sobbing had finally subsided, lingering like the cloud of working Monday morning on a lazy Sunday night.

'We don't have to do this now. Mr Thorne could—'

'No,' she interrupted. 'I'm okay. I just want to get it out of the way.'

'Well. If you need to stop for anything...'

The sentence just tailed off. They both knew that anything meant crying.

THE WILDE DIARIES

The detective cleared his throat and said something to the recorder. The intonation didn't rise, so she knew it wasn't a question, then he said something else.

'Mrs Thorne?'

She didn't think she'd heard the question, but the answer tumbled out, her brain on autopilot.

'Yes, that's right. We're... we were twins. I'm younger. Seven minutes.'

Another question came and again she let her autopilot take control.

'He was always quiet. So it was difficult to get a read on him.'

Usually. Until that phone call earlier tonight. Then you knew something was wrong.

'We'd talk once a fortnight. Maybe once a month if he was writing. He was usually writing. But, no. I can't think of any reason why he'd kill himself.'

The thin veil of steam had stopped rising from the tea, not that she had any intention of drinking it. Another question came.

'Seth was afraid. He lived in London for a good few years after we left uni, until he was mugged at knife point. He moved up here not long after. He probably bought it for protection, but no, I had no idea he had a gun, and I don't know where he got it from.'

The tea had started to darken in the middle as a skin formed.

'Yes I know him. He's an old friend. We were at uni together. Me, David, Seth and Joel. Joel was probably the closest thing Seth had to a friend. I was surprised to see him at the house. I had no idea he'd be there.

'Why were you there?'

Now you have to tell him.

'We spoke on the phone. Seth and I. A couple of hours before...'

'And he asked you to come?'

There was a pause. The crying was gone now. Over. At least for the time being. A numbness had started to take over.

'Mrs Thorne, if you'd like...'

'There was something wrong. He sounded... different.'

'Different how? Sad? Morose?'

It wasn't him though, was it? It was you. He sounded the same and you knew something was wrong.

'I just... He sounded... I just had a feeling there was something wrong.'

'Have you had these feelings before?'

She looked up. The detective was younger than her. There was nothing in his eyes. No sympathy. Trained that out of them she supposed. Cool impartiality.

'No. Never.'

'But this feeling you had was strong enough to make you drive from...'

'Amersham. Yes. I know how that sounds, but he wasn't answering the landline and there's no mobile signal at the

THE WILDE DIARIES

house.'

He scribbled something on the notepad in front of him.

'And can you think of any reason Joel Brewer would want to hurt your brother?'

She just looked back down and shook her head. The detective carried on talking as she stared at the cup of tea, dark circle of skin forming over the top. No more questions came. The detective spoke again, and she now realised he was standing beside her.

'Mrs Thorne?'

She didn't look up, just stood and walked outside as the detective opened the door for her.

***

David hugged Edie and asked if she was okay. He barely recognised the woman in front of him. Edie was usually bright eyed, a trait that showed off her keen intelligence and wit and the thing that had attracted him to her in the first place, aside from her natural beauty. Now she was a shell, that brightness in her eye had dulled and for a frightened moment, he wondered if it would come back at all.

'When you're ready, Mr Thorne.'

David glanced across and nodded.

Inside the interview room David sat and stared at the box of tissues. He wouldn't be needing those. He was sad about Seth, that wasn't in question, but theirs was the kind of relationship where they spoke or met infrequently. Seth had removed himself from David's life not long after university and it only became clear that they would have more interaction as his relationship with Edie flourished. To him, Seth would now be an empty place at the Christmas dinner table. Someone they saluted with a drink on birthdays. More often than not he supposed Seth would be someone he thought of when he saw that look of sadness in his wife's eyes.

'I shan't keep you long, Mr. Thorne. Just a few questions. I understand that the deceased is your brother-in-law, is that correct?'

'Yes, that's right.'

'In your own words, can you tell me a bit about Mr Haywood?'

There was one of those expressions he hated. An empty phrase that, as an editor, he'd have crossed out with glee. Whose words was he supposed to talk in?

'We... er... didn't talk much. I shouted a 'hello' whenever he'd call Edie. We'd meet at birthdays, Christmas. That sort of thing. He was a nice chap. Intelligent. Quiet. A great writer. Did biographies. Musicians. Did you read any of his—'

'Can't say I did, sir. More of a movie kind of guy.'

Another Americanism sneaking into the UK vocab. Red pen. NOT movie - FILM.

'Can you tell me what brought you to his house this evening?'

He shuffled uneasily in his seat. Was he supposed to tell him about Edie's weird "feeling"? Something she herself said

THE WILDE DIARIES

had never happened before.

'Edie got a phone call a few hours ago and was concerned. He wouldn't answer the landline, think it was off the hook, and there's no mobile signal so we came as quickly as we could.'

'So you didn't hear him yourself?'

'No. Just Edie. Like I said, we barely spoke—'

'And did Mrs Thorne say exactly what it was that led to her concern?'

'It wasn't what he said exactly, it was more of a feeling—'

'A feeling?'

David swallowed. 'Yes. She could tell something was wrong.'

The detective scribbled on his pad.

'I see. What happened then?'

'We were driving, I was driving, and Edie kept trying the landline, as I said, we couldn't get through, and then we got to the house. When we got there, Joel was outside. He didn't look too clever...'

'In what sense?'

'It might sound like an exaggeration, but he looked like he'd seen a ghost.'

More scribbling. 'Go on.'

'We were surprised to see him. Joel, I mean. He was loitering by his car. We got out and Edie knew something was wrong. She tried to get into the house and Joel stopped her. That's when I went in and saw him. Seth.'

The image of Seth with his brains blown out flashed into his mind as it had many times already since they'd arrived. This time he managed to shake the image out before the moment Seth's dead body opened its eyes and looked up at him.

The young detective motioned to the glass of water. 'Take your time. Can you think of any reason that Mr Haywood would want to kill himself?'

'None. None whatsoever.'

'You seem certain.'

'Seth was an odd character, but never did I get the impression he would take his own life. Not once.'

'Mr Haywood died by gunshot wound. Can you think of where he may have obtained a firearm? Or why?'

David shook his head. 'No.'

'Okay.' More scribbling. 'You said you were surprised to see Mr Brewer at the house...'

'We all knew each other, but visits to Seth were rarities, to say the least.'

David paused and the detective sat quietly, experienced enough to know when to let someone speak. The pause went on for longer than was comfortable. David had to break it.

'What was he doing here? Joel, I mean.'

The detective again said nothing.

David went on. 'I suppose you can't say. But I find it odd. That's all.'

'We're exploring all avenues of enquiry at this time, Mr

Thorne.' The detective wrote something and underlined it. 'Is there anything else you can think of that might be of importance?'

David shook his head. He'd already said enough.

The detective rose and handed a business card. 'If you think of anything.'

David took the card as he stood and nodded his head.

'Will you be going back to...?'

'Amersham. No. We'll be staying in town for a couple of days to sort things out, if you need us.'

'Thank you. Let me know if you decide to go back.'

'I will.'

Edie slept on the journey back into town. Stars peaked out from behind scattered cloud and crops swayed in the gentle breeze. They would get a room at one of the hotels in the city which allowed late check-in. Tomorrow, he would talk to Edie about Joel's being here. He couldn't be sure Edie had noticed, but he was up to something when they arrived. It didn't add up. The police thought as much. And if they didn't before speaking to him, they would now.

11th October 2015

That night, I barely slept. I wanted to know why Seth had done what he had done more than Ellison could ever imagine. I didn't have to stay, but now I couldn't leave. I owed Seth that much. I had to find out what happened. It would be easy for me to sell his house, go back home, and go back to my old life. But I couldn't. Not really. I would be able to get on with things, after I'd got tonight's nightmare out of my system, but for how long? How long would it really be before my curiosity came back? At some point it would start eating at me. I'd have to find out what happened to Seth, even if it was dangerous. Seth was the most level-headed man I knew. For him to take his own life like that...

Run. That was the easy option. Maybe I should have. But I didn't. I wanted to know what had happened to Seth. And I had to find out what was in that box.

***

The rough tweed scratched at my face as I drifted out of the latest exhaustion induced nap. Bright sunlight burst through the narrow, frosted window that ran high along the wall and warmed the room past the chill that had reigned all night. For a panicked second, I scrambled to get my bearings, before recognising the police station. The door swung open and Ellison breezed in, holding a mug.

'Morning. How did you sleep? That thing's more comfortable than it looks, eh? Spent many a night on there myself.'

I didn't get a chance to answer any of his questions. I just rose up from the settee, and rubbed my swollen face, feeling like I hadn't slept at all.

THE WILDE DIARIES

Ellison thrust the mug towards me. 'Here's a coffee. I've ordered you a taxi. Be here in twenty. Give you time to get yourself together.'

'So that's it?'

Ellison nodded. 'For now. But, do me a favour,' Ellison said. 'Let me know if you plan to leave town.'

I nodded. He left the room. I dropped back onto the settee and grabbed the coffee. I had to figure out what I was going to do next. Although I was certain it would involve the object sitting in the footwell in the back of my car.

I stared at the business card as the taxi weaved its way back to the house in the morning sun. Ellison had insisted I take it in case I needed to let him know of something I'd forgotten. The one thing I hadn't forgotten was sitting in my car. I wanted to pick it up and get to a hotel as quickly as possible. The house was technically mine, but I wouldn't be allowed in for a few days while forensics finished up. Staying there now was unthinkable anyway. I didn't believe in ghosts, but that didn't mean I rejected the idea of hauntings. I would be haunted at every turn by the image of Seth; drawn, haggard, and sleep-deprived to the very edge of his sanity – maybe beyond. I'd see his shambling figure leading me to the reception room every time I walked down that dim hallway. Or see his gaunt figure waiting to let me in every time I approached the front door. I just wanted to get my hands on the box. It would at least hint at why Seth did what he did.

As one inane pop song replaced another on the radio in

the taxi, I finally peered up to see where we were and was surprised to see the house on the horizon. The car weaved through the countryside and my eyes were drawn to the house. Just a building. Just bricks and mortar, and yet, I couldn't escape the feeling that it was watching me. Surveying my every move, like a cat toying with a wounded mouse. The taxi drew to a stop at the end of the short gravel driveway, and a weight lifted from my shoulders as I set eyes on my car. Safe, reliable, and waiting for me, with a gift inside.

I paid the driver and muttered thanks before stepping out into the fresh morning air, keeping eyes on my car the whole time. I stood at the entrance to the driveway until the taxi left. I wanted to get to the car alone. He didn't need to know about the box. My box. After waiting a few seconds I strode along the drive with the crunch of gravel underfoot for company, into the chill shadow of the house. I needed to get to town and into a hotel, then I could check the contents of the box. Out here was too exposed. I glanced at the comforting bulge beneath the jacket behind the driver's seat, got into the car, and drove.

***

Town was a dull affair. A main road curved in and straightened into a high street of small businesses. A café, a betting shop, a post office, a ladies fashion shop. Glancing down the side streets there were more signs of life. No people, but an Indian restaurant and a pub. Winding through the

THE WILDE DIARIES

country roads, it was a minor miracle that I'd got here at all. The weight of curiosity pressed down on the accelerator all the way, and even though I knew I couldn't see it, I'd glanced in the back to check the bulge under the jacket was still there more than I'd checked the mirrors. Between that main road and the shops at one side was a war memorial and car park.

The war memorial was three levels of steps leading to an obelisk with inscriptions of the names of local fallen World War II soldiers. I parked beside it. I wanted to get into that box, but I wanted to do it in the privacy of a locked room, and after I'd eaten. Once I started, I wanted nothing to stop me. Between the long trip and then the loss of appetite brought about by Seth's suicide, it had been well over fifteen hours since I'd had anything to eat at all. The café staff would tell me where I could rent a room. I just had to hope that my budget would stretch far enough to cover my research into the box while I looked into Seth's death. If time ran out I could always move in to the house, but the idea of staying where my friend had taken his life chilled me to the bone.

A small bell tinkled overhead, signalling my entrance to the café. Bright sunlight made it a welcoming sight, a handful of small tables leading up to a counter with an old wooden case stacked with homemade cakes and treats.

A voice from behind me spoke. 'Good morning.'

I hadn't seen the woman in the corner, wiping the table clean after some unseen customer who'd vanished into the ghost town outside. There had been somebody there though.

The smell of bacon over the fresh coffee was testament to that. My mouth watered at the thought of a fry-up.

'Good morning,' I replied, forcing a tired smile. The woman smiled back, her own smile forced much more professionally than my own. She gestured with a slender hand, fingers knotting with arthritis, to a clean table.

As I sat, she squeezed one eye to a slit, sizing me up: 'Let me guess.' She paused momentarily. 'Full English, coffee – black, one sugar, and maybe a blueberry muffin after, if you've got room.'

'Yes. Yes, that sounds perfect.'

She nodded, winked and disappeared into the back, leaving me baffled, but sure I would have room for a muffin after I'd polished off breakfast. I picked up a menu, more out of boredom than anything, as she started singing tunelessly in the back, the sizzles and smells of cooking drifting along shortly after. It wasn't long before she reappeared with my breakfast, everything cooked just how I liked it.

'That looks wonderful. Thank you.'

She went on doing chores as I ate, humming songs I didn't recognise the whole time. The tuneless humming struck me as oddly soothing. Normally I'd find it annoying, especially operating on so little sleep. It left me with the impression that she was reading my mind, without it feeling invasive. She left me to eat, not asking if I wanted any sauces (I didn't), or if everything was okay (it was).

The moment I finished she turned, as if she were fluent

THE WILDE DIARIES

in the language of cutlery on ceramic. 'You thought you'd have room for that muffin but it turns out you're full.'

'That's right,' I said, not in the least bit surprised at her latest bit of mind-reading. 'I'm looking for somewhere to stay. Is there a hotel in town?'

She smiled knowingly as if she anticipated the question, (and who knows, maybe she had), 'You need to speak to John. At The Ship.' She threw a thumb over her shoulder, in the general direction of a side street. 'Not a hotel, but he's got rooms. Nice, too.'

I paid and left, feeling that no time at all had passed since entering, but full and more alert after the coffee. Despite that caffeine kick, I still felt that I could sleep for days. As soon as I'd checked the box, of course.

I crossed back over the road to where my car sat waiting. I reached into the back and peeled back the jacket. The black gap in the side of the box still stared back at me. I grabbed it, locked up, and headed back across the road, to the side street where The Ship Inn waited. The Ship was the size of a large, detached property, white with black panelling, with one large door in the centre. I ignored the lack of signs of life and knocked.

Within a minute the door opened.

'John?'

'You just come from the café?'

Christ, can everyone in this town read minds?

His face broke into a smile. 'Carol called ahead. I'm

guessing by your reaction she did her telling-you-your-order trick.'

I felt a relieved smile break onto my own face. 'That's right. I just need a room for a few nights. Maybe a week.'

'Course. Come in.'

Inside the place was a traditional pub, decorated with nets and compasses and many-pointed steering wheels. He patted himself down until he located a bunch of keys, before doing the same in search of a pen. I pointed behind his ear and he smiled.

'Ah... So tonight, with the option to extend?'

I replied tapping my credit card against my palm. 'Sounds about right, yes.'

'We'll talk payment later. I can leave the tab open for food then. That okay?'

I agreed and was almost running as I went upstairs, leaving John shouting directions at my back. I perched the box into the crook of one arm and grabbed the handle of the door at the top of the stairs and entered the passageway that led to the rooms. The box felt lighter the closer I got. The idea of sleeping suddenly seemed ridiculous, now I was this close. Room 4 was the last at the far end of the hallway, next to the fire escape, something I usually searched out when staying at a new place. Now I didn't care. The key to Seth's suicide was in my hands and I wanted so badly to unlock the secrets within.

Again balancing the box on one arm I snatched the key

THE WILDE DIARIES

from my pocket and entered my new home. A small, narrow, double room (all the rooms here had double beds, according to John), a TV perched in the corner next to the ceiling and a dresser opposite the bed. I threw the keys onto the dresser and dropped onto the bed, setting the box down beside me, that black empty space staring out from the torn side. The worn corners of the box hinted at its age, and the sights it must have seen. More with intuition than certainty, part of me felt that this box was once owned by Lucas Wilde, a man whose name would have been etched into music history but for a combination of horrible luck and his untimely death; a death that came just as it seemed certain he and his band *Soothsayer* would hit the big time.

Yet all of these things made opening the box more difficult. Like there was too much pressure. Too much to lose. What if the box did have all the answers? About Lucas Wilde's cursed bad luck; about Seth's strange behaviour and appearance; about why the police thought I was involved in his death. What if all of those things could be answered and I just didn't have the nous or savvy to put the pieces together? I was always one step behind Seth when it came to intelligence. This box could confirm exactly that.

But it could give me the chance to prove all of that wrong. Maybe I could piece everything together. Succeed where he'd failed. If I could do that, the financial rewards could be significant.

As I grabbed the nearest edge of the lid, a smattering of

excited gooseflesh crept up the arm. I pulled it back and peered over the edge. I was not disappointed. I reached in and grabbed the first thing that caught my eye: a dark blue, hard-backed notebook, with a lighter blue linen-taped spine. As I lifted it out, I realised that it was one of a set, each marked with masking tape and handwritten labels. The writing did not belong to Seth.

The book in my hand was marked with a number one. Inside were a series of sketches, doodles and notes. The notes were sometimes single sentences, or phrases, perhaps ideas for song titles or lyrics, and then there were poems, and blocks of text marked 'verse' or 'chorus'. The first page was signed at the bottom in looping scrawl. Lucas T. Wilde. I closed it, wanting to read on, but like a child on Christmas morning eager to see what other gifts were ready for unwrapping.

There were more notebooks, of the same style, and a lined A4 notepad. The notepad was modern, but well used. Some leaves were torn lose and simply slotted back into the book itself. I lifted the cover to see something I recognised immediately. Seth's handwriting. As with Lucas' notebooks, the pages had doodles and sketches, all of which seemed random and insignificant. Reading the first lines, Seth had printed:

NOTES: Accompaniment to Lucas Wilde's notebooks. (More notes on memory stick.)

THE WILDE DIARIES

The notes were Seth's ideas and opinions about the diaries that Lucas had written across four notebooks. Like a television-series junkie afraid of spoilers, I turned the pages away and closed the book. I didn't know the ending to this story and I'd much rather hear it from the horse's mouth than second hand. Plus, doing it this way I could draw my own conclusions and see if there was any deviation from Seth's. As I lifted the A4 pad back into the box loose pages slipped out and see-sawed to the thin carpet of my room. I reached down and turned the first over, and when I did a wash of icy droplets splashed down my spine.

It was a sketch of a door shrouded in darkness; boards nailed across with stark white lettering painted across: *WARNING! KEEP OUT!*

Seth had sketched this and written underneath. 'The attic room'. The drawing itself was plain enough, but something about it unnerved me. This room clearly sat at the top of Seth's house and I had to question if it was in any way connected with his death.

I turned the second loose leaf over to reveal a sketch of ragged lines: a man, almost silhouetted against the background. But the background was no longer white. Seth had shaded the empty spaces around this strange figure a darker shade of grey. The figure almost looked like an outlaw. A gunslinger from the Old West; long coat reaching down to his ankles and wide-brimmed fedora hung down over the eyes. I only knew this sketch as Seth's work by the handwriting. Three words were printed below the image in letters drawn so hard into the page they were almost carved:

WHO IS HE?

I swiftly slid the page back into the notepad and peered back into the box. An A4 notepad, diaries, a memory stick, and an old key. The key looked like it might fit the front door to the house. Seth knew he was going to kill himself and he wanted me to be able to get into his place. What sat before me was of some historical and monetary value but held little in the way of revealing what happened to Seth. All I had for now was a few pages of diaries, notes and scribbles. For the next few days I would scour those diaries for clues and learn one hell of a lot about the final few weeks in the life of Lucas T. Wilde. Those weeks which lead to his tragic death on Sunday 18th September 1977.

From the first page of Lucas Wilde's first notebook:

This is a diary. Of sorts. Shit has been so weird lately that I want a record of it. In my words. Partly as a reminder, partly to try to sort out the ~~truth~~ real from the unreal.

I can't make sense of it all without this.

Things have happened that I can't explain. Things that shouldn't be happening. We (the band) have arrived. We've

THE WILDE DIARIES

"made it" as they say. It (life, writing, whatever IT is) should be getting easier. Doors are opening for me now that before I could only dream of. But as each door opens, it's like more shit comes through to me, rather than me stepping through and seeing what's on the other side.

Regrets? I have a few (ho-ho). Yes. If I could go back I would. I would do it differently. But I can't. I've made my bed and I have to lie in it.

(If only I could fucking sleep.)

And from that moment on, I was drawn into the world of rock and roll. Fortune, and fame. What I found was not what I expected.

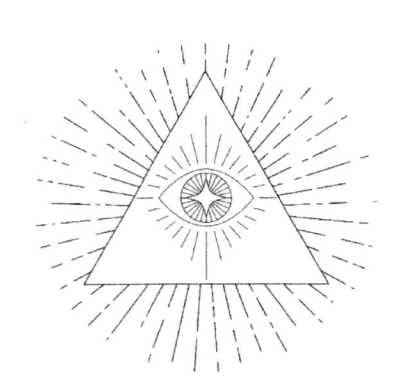

LUCAS WILDE'S DIARY #1

30th August 1977

The gathered masses gazed through the darkness towards the light, all enveloped by the feeling they had just witnessed something special. Twenty thousand souls gazed as one towards that stage, some clapping, some cheering, a few just standing soaking the whole thing up, but all of them emotionally exhausted and invigorated in equal measure, the same way someone who's never experienced this would equate to the aftermath of an earthquake orgasm. A real toe-curler. The way these things always go, the crowd seemed instinctively aware of movement backstage as the noise swelled and the elfin, angelic figure of Derek Boyd appeared onstage, arms aloft waving to the post-orgasmic audience. The swell became a roar and the rest of the band followed Boyd out, but where the fourth member should appear was a gap. An invisible band member followed guitarist Jack Mayberry leaving a split second for the crowd to wonder, *what if? Is he going to come out?* Then the deafening roar doubled in volume as Lucas Wilde appeared. Not waving. Not saluting. Just walking, head down, oozing cool and sex-appeal as he took his place at the mic stand.

The crowd volume dropped a few decibels awaiting for their new hero to speak.

'We're gonna do one more song.'

The volume rose again, and Jack Mayberry plucked the first few notes to their final tune of the night. The notes soared out into the crowd, imbuing them with new energy as Boyd's thundering bassline and Joey Gillespie's machine-gun drums drove the crowd higher than they could have dreamed a few hours before.

Lucas Wilde threw a lock of corkscrew hair back and moved with the beat waiting for his cue. He'd never felt this good before. He never would again. But this one moment was the culmination of years of hard work. Touring dives, bars and clubs. Arguing about song order and guitar solos and band leaders. Tonight it had all come together. There was no posturing about who should be centre stage. It didn't matter. It was as if tonight he and Jack had shared the limelight, and each one was happy to let the other take it, because that's what the crowd wanted. They were supposed to be here to warm the crowd up for *Burning Bridge*, now he almost felt sorry for them. Burning Bridge were one of the best live acts around, but tonight had proven to Lucas what he'd always known in his heart: when *Soothsayer* were on form, nobody could touch them. Tonight, they had arrived. It had taken two albums, and

THE WILDE DIARIES

up until this final night of the tour for them to get here, but this was it.

It came to the surprise of nobody. As the tour had progressed, the numbers arriving early to catch the support had grown and grown, until, for the past few weeks, there were as many coming to see *Soothsayer* as there were *Burning Bridge*. And the crowds were becoming amped as much for *Soothsayer* as they were for the main event. On those nights they'd played well. But tonight they had knocked it out of the park. Everyone was on form. Lucas knew it was coming too. Tonight had that magic feeling, like the crackle of energy in the air before you did that perfect take. Only tonight it had gone on and on. They band had drawn energy from the crowd and given it back tenfold. Back and forth it went until this crushing avalanche of emotion.

It should have been the start.

It would never be this good again.

Lucas had written the first two Soothsayer albums with relative ease. Like the songs had flowed through him. He was a conduit channelling the energy, but now, as he stood onstage celebrating his greatest moment, just for a second, the reality hit him. This tour had seen the reputation of Soothsayer grow and grow. Burning Bridge were getting jealous of the attention Lucas and company were receiving, not only from the reviewers, but more obviously, from the crowds. The apprentice had become the master. Both bands knew that when Lucas and company were on form, they were better. Now everyone else had caught on. As if it weren't enough that the numbers were growing to see the support, now too the groupies were more interested in them. Tonight it actually looked like some of these people may leave after this song. But now they had made it, something else had come with the fame and popularity. Expectation.

Lucas had fired off two albums in eight months. He'd written most of the second one whilst touring the first. But it wasn't the hard work that scared him: touring, writing, recording, partying, that was what he'd signed up for. That wasn't just part and parcel of the life - that *was* the life. No, it was something much more troublesome bothering Lucas Wilde. He hadn't finished a new song in almost four months. Three months and twenty-six days to be exact.

His cue came along and he drew a deep breath, just as it seemed the crowd was holding theirs, and screamed. Tonight wasn't a night for worry. It was a night for celebration. That part always came easily.

***

'Thank you. And goodnight!'

The crowd roared again and some were already trickling away, not waiting to see the main attraction. Lucas and the band lined up and bowed to the audience before waving and filing off stage, the buzz of adrenaline coursing through his veins now just like it had the first time. That elusive high that, as entertainers, they were forever chasing. Offstage, roadies

THE WILDE DIARIES

were waiting in the wings to change the guitars and drums over for Burning Bridge. And band manager Johnny Bateman was grinning like a fool.

Lucas saw the grin. While lead guitarist Jack Mayberry might have seen it as rampant opportunism and greed – the wheels turning and him imagining the sackloads of money he was going to make; Lucas saw it for what it was – genuine happiness.

Soothsayer was as much his band as it was theirs. He'd been there from the start. He was their fifth Beatle. The band's success was his success. He'd tasted the lows too, of course. Mayberry was quick to forget that it was Johnny who practically saved his life after the heroin overdose he'd taken in Atlanta. The heroin overdose that railroaded their first tour to the States. Just when they'd been gathering momentum. Just as the crowds had been growing. As their airplay was on the up. As sales were starting to touch the tipping point between where they were and the big time. It was Johnny. It was all Johnny.

Not tonight, Lucas, for fuck's sake. Tonight was good. Great even. Get out of the past. Enjoy tonight. Enjoy now.

He felt his frown melt at the warmth of his smile as he hugged Johnny. Bassist Derek Boyd joined in with a scream of delight, even sheltered drummer Joey "Dizzy" Gillespie joined in. They broke the huddle, Johnny staring ahead. One by one the band turned to see Jack Mayberry looking at them. Staring at them. At Lucas. It seemed like a moment frozen in time. If it wasn't, it should have been. This was an all new tipping point for the band. Could the lead singer and guitarist put their jealousy and petty differences behind them and focus on the band? On the *music*.

Lucas stared at Jack who stared back. Lucas felt a smile warm his eyes, though his mouth remained frozen, not wanting to lose ground in this Mexican stand-off. Then he saw it. His own body-language mirrored by Jack. The fucker was trying not to reveal his own hand. Both men smiled and the world around them exhaled. Mayberry strode towards the band, arms out wide, smile even wider. The huddle resumed.

'Drinks?' the drummer, of course.

'The after party.' Boyd said, almost as if it were a given.

There was to be a huge end-of-tour party. It was supposed to be Soothsayer worshipping the ground that Burning Bridge walked on. A few weeks ago, Soothsayer might have been welcome at such an event. That was then. There followed a split second of silence, broken by Lucas, looking directly at Mayberry. 'Fuck the after party.' He smiled.

'Fuck Burning Bridge!' Mayberry declared, either unaware or not caring that their road crew and tour manager were within earshot.

Lucas grinned, 'Not sure they'd want to see us after that performance anyway.'

He was right. Soothsayer's growing popularity during the tour had become an issue. They'd started out very much in

THE WILDE DIARIES

the shadow of Burning Bridge, but as the tour had gone on, some uncharacteristic iffy performances from them, coupled with the rock solid Soothsayer shows meant that Lucas and Co had very much cast the shadow. In their world of huge egos where fame was a butterfly, the most delicate of creatures; alive for the briefest of moments, it had become a growing problem. Burning Bridge were sick of the sight of Lucas and Jack Mayberry and the line of groupies that used to crave their attention just a few months earlier.

They ended the night on the town. The whole band. The roadies. Manager. Everyone. And for the first time in a long time there were no arguments. None of the old bullshit seemed important. They were as one, and it was crystal clear they were on the verge of something huge. It didn't matter who was the band leader. Who was the most popular. There was more than enough popularity to go around. Jack even spoke to Malcolm and Sally without his usual trick of accusing them of riding Lucas's coattails and bleeding him (and by proxy, the rest of them) dry. Jack and Dizzy were tight, but then again, they'd known each other for ever, and they'd played together for ever. It must have finally seemed that all of their hard work had paid off.

They slept on the tour bus and the next afternoon they headed home and as the tour bus neared, the old issues of squabbling and jealousy and one-upmanship within the band seemingly dealt with, Lucas became starkly aware that he had a much bigger problem to deal with. The tired conversations and laughter faded around him and once again he was haunted by the problem that dogged the brief moments of quiet the night previous. He still hadn't finished a new song in months. More than the issues within the band, this was the thing he wanted resolving. His creative constipation. Writing was his life. He'd never dealt with writer's block before. Until a couple of months ago, he thought it was a myth. Something that those without a natural ability like his made up to console themselves and paper over the cracks where their talent had failed. In the beginning, it was fine. He just needed a break. A few days off. Even when a few days turned into a week he wasn't stressed. It was just his mojo recharging. He'd written two albums and a slew of B-sides non-stop for a few months. One week of inactivity turned into two, and he got the jitters.

A noise in front of him dragged him back to reality.

'You're quiet,' Sally said, leaning over the seat in front.

'Don't let Mal see you talking to me alone,' he replied with a soft smile.

'He can bollocks,' she replied with an eye roll. 'You okay?'

'Just hung over...' He glanced just over her shoulder and in a barked whisper said, 'Quick! He's coming!'

She flinched a little before sticking her tongue out. 'You can bollocks as well,' she said before sitting back down.

Lucas went straight back into his fog of self-pity. He needed to finish a song, and fast. But the chords never sounded right. He could never find the right one. When he did the melody was too plain. Too obvious. If that came

THE WILDE DIARIES

together, then it was the lyrics that weren't working. That or they were downright garbage. In fact. The lyrics were unfinished to all the half-songs he'd started lately. Some days he'd sit for hours, coming up with different variations, none of which worked.

That was the worst part. The frustration of not moving forward. And with it came the fear. Fear of stagnation. Fear that he'd lost the magic touch forever, just when he needed it most. It occurred to him that it must have happened to countless others, consigned to the musical scrap heap when it looked as if they were about to break through. That was his biggest fear. That his creativity was enough to get them so far. So *close*. Then it had dried up completely. A creative drought. Though he was never a religious man, that was the thing he'd started to pray about. He'd prayed for rain. His prayers would be answered. But, then again, that wasn't necessarily a good thing.

As the bus rumbled on, his mind drifted to happier times. To the summer of '72.

4th June 1972

'And you're sure you know the middle eight in Road House? Because it's tricky.'

Derek Boyd just shrugged. Seventeen years young and The Bluebirds number one fan was in the tiny storage room that stood in for backstage at The Ram's Head, moments away from playing his first gig for the band. For all intents and purposes, it was the final stage in a job interview that equated to three weeks' studio time. In all honesty, Derek hadn't needed weeks. From the moment he stepped in the transition was seamless. Lucas was five years older than the quiet, unassuming kid, but liked him immensely.

'He'll be fine, Sal.' Lucas smiled.

Sally nodded, nervous. Lucas was surprised at how well Sally had taken to her replacement. She'd even coached him on the trickier parts, not that he'd needed it. But she'd been there all the same, giving him pointers on transitions and working with a drummer. Sally sipped her rum and coke in the darkness of the club and Malcolm kissed her on the cheek.

'Go easy on those,' Mal said, nodding at the drink.

'I'm only having a couple,' she said, rubbing the swollen belly with her free hand.

'Well, that's what Luke's mum said when she was having him and look how he turned out,' Malcolm replied, grinning.

'Alright, twat,' Lucas said, smiling. He got serious and turned to the others, 'Are we ready?'

The band nodded and turned to go out on stage, but they all stopped dead when a shout came from behind.

'Lucas!'

It was Shelley. She ran over and kissed him.

'All right, all right, leave the man alone, he's got a gig to do,' Malcolm said.

THE WILDE DIARIES

She broke the kiss and stared at Lucas. 'You aren't going to believe who's out there,' she said, then, without pause to let anyone answer, 'Johnny Bateman.'

Lucas took a second to process the information before he could reply. 'You're sure.'

'Who's that?' asked Derek.

'Ninety per cent. Ninety-five.' Shelley replied.

Malcolm answered Derek, 'A talent scout. From Giddy-Up records. He's the one who signed Mayberry's band.'

Derek shrugged. He knew fine well who Jack Mayberry was, and the man who signed him to a major record label being in the crowd was a huge deal. But that was just Derek.

Lucas smiled and clapped him on the shoulder. 'Well. Let's go out there and give them a show.'

The anticipation rose as the four stepped out on stage. The crowd was a couple of hundred and just for a moment, Lucas tried to recall the last time they'd played for a crowd of less than triple figures. Whistles and cheers rose and fell as they took their positions.

Lucas glanced up at the crowd with a gleam in his eye. 'Alright?'

The crowd responded with a loud cheer, the days of the question being met with mumbling a distant memory.

'I've got a new friend,' Lucas said, arm stretched out presenting the bands' new bassist. 'Are you going to be nice to him?'

More cheers came and Derek, still only seventeen but as

cool as ever, nodded.

All the time he was talking, Lucas was searching out into the crowd beyond the lights burning onto the stage, a hand covering his eyes like a sailor searching out land. He was looking for Shelley. Not seeking a connection from her; just like the mumbled responses and smaller crowds, that was another long-forgotten tradition, but because she said she'd be standing next to the man she thought was Johnny Bateman. Lucas finally set eyes on the man in question, but he was half-turned chit-chatting to some leggy young thing. Shelley stood beside him, nodding theatrically.

Before the energy fell away Lucas spoke again.

'This one's called "Ghosts",' and amid the rising cheers, 'Three! Four!'

And that was that. So began the show.

The crowd were wowed by yet another Lucas Wilde masterclass. Once he was on stage, the crowd cheering, the band behind him, he was unstoppable. He was the presence of Morrison. He was the energy of Jagger. The magnetism of Plant. Malcolm's solos that night were special. He always improvised his solos, some nights they were wandering, meandering and lost. Not tonight. Tonight they were thunderous, rising and falling as if he were channelling Jack Mayberry himself. Derek was flawless. He'd learned every note of Sally's baselines and added a flourish of his own. Even Carl the drummer was playing well tonight, enjoying the new tightness Derek had brought to the table. And it was after that

THE WILDE DIARIES

count in that Lucas forgot that Johnny Bateman might be in the crowd. None of them knew it, but Derek's first gig with The Bluebirds was to be his last. The bands' last. For when Lucas finished the show, the man standing next to Shelley approached the stage grinning from one ear to the next. Shelley was right. It was Johnny Bateman.

***

Lucas, Sally and Malcolm were all crammed into the "backstage" cupboard at The Ram's Head and the atmosphere was charged.

'You don't get it, Luke,' said Malcolm, drenched in sweat and stinking of whiskey, 'this is what we wanted.'

'I can't. I won't.' Lucas replied.

Sally stepped closer, hand still cradling the bump that would join the world in a matter of weeks and placed a hand on Lucas Wilde's shoulder. 'Lucas, we knew that this time would come. We've been expecting it. For years now.'

'Johnny Bateman is waiting outside. He won't wait forever,' Mal said.

'I don't care,' Lucas replied, his tone almost petulant.

Mal stood square in front of Lucas and grabbed his shoulders. 'Mate, this is once in a lifetime stuff. You are going to be in a band with Jack Mayberry. Jack fucking Mayberry.'

'And what happens to you two? You've got a baby on the way.'

'We'll be fine. We always are.'

Lucas thought back to the early days, arguing with his dad about getting a real job and that his "silly little band" wasn't a living. Sneaking out to practice with Malcolm and Sally, playing Stones and Creedence songs. The first time as a band they met Carl, Sally's cousin who could play the drums, and Lucas remembering thinking that when they played together this was what he was supposed to be doing. It felt right, like a needle in a groove, in a way that nothing else he'd ever done had. But those were experiences he'd had with Malcolm and Sally. Going through that all over again with another band would be weird. Would it be wrong? It felt like a betrayal.

'Luke, mate, we'll look back at this one day and laugh. The difference is you'll be famous as fuck and rolling in money, but we'll laugh.'

Lucas smiled.

Sally rubbed her swollen belly again. In a couple of months, their lives would be totally different anyway.

'Luke, just have a chat with him.'

Lucas nodded, then pulled his friends in for a hug.

***

Johnny Bateman was sitting with Shelley when Lucas walked out into the bar. A few drunken stragglers left behind congratulated Lucas on a great show as he neared the man checking his watch. Johnny looked up from his watch and saw Lucas and beamed a wide, genuine smile. He stood

THE WILDE DIARIES

immediately and for the second time that night, shook Lucas by the hand. A firm, trustworthy handshake. When Lucas thought back to this moment in years to come, he'd feel bad at the notion that Johnny Bateman had his nice-guy persona polished to a T. He'd feel bad because from his point of view in the future, it wasn't an act. This wasn't some portrayal, it was the real Johnny and he was actually exactly as likable and warm as the first impression he gave you.

'Hiya Lucas, want a drink?'

'No thanks.'

Guard up.

'Have a seat.'

Shelley motioned to go, so she could let the men talk business. Lucas wanted her right there. An extra pair of eyes on the slippery snake-oil salesman. Johnny surprised both of them when he signalled he was having none of it.

'Please, if it's okay with you, Lucas, you don't have to go.'

Lucas nodded and Shelley shifted her weight back into the seat, Lucas squeezing her leg under the table in a "thank you".

Johnny did most of the talking. How he'd recently taken over Jack Mayberry's band Second Sight, but there were concerns within the record label over the quality of the vocals. Not only that, but he was a liability. High all the time (on whatever he could get his hands on, if the rumours were to be believed), difficult to deal with, a bit of a diva. Tommy D's reputation preceded him. Most of the vocalists on the local circuit cared little for him. He was nowhere near good enough for the kind of diva shit he was trying to pull. The conversation had moved to how Jack Mayberry and Joey 'Dizzy' Gillespie, Jack's drummer, had a list of singers to replace Tommy. The list consisted of one name. That name of course, was Lucas Wilde.

'I've got some concerns.' Lucas said, after listening to Johnny's speech.

'Fire away,' Johnny replied, a man confident he had all the answers.

'I've been with Malcolm and Sally since the beginning. She's about to have a baby.'

'Two months,' Johnny replied.

He'd done his homework.

'Leaving them now would feel like a shithouse move.'

Johnny nodded. 'Lucas Wilde and Jack Mayberry. You guys are generational talents. I'm not saying that because you're sitting in front of me. Jack and Joey know you're the real deal. They prefer your songs to Tommy's. They prefer your voice to Tommy's. This isn't coming from me. I'll be honest, when they said they were pissed off with Tommy's nonsense I was delighted. And when they said your name, well, that matched my ideas. You guys have "it". The potential for you working together is huge—'

'How does that fit in with Malcolm and Sally?'

'Lucas, this band is going to be massive. There will be tour managers, roadies, PR teams—'

THE WILDE DIARIES

'PR?' Shelley asked.

'Public Relations,' Johnny replied.

Sally did any promotional stuff for their band at the moment. She could fill any number of roles, when the time came.

'Guitar technicians?' Lucas asked.

Johnny smiled. 'You've got it.'

Lucas leaned forward in his seat. Spending this time with Johnny in person, he saw how easy it was to get on with him. Working with Jack Mayberry every day and dealing with someone like Johnny... It was all starting to make sense.

Lucas narrowed his eyes and decided to push a little further. 'I've just got one more question.'

Johnny nodded.

'You've spoke a lot about Jack Mayberry and Joey Gillespie tonight, but I haven't heard you mention a bassist.'

Johnny nodded again. 'That's another thing. The bassist we've got isn't sure that he's ready for the big time. He's a lovely guy, and he can play, no doubt about it. But when there's talk of playing arenas and crowds of thousands, rather than hundreds he breaks out in a cold sweat. Cards on the table, he's thinking of quitting.'

Lucas held out a hand. 'I'm in.'

Johnny reached across the table and took it. Before he could shake it, Lucas spoke again.

'On one condition.'

And that was how Derek Boyd joined the band. That's

how Soothsayer were born.

28th August 1977

It was two days before that final show with Burning Bridge and Lucas, Malcolm and Sally were heading through the northern English countryside.

Sally shouted from the back seat. 'Tell us where we're going!'

'Well that would take all the fun out of it, wouldn't it?' Lucas replied.

Sally stuck her tongue out theatrically in the mirror. Lucas smiled.

Where they were going already stood out on the horizon. There wasn't much else around at all, just that magnetic, alluring old house, drawing you in like the tide.

Malcolm fidgeted in his seat and moaned, 'There's nothing here.'

'That, my friend, is the point.'

The house rose from the horizon against the blue skies, and Lucas glanced at it from time to time, forcing himself not to grin with pride.

Sally had twigged. 'Hang on, is that it? Is that where we're going?'

'That, my friends, is my new house.'

Malcolm perked up, 'Shit... The parties we could have in

THE WILDE DIARIES

there.'

Lucas clapped a hand down on his knee, 'By Jove I think he's got it!'

Lucas sped up, wanting to get there sooner, the house watching them all the way. They'd been driving for an hour by the time Lucas pulled into the driveway and they all jumped out. Inside, Lucas gave them the tour: the room where they'd probably do most of their partying; the room where he planned to do recordings of his new songs, reading and chilling out; kitchen. They bound upstairs excited and after showing them the master bedroom and the guest rooms, Lucas had one final surprise for them.

'And in here—'

'What's up there?' Sally interrupted, pointing to a small, narrow, crooked stairway.

Lucas turned and stared into the darkness where the stairs vanished. 'Oh that? Nothing interesting. Just the attic. Couple of rooms.' He turned back, ignoring the shiver that ran down his spine. 'Anyway, in here is much more interesting, come on.'

He pushed the door open and let Malcolm and Sally go in first, following them in with a grin. Sally shrieked in excitement and Malcolm's mouth fell open, for once, he was speechless.

'Ta-da!' Lucas shouted.

The room was as big as the master bedroom, but looked bigger because there was no bed. In each corner were guitars and amps. Between the guitars on one wall was a fridge, and along the other, a three-seater settee.

Sally ran across to the bass, an orange Fender Mustang, 'Is this for me?'

'That it is, milady!' Lucas smiled.

Malcolm wandered slowly over to the Gibson SG like it was a wild animal that might get spooked if he made any sudden movements. He slowly reached out a hand.

'That one's mine actually Mal,' Lucas said.

Malcolm slowly turned back, trying his best to hide his disappointment.

'Just kidding,' Lucas said, grinning.

'You twat!' Mal shouted before shoving Lucas away with a grin forming on his reddening cheeks.

Between Mal's new SG and Sally's Mustang was a fully-stocked fridge. Beer, mixers for the stronger stuff.

Lucas grabbed his acoustic. 'Well, are we going to play?'

***

The three of them played old Bluebirds songs until the sun had gone down and the fridge was half empty. By then, they'd retired to the settee, Sally sound asleep against one of the arms. Lucas sipped at his beer.

'Funny how stuff works out, isn't it?'

'Hmm?' In the silence, Lucas' thoughts had drifted back to the same thing they always did these days - his inability to finish a new song.

THE WILDE DIARIES

'I said it's weird how things turn out. You never know.'

'Right.'

'Remember that gig we played in Leeds? There were only seven people in the crowd—'

'And a fight broke out!' Lucas finished.

Malcolm took on the voice of a shrieking woman, 'Don't you touch my arse!'

Lucas followed with a deep Yorkshire accent, 'I've bin touching it all night you've said nowt, ya fat cow!'

The two men screamed with laughter, Sally not stirring at all.

The laughter subsided and Lucas spoke. 'Any regrets?'

Mal thought for a second. 'No. Not really. I think The Bluebirds had gone about as far as we were going to. We're all still together, sort of. We've both got jobs, security. Our health...'

He tailed off and the silence hung there. For once, Lucas didn't turn attention to his writers' block, but to the time just after the first Soothsayer practice when he got the news to rush to the hospital. Sally had miscarried. Lucas shuddered at the memory of the dead look in Mal's eyes. He looked lost. Terrified.

'Health. That's the most important thing.' Mal finished.

Lucas clapped his hand on his friends leg.

'Young Derek did okay for himself, didn't he?'

'One gig! And Johnny Bateman's there. I don't think he knows what to do with all the attention he's getting.'

'He's doing alright.' Lucas smiled.

'Mandy?' Mal said.

Lucas nodded. 'Oh yeah. Sweet little thing that is.'

There was another silence. Sally shuffled position and the men were silent until they heard the light drone of her snores again.

'What about you?' Mal asked.

'Me?'

'You're quiet. There's something on your mind. Tell uncle Mal.'

Lucas smiled. "Uncle" Mal was two months older than him.

'Yeah, I mean, things are going great. Tour's going well, but I don't think Burning Bridge would agree.'

'Fuck 'em,' Mal interjected.

'Fuck 'em,' Lucas agreed. 'Two albums in. Bought a new house. And I keep having dreams where I'm at these massive parties and everyone's there. The Stones. Beatles. Even Jimi and Janis are there. And they all know me. By first name...'

Mal swigged his drink, waiting for Lucas to carry on. But he didn't.

'So why does your face look like a smacked arse?'

Lucas finished off his drink. 'I haven't told anyone this.' He looked straight at Mal. 'Nobody.'

Mal nodded for him to continue, his confidence tacit.

'I bought this place for a change of scenery. Peace and quiet. To get away from it all. I'm hoping it will help. We've

THE WILDE DIARIES

got a band meeting in a few weeks, when the tour's done, for me to present the new songs—'

'Can't wait.' Mal replied with a confidence in Lucas ability that he himself could only dream of.

A sigh escaped. 'That's the thing... And you can't tell a soul this... There are no new songs.'

Mal's faced dropped, just for a second, before the poker face mask was replaced. But he'd seen it.

'I've been trying and trying, but I can't do it. I've got the beginnings of about twenty songs. Twenty-odd songs I can't finish. I've never had this. I usually write while we're touring, but this time...'

Mal sat silently. When he realised that Lucas had disappeared into the fog of his thoughts, he spoke.

'It's been a long tour, mate. A lot of shows. Harder than it usually is. Even me and Sal have felt it. How does this sound? Get the last show out of the way, give it a few days, and we'll have a party. Celebrate the end of the tour, and it can double as a housewarming for this place. Let everyone relax and unwind. You'll see, everything will come back. It'll be fine.'

Lucas nodded. Relax, unwind, unblock. It sounded like a good idea.

It was not.

MARC W SHAKO

1ˢᵗ September 1977

The party was winding down and Lucas felt good. The band were here, with plus ones, Malcolm and Sally were somewhere or other, christening one of the beds upstairs more than likely, and Johnny was here, as always, alone. Lucas was sitting in the same room where, some forty years later, a writer would put a gun to his head and squeeze the trigger, blowing his brains onto the wall behind. He'd come for a bit of quiet, but for once his mind was not on writers' block. Maybe Mal had been right. Unwinding might just do the trick.

'You alright mate?' Derek asked, dancing into the room, Mandy and the sounds of The Rolling Stones following behind.

'You seen Johnny and them?' Lucas asked.

"And them" was Jack, Joey and their girls.

'Other room, asking where you are. Well the girls are. The others are asleep.'

'Why what time is it?'

Mandy checked her watch. 'It's nearly three in the morning.'

Mandy was a quiet, sweet girl. A great match for Derek. She never said much, but always jumped at the opportunity to speak to Lucas. Lucas had noticed, and he was sure that Derek had too. Derek was growing a little tired of it, he could see. The jealousy from other partners was something he'd had to get used to himself over the years. He'd had exactly the same with Sally, and even now, from time to time, it would bother

THE WILDE DIARIES

Malcolm, and that despite Mal's flirtations with anything with a pulse.

Just as Lucas was about to ask where Malcolm and Sally had got to, the door burst open and they fell into the room.

'Where the fuck have you two been?' Derek asked.

'Don't answer that! I can imagine.' Lucas said, only half joking.

Sally laughed, 'Cheeky sod! We've been up in the attic.'

Derek leaned trying to see whatever Mal was hiding behind his back, 'What you got there?'

'Well...' he started, 'While we were up in the attic, we found this.' Mal produced a piece of board and turned it over to reveal a set of letters and numbers drawn in gothic writing.

Derek frowned, 'The fuck is that?'

'Haven't you seen *The Exorcist*?' Mal said, crossing his legs in the middle of the room and setting the board down in front of him.

Derek shrugged. He hadn't. If it didn't involve playing music, he wasn't interested.

'It's a Ouija board, man,' Lucas slurred.

Derek shrugged again.

'And that was in the loft? My loft?'

'Yep. It's for talking to dead folks,' Malcolm said, wiggling his fingers to suggest something spooky was imminent.

Derek's girl Mandy, who had barely said a word all night and only laughed when Lucas made a joke, finally spoke. 'What do you want to mess about with that for?'

Derek's face lit up, 'We'll fucking have some of that. Turn the lights off, Mand.'

But Mandy had shrunk away, holding her elbows like the temperature had dropped a few degrees and for a second Lucas felt sorry for her.

'I don't want to do it, Derek.' Her features had darkened, as if she'd had some previous experience.

The mood in the room shifted. Any tension between Lucas and Derek had gone, their energy focused entirely on this new macabre plaything. Mandy's fear had done nothing to dissuade the group from testing its abilities, on the contrary, the air crackled with excitement. If this board was going to do something extraordinary, they wanted to see what it was, the weirder the better.

Derek's eyes hardened. 'Well the rest of us want to do it. If you don't want to, turn the lights off on your way out.'

Lucas had sat himself down across from Malcolm and was staring at the board. None of the others knew that he'd started praying at night, praying for an end to his misery at the hands of writer's block. If they'd seen him in prayer, then seen his staring at this board, they'd have been hard pressed to tell the difference.

The room fell silent. Without taking his eyes from the board, Lucas spoke.

'Let's do it. Kill the lights, Sal.'

Derek gleefully plopped on the floor beside Lucas, waving Mandy over to sit beside him. Whether it was because

THE WILDE DIARIES

Lucas was into the idea, or just because she didn't want to listen to any more of Derek's complaining, she reluctantly shifted herself from her spot in the corner and slouched over to where a drunken half of Soothsayer sat, cross-legged in the centre of the room. Sally turned out the lights and she and Malcolm gathered the candles and placed them between the members of the group in a circle. With the room in darkness, the silence from before was now pregnant with expectation. A heaviness fell, flickering the delicate candle flames, motes of dust dancing in and out of their soft halos of light.

Sally and Malcolm sat in the final spaces around the board, the final points in a star. Malcolm reached two fingers into his shirt pocket and withdrew a pointed piece of wood, placing it in the centre of the board.

'What's that?' Derek asked.

Sally replied, 'It's called a planchette,' and placed a delicate finger atop the pointer. Malcolm did likewise, his eyes drawn to the board the same as Lucas'. Mandy, then Derek followed suit. Malcolm glanced up at Lucas, who leaned forward and slowly moved his index finger to the planchette. As he made contact, whether by consequence or coincidence, the flames on the candles bobbed, and the air changed again, as if the room had sighed. Sally and Mandy exchanged a sideways glance.

Derek's eyes darted amongst the others. 'Did you feel that? You felt that, right?'

Nobody spoke.

'Right?' he repeated.

'I felt it,' Lucas said, not taking his eyes from the planchette.

Malcolm cleared his throat and spoke in a half whisper, 'Let's start.'

'How do we do that?' Lucas asked, still not looking up.

Sally replied in that same half-whisper used by Malcolm. 'We ask a question.' She stared at the planchette. 'We're here to talk to anybody in this room who is in the spirit realm. Is there anybody there?' Her voice was clear and confident.

The planchette stayed put.

'What if it says 'No'?' Derek asked, smirking. Mandy elbowed his ribs, finally smiling.

Sally ignored him, 'If there are any spirits in the room, we'd like to make contact with you. Is there anybody here who would like to talk to us?'

Though it hadn't moved, the planchette gently vibrated with an energy all of its own. Then, slowly, briefly, it moved. Glances were exchanged, but Lucas just stared. Then, the pointer slowly set off again, scraping along the wooden board, feeling like it was being pulled by an unseen energy. It finally came to rest, at "Yes".

'Fuck off,' said Derek, lifting his finger. 'That was you Mal.'

Malcolm shook his head. His face was deadly serious.

'Have you done this before?' Derek asked.

'Yes.'

THE WILDE DIARIES

'What happened?'

Malcolm looked at Derek. 'Nothing. Nothing happened.'

'Put your finger back on, Des.' Sally said, in that half-whisper.

He did.

Sally spoke aloud, addressing the spirit. 'Thank you. Can you tell us your name?'

The planchette vibrated again, before sliding over to "No".

Mandy jumped back this time. 'Fuck off now, Mal.'

'I swear to God. I'm barely touching it.' His touch on the planchette was so light it was almost like he was afraid to leave a fingerprint. 'Everyone do the same.'

The others lifted their fingers so there was barely any pressure at all. Again the candle flames danced, moved by an invisible breeze.

'Ask it something, Des,' Mal said. 'Something only you would know.'

Derek paused for a second, then his eyes lit. 'When I was a kid, I had a dog. What was it called?'

The air shifted, candles flickering in unison, then the planchette moved. Slowly, surely, to the middle of the board. It moved not like someone was pushing or pulling, but as if the movement were magnetic, setting off with a jerk before settling into a uniform movement. Derek looked up, his face pale. Everyone else was focused on the board. Mandy gasped as the planchette jerked across the board.

'Jesus.' Derek said, leaping back, the words falling from his mouth. The pointer was at "No".

'What?' Lucas asked. But Derek was frozen. 'Des.'

Derek spoke as if he couldn't understand what was happening. 'I lied. We didn't have a dog. I always wanted one, but we never had a dog.'

Before anyone could react, the planchette moved again. Slowly, deliberately, stopping at the letter *L*.

'Is that "L"?' Sally asked.

It slid again, stopping at *U*.

Lucas looked up, again at Malcolm. Malcolm gaped back. 'Look at my finger. I'm barely touching it.'

Before Lucas could speak, the planchette jerked again, stopping at *C*.

'You want to speak to me?' Lucas said aloud, addressing the hidden figure in their midst.

The planchette slid again, faster now, across the board, coming to rest at "Yes".

Lucas looked at each of the people around the board in turn. They all took turns at gesturing that they had nothing to do with what was going on.

'What do you want?'

The planchette set off again.

...*A*

...*S*

...*K*

Then stopped.

THE WILDE DIARIES

'Ask? You want me to ask a question? Is it because I don't believe?'

YES

'Okay, I'll ask. Is it Mal? Is Malcolm moving the pointer?'

Malcolm lifted his finger from the planchette altogether. Throwing a questioning glance at Lucas.

The pointer slid again.

NO

Lucas looked back at Malcolm. 'Put your finger back on.' Malcolm placed his finger lightly back onto the pointer. Lucas projected his voice to the room again. 'How do I know you're not one of the others messing around?'

The pointer took off again.

...S

...E

...C

...R

...E

...T

Lucas nodded. 'I understand.' He set out to trick the board as Derek had. 'What am I afraid of most, spiders or heights?'

If it was the others fucking around, they would now have to guess. He cared for neither spiders nor heights, but he'd never told anyone what his real phobia was. Ever since he'd been a boy, the one thing that had terrified him the most was birds. He'd named the first band The Bluebirds in a bid to get over the fear of those beady little eyes and fluttering horror. None of the others in the room had a clue, as far as he knew. He given them options A and B, and the answer could have been anything from C to Z. The planchette moved slowly, clearly, again pulled by that invisible force that felt like magnetism.

...W

...R

...I

...T

Writing? He'd never been scared of writing. That was the one thing he loved. Even recently, with his problems, he'd never call it a phobia.

...E

...R

Lucas spoke to the invisible figure, still not convinced it wasn't one of the others. 'Yes, I'm a writer. A songwriter.' If he had a thought beyond that he never got a chance to express it. The planchette jerked around the board, quickly spelling.

...S

...B

...L

...O

...C

...K

The planchette flew out from beneath their fingers, striking Lucas hard in the stomach.

THE WILDE DIARIES

'Writer's block?' Sally asked aloud.

Lucas looked up at Malcolm, and Malcolm saw a look in his eyes that he'd never seen before. A look of pure hatred.

'You cheap cunt.'

'I swear, I nev—'

Lucas launched himself at Malcolm. The others flew back in shock.

Sally screamed. 'Lucas! What the fuck are you doing?'

Malcolm was on his back, eyes bulging, Lucas' hands wrapped tightly around his throat. Derek launched himself at Lucas, knocking him sideways. The women were screaming. Mandy jumped up and hit the lights, flooding the dim room with bright colour. Lucas was struggling with Derek, trying to get at Malcolm, who had backed away, eyes wide with fear.

'I fucking told you that in confidence, you cunt!'

Malcolm was almost in tears, 'I swear to God, Luke, that wasn't me.'

Sally hugged herself to Malcolm. Lucas threw off Derek's grip and launched himself at Mal. Sally tried to get between them, but Lucas threw her aside. She hit the floor hard, and Mandy screamed again, backing further into the corner.

Derek screamed, 'Lucas, what the fuck are you doing, man?'

Lucas was swinging punches at Malcolm, who was on his back, desperately trying to put his hands in front of his face. Derek tried to grab him and was caught in the mouth by a flailing elbow. He staggered back, falling into the far wall before crumpling to the floor. Mandy and Sally were crying, and Malcolm was still pleading, refusing to fight back.

'Lucas!' Sally jumped in between them.

Lucas grabbed hold of her, about to throw her aside once again, enraged by Malcolm's betrayal.

'Fire!' Mandy screamed. 'The fucking curtains!'

Lucas finally let go. He jumped to his feet and whipped round to see one of the candles had been overturned in the fracas, fingers of flame reaching up from the bottom of the curtains. Lucas jumped up and ran over, yanking at the burning curtain. Mandy and Sally screamed. The whole rail came crashing down and he smashed it through the window. A light breeze blew into the room. Lucas heard a sniffle behind him. He turned again to see four pairs of eyes burning into him, all from their places pressed against the far wall. Mandy and Sally's red and puffy. Malcolm's peering out from his marked and swollen face, filled with fear. Derek's burning with anger over his bleeding nose.

The door burst open and the rest of the band fell in.

'What the hell's going on in here?' Jack Mayberry asked.

Derek stared at Lucas, shook his head and held out a hand to Mandy. She took it and they silently left. Sally grabbed Malcolm's hand and led him out behind the others. As he got to the door, he stopped and turned to Lucas, his eyes filled with tears.

'It wasn't me.'

Lucas couldn't speak. Nobody could. Now it was Lucas

THE WILDE DIARIES

and the rest of the band in the room, net curtains fluttering in the breeze. Whatever happy party atmosphere there had been before, it was gone.

Dizzy turned to Jack, 'Maybe we should get a taxi.'

Jack held Lucas' gaze, before nodding. They called from the hallway and waited outside for the car to arrive. Lucas was left alone.

***

Lucas stood alone and turned on the light. The burning smell of curtains hung in the air, blown gently on the breeze coming in through the broken window. He surveyed the room: smashed glasses and spilt drinks; knocked over candles beside cooling, hardening wax; that stench of singed fabric. And yet, despite the mess, the feeling in the room was *different*. Before the fighting, during the séance, the mood had been heavy with the same static oppression you'd feel before a thunderstorm. It had the same excitement, he recalled distinctly feeling it, through his rage. That was *why* he remembered it. He wasn't much of a fighter. He'd been *in* fights, but he was never the kind of person who'd go out looking for trouble. In those few moments of battle he'd experienced before, the feeling during the séance was like that before a fight. Oppressive. Electric. When the fighting started tonight the overriding emotion, above anger even, was excitement. Now the fight was over, the air was lighter. Not like after a storm. This was different. He'd felt it before, but now he couldn't place it. Then it struck him. Malcolm and Sally's house. Just after they announced they were going to have a baby. It was the air of celebration.

The house. The house is celebrating. Before the thought could fully form, it evaporated.

'Lucas, you're drunk. Go to bed,' he slurred to himself.

Christ, what was he thinking? The *house* was happy? He'd imagined it. All of it. There was no feeling before but his own anticipation. The excitement at the idea of freeing himself from the grip of writers' block. He stared at the Ouija board. Before the séance, it stared back. Now it just sat there, lifeless. Because it *was* lifeless. There was no séance. Just a guy who used to be his friend spilling his secrets because he thought that Sally had the hots for him. Fuck Malcolm. This was the first time Lucas had ever experienced such a betrayal. He'd shared something so intimate, something that could really hurt him, to the one person he thought he could trust above all others.

'Fucking Malcolm.'

His voice sounded petulant and heavy with alcohol. He hated it. It was more than time to go upstairs. He left the room, desperately trying to avoid looking at the mess that was there. On the way out he grabbed the key from the inside of the room and switched it to the outside of the door, locking the smell of burning in there for the night, and sealing the new entrance in to the house via the broken window to the outside world. He locked the front door and trudged upstairs

THE WILDE DIARIES

to bed, trying not to think of what had just happened. He cursed his luck. Just as the band looked like it was going somewhere, finally about to break through the glass ceiling that had held them for so long, he had a fight with the bassist. The one real ally he had in the band. Whenever divisions appeared in the band, he and Derek always had each other's backs. Now they were fighting.

There was always something holding him back.

Before they didn't have the songs. Or the drummer was no good. Or their look was wrong. Or one of the million other reasons a band doesn't 'make it'. Finally now it had all come together, writer's fucking block aside, and he'd had a punch up and bloodied the nose of a bandmate.

He tramped along the corridor to his bedroom, the one open door at the end of the hall, thinking of the other bands he'd known that had all of the right ingredients to hit superstardom, but never quite got there. He tried, as he always did when he felt sorry for himself, to work out what those bands lacked that the Rolling Stones and Elton Johns had. As usual, he couldn't. Not that he had anything against the Stones, or Elton for that matter: he loved them, but the bands he knew who deserved their seat at the top table (including his own) were no worse than those guys. Even when it came to levels of musicianship, which was saying something.

He closed the door to his room, 'Ah, fuck it,' and slumped onto the bed.

MARC W SHAKO

Maybe he just needed to sleep. Maybe all this would look better in the morning. Probably not, but maybe. Yes, sleep would help. Sleep always helped. Tomorrow everything would be fine.

***

The streets in town were empty. The glorious weather had him expecting the opposite. The high noon sun shone down with the kind of heat you'd expect in July, but when he slipped off his jacket the gentle breeze swayed the fine hair on his forearms, the same way it would a field of wheat. The empty streets reminded him of the siestas they had in Pamplona. But despite what the weather would have him believe; this wasn't Spain. This was England. He looked up at the red, white and blue bunting that crisscrossed the street as it fluttered in the gentle wind as if to confirm.

Then he heard a sound. Distant, but there all the same, upon that gentle wind rode the lightly plucked notes from an acoustic guitar. Too faint to recognise a tune, but unmistakable. He tried to get his bearings, there was not a soul in the high street, unless they were hiding behind the war memorial, so the mesmerising sound must be coming from one of the side streets. He walked along, head cocked, trying to locate the source of the wonderful playing. He passed the café, and the ladies fashion shop (both of which were closed), and the sound of music rose. Oh so slightly, but now he could make out a melody. An unusual, haunting melody. Unusual

THE WILDE DIARIES

not because the melody was so beautiful, which it undoubtedly was, but unusual to Lucas because for all of his years of studying music as a scholar, and listening as an admirer, he'd never heard this particular arrangement of notes before.

He turned and faced the deserted road that sloped away, The Ship Inn at the bottom, and the music rose again. He walked faster now, eager to meet the one who was playing such a tune with such grace and dexterity. As he reached the bottom of the block, those colourful bunting triangles fluttering overhead, the source of the sound seemed to move, and he felt like he was chasing a rainbow. He quickly turned right, into the next empty street, following the music all the while. The music was coming from around the next corner. From the high street. He stopped. It couldn't be. The street had been empty just moments before, and yet, as the light wind drifted down, it undoubtedly carried with it the most beautiful music he'd ever heard. He turned the corner and stopped again. At the top of that incline, in the gap between the buildings, he could see the war memorial. And around it a crowd of people, all facing away, blocking the view of whoever it was playing this delightful tune. As he raced along the street, he couldn't escape the feeling that when he got to the top of the hill, the music would stop. The music would dissolve into the breeze and when the crowds parted, there would be an empty space. Nobody playing at all.

But the music did not stop. It still played as he reached

the crowd. He muscled his way through to see who was playing. As Lucas reached the front, in the shade of the war memorial sat a man, a little older than himself. Despite the heat, he wore a long black coat, like a gunslinger from the Old West. Only the lower half of the man's face could be seen, smooth skin on a slender jaw that came to a pointed chin, his eyes obscured by the wide brim of his fedora hat. His thin fingers moved lightly on the fretboard as the notes floated towards Lucas, the clarity of sound and hypnotic melody drawing him in closer. The crowd was now behind him and they were stony silent, as captivated by this man's playing as he was.

And when the busker started to sing, the voice was timeless. Neither the voice of a young man, nor an old man; not in fact sounding like a man at all. The voice was that of some ethereal being, never confined by the physical form. Lucas felt the hairs on the back of his neck rise to meet the sun, the same way flowers reach to touch their faces with its warmth.

The busker looked up and his eyes instantly warmed in recognition as they fell upon Lucas. A smile formed as he sang and Lucas couldn't help but smile himself, the words a poem not unlike one of his own compositions. For that moment, time around him stopped. There was nobody else there but him and the busker, because *they themselves* weren't there, and for the first time since that perfect moment at the concert, he felt a sense of belonging that moved him to the

THE WILDE DIARIES

verge of tears.

In the blink of an eye it was over. The song ended but Lucas could remember all of it. Every word. Every chord change. Each perfect melody. Lucas clapped enthusiastically but was stunned to realise he was clapping alone. He turned and saw the backs of the crowd again, as they silently dispersed back to their humdrum existence. Lucas clapped still and approached the busker.

'You get used to that,' said the busker, his voice sounding exactly the way it had when he sang. His accent was faintly American, but not strong. No harsh New York tones or Scandinavian Minnesota twang.

Lucas turned again and saw the people disappearing into shops and down side streets. He shook his head, 'They don't know anything.'

'Sometimes,' the busker started, his voice sounding a little older, 'I wonder what it is, makes one man famous and another not.'

Lucas felt a warmth in his heart. He'd met a kindred spirit, and felt again that connection, like home. 'I ask myself the same question. All the time.'

'That so?' The busker was surprised.

'I write myself.'

'I know you do, sir.' He smiled a perfect set of teeth, 'Lucas, right?'

Lucas nodded. 'That's me.'

The busker looked serious. 'You've "made it", haven't

you? People know you.'

'Some people. We're not household names just yet. Feels like there's some kind of...'

'Glass ceiling.'

Lucas nodded. 'Exactly.'

The busker took a step closer and Lucas realised he couldn't remember the man standing at all.

'Actually, Lucas, that's why I'm here.'

The busker was tall. Taller than Lucas realised. He now loomed over him, and Lucas felt that feeling of home dissipate. 'I can help you Lucas, if you want me to.'

'Help me?'

He nodded. 'That song I just played. You heard it before?'

He shook his head. 'No. Never.'

Lucas was gripped by recognition. He knew this man, as surely as the man knew him. They had met before. It was he who had contacted him through the Ouija board. He couldn't say *how* he knew, but the same way he knew the sound of a chord before he strummed it, the knowledge was there.

'And you've heard all kindsa songs, right?'

He was right. 'Yes. I think so.'

He thought back to the song and he could still recall every bit of it. The melodies, the changes. He was struck by how much it sounded like one of his own. Now the meeting lost its sense of coincidence, and as happens so often in dreams, a feeling of fate took its place.

The busker smiled, as if he felt the same, though he

seemed to be enjoying the experience much more than Lucas ever would.

'That song sounds like something you'd write, don't you think?'

'Yeah. Very much so.'

Lucas now got the feeling he wasn't talking to a busker. More like a salesman. A snake-oil salesman who'd wormed his way past the front door and would be difficult to remove, like a wine stain.

The busker smiled that perfect set of teeth, 'You want it?'

'The song?'

'Take it. It's yours.'

Lucas suddenly felt uncomfortable. He got the feeling he was in a room he shouldn't be, rifling through drawers of private possessions. But the song... It was so beautiful.

'I couldn't...'

'You don't like it? The busker asked, his cheeks reddening.

'No, no. Don't get me wrong. It's an incredible song.'

The busker locked eyes with Lucas, 'The kind of song you've been struggling to finish.'

'Well, yes.'

His eyes softened, 'The kind of song that would break the glass ceiling?'

'Yes.'

Until they were no longer the busker's eyes, but his own, 'The kind of song that people will listen to in years to come?'

'Yes.'

'So take it.'

The busker again stepped forward, hand held out, awaiting a handshake, his eyes once again a mirror reflection of his own. Lucas never broke the busker's gaze, but felt his hand reaching out, despite his whole body pleading with him not to do it. He felt the same electricity that he had during the séance, only now it was concentrated within that shrinking space between their hands.

'Lucas!'

Before their hands made contact, a female voice snapped him from his trance. He recognised it at once. His eyes were drawn above, to the tall column stretching out from the war memorial.

'Mandy? What are you doing here?'

Mandy smiled. Wearing the same flowing summer dress she had when they'd first met, it swayed in the breeze. Mandy wobbled. Lucas looked at her feet. She balanced with one bare foot on top of the memorial, she stared down, her eyes never leaving his.

'I love you, Lucas.'

For a moment, balance left her and she shot out an arm instinctively, redressing the equilibrium and stabilising herself. Then Lucas saw the rope. Thick, rough rope - coiled around her fragile neck.

'Come down Mandy. Please.'

She didn't speak, just smiled. Her eyes wild with

THE WILDE DIARIES

madness. Again, her balance failed, just for a second, and again she was able to recover.

Lucas looked down to the busker. He was gone. Lucas looked around, but he was alone, the streets completely empty. He turned back, to see Mandy still smiling. But the smile wasn't natural. Her eyes told a different story. She was afraid. A tear was building in the corner of her eye. Swelling inexorably, until it fell. As it did, so did Mandy.

All the way down she never took her eyes off Lucas. Lucas ran towards the memorial, arms outstretched, trying to catch her. Small pebbles scraped the asphalt beneath his feet as he scrambled ever nearer. Then he was below her. He reached up, and swung his arms to catch her feet, but the rope jerked taught. Lucas heard a sickening snap. Her head at an impossible angle, she looked at him, eyes wide, a thick gurgling coming from her throat. But Lucas could make out no words. Her eyes grew wider as her face reddened, and her lips slowly turned blue. He couldn't take his eyes off her, holding her stare as her eyes bulged.

'Lucas?' A heavy hand fell upon his shoulder.

INTERLUDE

11th October 2015

I closed the first of Lucas Wilde's diaries and sat back on the lumpy bed in my room at The Ship. Daylight had faded outside and below me in the pub were faint sounds of life. The idle smatterings of conversation and brief bursts of laughter. I tried to absorb what I'd read about the man Seth had drawn in his sketch appearing in one of Lucas Wilde's dreams, but the faint noise below and my rumbling stomach were having none of it. I checked my watch and realised it had been hours since my café breakfast. In the reception area I'd spotted a sign for the restaurant. I wanted to carry on reading, but I knew once I started, stopping would be nigh on impossible. Taking the next diary with me was an option, but the idea of reading them in public was unthinkable. They were a secret. For my eyes only.

Just as I closed the first of Lucas Wilde's diaries, a slip of paper revealed itself in familiar handwriting. So focused and drawn into the world of Lucas Wilde was I, it had momentarily slipped my mind why I was here. Why I was doing this. My friend had taken his own life, something I would never have imagined saying about Seth. But when I read what he'd written, I got an insight into his mind in those final weeks of life. Even if he didn't look sane and balanced when I saw him, the notes scribbled on that slip of paper confirmed that his mind had been on the slide for some time.

Who is Busker?

Is there connection between Busker and symbolism (666/all-seeing eye/black and white chequer etc.)?

Point of symbolism?

Symbolism hints at secrecy. Silence. How is this maintained? Blackmail? Why?

Is there connection between him and ritual sacrifice/leaps in popularity?

Was Mandy a sacrifice?

Were these things that my friend truly believed? I was weighted with a sadness for my friend, that he'd even entertained such possibilities. The next diary could wait. I changed clothes and went downstairs to eat.

***

The dining room was devoid of customers, though the sounds I'd heard from upstairs drifted in to kill the silence. It was just me and the bored waitress who looked delighted to see me

THE WILDE DIARIES

and the break from monotony I represented. The room was dimly lit and reminded me a little of Seth's house. *It's your house now, remember?* In amongst the fishing nets and paintings of galleons I immediately spotted something out of place and the sounds from the barroom faded. A photo of a young man with a tired looking Lucas Wilde. The young fan was the landlord John, a little wider around the middle and thinner on top now, but it was undoubtedly a young version of him.

'Fan, are you?'

I jumped and turned to see the waitress beside me. She nodded towards the photo.

'Soothsayer.'

'Yes. Yes, I'm a fan.'

The waitress was a little older than me, but probably too young to have been around when Lucas was.

'Taken a few weeks before he died, that was.'

I turned back to the picture. Lucas Wilde was tired, drawn, ragged.

Like Seth.

I shuddered and turned back to the waitress, silently waiting for her to tell me what I wanted before I remember that this was the wrong eatery.

'Sorry,' I said absent-mindedly, 'I'll have the steak pie.'

'Chips?'

I nodded, not really caring.

As I awaited my food, all I could think about was diving back into the diaries. I now knew who the mysterious busker was, but I wanted to know more. Lucas Wilde was dead. He died in September of 1977, just weeks after the diaries were written. How much of his death was to do with this busker?

I glanced again at the photo of Lucas with the landlord. I couldn't put my finger on it, but there was something wrong with the way Lucas looked, aside from his exhausted appearance. Then I was struck. The eyes. The face was undoubtedly that of Lucas Wilde, but the eyes... Empty, haunted, ringed with dark circles of tiredness. The eyes were Seth's.

'One steak pie.'

The waitress had again appeared from nowhere, jolting me out of my thoughts. I nodded thanks and ate. Throughout the meal, I kept my eyes forward, avoiding the haunting image of Lucas to my right. A reminder of Seth was sure to ruin what little appetite I had.

Seth. A sob started to thicken my throat and it took a deep breath and every ounce of self-control to subdue it.

Get yourself together. Seth wants you to solve this thing. There will be a time for grief later. You are here because Seth wants answers. Find them.

Although Seth wasn't the only thing on my mind. I kept asking myself if the photo I was avoiding was taken after Lucas had dreamed of the strange busker. And if he'd dreamed of him, then had Seth too? There was a connection between the mysterious songwriter and the death of my friend, surely: I could think of no other reason Seth would

THE WILDE DIARIES

make a sketch - why he would want me to have the information.

My racing mind took me to the story of the Ouija board. It sounded far-fetched, even to a horror writer, but despite my healthy scepticism, I've admitted on more than one occasion in the past that I'd be reluctant to use a Ouija board myself. It would be easy for a believer to say the board had an effect on Lucas; a sceptic would posit it was just his frustrations coming to the surface after weeks of trying to deal with (and hide) writer's block. Either would explain his treatment of Mandy, and Malcolm and Sally.

Glancing at my watch, I realised that if I went upstairs and read on, it would be morning by the time I finished the next of the diaries, and I needed sleep. But the diaries didn't want me to sleep. They wanted me to know something. So I went upstairs. And I read.

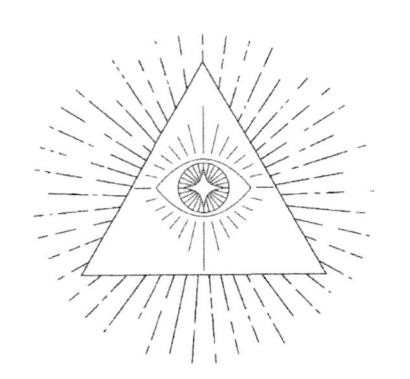

LUCAS WILDE'S DIARY #2

2ⁿᵈ September 1977

Lucas bolted upright in bed. His clothes soaked with sweat, warm sun pouring through his curtains. Gasping, he sat, disturbed by his dream, but unable to remember what it was that had left him so shaken. A noise here in the real world had dragged him from his sleep. The wooliness of his hangover blocked any memory of his dream, but the horror of it lingered, momentarily turning his blood to ice. He swung his legs out of bed, and just before they hit the floor, there was a noise from downstairs. The harsh ring of the telephone.

'Who the fuck is that at this fucking time? Fuck off!'

He raised himself and tottered out into the hallway, moving slowly towards the shrill tones peeling at the bottom of the stairs, all the while hoping it would stop. But it didn't, until he answered.

'Hello?'

A trembling voice spoke. 'Is Mandy there?'

'Derek?'

Shit. It all came flooding back. The fight. But that was between them. Nothing to do with Mandy. He'd never heard Derek talk like this. The calm cool Derek was gone, but it wasn't anger or hatred causing the tremor in his voice. It was fear.

'I woke up at three and she was gone. I've been looking all night. I can't find her.'

'Mate, slow down.' It was far too early for this shit. 'Where are you now?'

'We're in town. At The Ship.'

We? Malcolm and Sally. They'd all left together.

'The Ship?'

They were supposed to be staying at the house. Plenty of room. The argument. It was too far for them to drive back home, even though that was what they were probably planning to do. They went through town and saw lights on in The Ship. John liked to have lock-ins, he'd already been to one himself. They stopped by and John had put them up. Like *he* was supposed to do.

'Lucas. Mandy is missing.'

'I'll meet you in town. Are, er...' this was getting more awkward by the second, 'Sally and Malcolm still there?'

'They've gone back home, see if she somehow got a lift back.'

Thank fuck for that.

'Okay. I'll see you at the café in fifteen minutes.'

***

THE WILDE DIARIES

When Lucas pulled into the high street, Derek was standing outside the café. Lucas waved. Derek did not. Lucas wasn't surprised. Before he'd left the house he'd inspected the damage done to the reception room. A mess of sticky drinks and hardened candle wax, the smell a mixture of the country outside blowing in through the broken window and stale beer. That same feeling of humiliation washed over him afresh as Lucas saw the redness at the bridge of Derek's nose where his own elbow had made contact, and gentle blueing where the eyes were starting to bruise. His neck prickled.

'Shit.'

He pulled into the car park opposite the café, surprised at how few cars there were (as Saturday night was for drinking, he'd never been into town on Sunday morning). He looked up at the top of the war memorial. It made him shiver, though why, he knew not. The warmth of the sun struck him as he opened the door, a thin layer of beer sweat forming instantly on his skin. Derek crossed the road to meet him.

'Have you heard anything?' he said.

Lucas shook his head. He wondered why Derek thought he might have, but this probably wasn't the time to ask. 'What's going on?'

Instead of looking Lucas in the eye he surveyed the deserted street as he spoke. 'We left your place. Mal drove, even though he was pissed up. He was shaking as well, after...'

After I beat the shit out of him.

'Anyway, he said he didn't fancy driving all the way, and

MARC W SHAKO

I was too drunk to do it. And as we passed the street, I saw the lights on in The Ship. So we stayed there. We had a few more drinks with John. The landlord. Then we went to bed. About two o'clock it was.

'I fell asleep straight away, you know me, but then about three, I woke up. And she was gone. I thought she'd gone for a piss, but the light in the bathroom was off, and she always turns it on, even though she's sitting down. So I shouted: no reply. And I knew. I just knew that something was wrong.'

His eyes glistened in the sun and he drew a deep haltering breath. Lucas didn't speak, he knew there was more coming.

'I went to Mal and Sally's room, and I don't know why, but a horrible thought popped into my head.'

Lucas knew exactly what it was. Malcolm and Sally were very open, sexually. It didn't take a rocket scientist to see what was coming next if you put together Derek's jealousy with Malcolm's constant little remarks to Mandy, who knows, in the same situation, maybe even he would have come to a similar conclusion.

Derek continued, 'I felt sick. And angry. I started beating on the door. And after a minute Sally popped her head around the door. I burst in, but she wasn't there. Malcolm asked what was going on. I told him Mandy was missing, and they knew something was wrong.'

Lucas felt his eyebrows draw together, 'How did they know?'

THE WILDE DIARIES

Derek swallowed hard, fighting tears. 'They saw how upset she was. I tried to tell her that it wasn't you. That it was the drink...'

Jesus, she was young, but if she'd never seen a fight before, that was a sheltered upbringing.

'I'm sorry, mate. About the fight.'

Derek turned to him, eyes lost. 'It wasn't the fight.' His head jerked back in surprise. 'You can't remember, can you?'

'Remember? Yeah I remember. Listen, I was out of order, I accept that, but the truth was, what I told Malcolm I told him in confidence. And he—'

'Malcolm? I'm not on about Malcolm.'

What the fuck was this madness? A blackout? Now all kinds of thoughts and images were swirling around his mind. He'd got blind drunk in the past and done stupid things, usually involving climbing things, nudity, or sometimes both. Last night was the first time he'd lost control and raised his hands in anger, but considering the way Malcolm had betrayed his trust, he felt it was justified. When he was whiskey drunk, he'd do stupid stuff and forget, only to be reminded the next afternoon. The thing was, last night, he was only drinking beer. He'd remembered everything. Hadn't he?

'Wait a minute, are you saying that it wasn't the fight? It must have been. I wasn't *that* drunk. I remember everything.'

Derek shook his head. 'That's the thing. I don't think it was the drink. I think it was the Ouija board.'

Shit. He'd completely forgotten about that. That had just

been a laugh though...

'In the middle of the fight, just after you'd elbowed me, you screamed and ran over to the curtains.'

So far so good. One of the candles had turned over and set a curtain alight. Thank God Mandy had noticed it when she did, or the night could have been much worse.

'You pulled them, the whole rail came down. And then you smashed the rail through the window.'

'Yeah, I remember that. The curtains had caught fire.'

Derek shook his head, 'No. They hadn't.'

'What?'

His stomach lurched and for the tiniest fraction of a second all the strength went from his knees.

'You thought they had, but they were fine.'

'Bollocks... Fuck off...' He smiled at Derek, his young friend taking advantage of his drunkenness to poke fun at him.

But Derek's face was stony. Derek Boyd had many skills. Keeping a straight face while lying was not one of them. Lucas went cold.

'We can go back to my house now, the window's smashed, and the smell...'

He thought back. The room was smashed up, there had been a fight. The window was broken, the glasses overturned with sticky puddles of drink drying beside them. The fallen candles too had pools beside them. Hardened wax. He could smell the booze. But the curtains... He didn't even bother to

THE WILDE DIARIES

look out of the window, he'd been in such a hurry to get out of there.

'That wasn't the worst part.' Derek's face was paler, his eyes animated, like he was reliving the experience, still unable to fathom what he'd seen. 'It was when you turned around. I didn't recognise you.'

Lucas felt the skin on his testicles shrivel. His stomach writhed with sickness. Maybe it was just the breeze against his sweat, but the air felt a few degrees colder.

'I knew it was you, but you looked different. Scary. So *angry*. We were all just staring at you, because of the business with the curtains, but when you turned your eyes were fixed on Mandy. And she was crying, because of everything that had been going on, you know. Then you spoke... only...'

Lucas was growing frustrated, being told of things he couldn't recall. 'What, man? Out with it.'

Derek's eyes were filling with tears. 'It wasn't you.'

Lucas swallowed hard. He was trying desperately to hide it, but he'd never been this scared in his whole life.

'Mate what the fuck are you on about?'

'You *growled*. I heard it. Mal and Sally said I'd imagined it, but I heard you. And so did Mandy. You were staring at her and this voice came out.'

The world fell away from beneath his feet, and it suddenly felt like he was experiencing this conversation from outside his body.

'What did I say?' his own voice distant as he stared at the

cracks in the pavement, trying to draw them into focus.

'You stared at her and this growl comes out. You said: "What the fuck are you staring at, you silly little cunt". But it was the *way* you said it. Fucking venomous.'

Lucas wanted to correct Derek. Surely there was some mistake. He looked up to question him, but Derek was just staring. Whatever he was saying, he believed it.

'Jesus, Des, I'm so sorry. So *embarrassed*.'

Derek shook his head, 'Mal and Sally said it was out of character, but they were nowhere near as spooked as me and Mandy. The thing is, I know it wasn't you, mate. I tried to explain to Mandy. She was so shocked. So disturbed. She thought you liked her.'

'I do!'

'She was devastated. She really looked up to you. She hardly spoke for the rest of the night. Then, like I said, I woke up and she was gone. And I knew something was wrong. So did Mal and Sally.'

'Where are they now?'

'One of the few things Mandy did say, all she said, was that she wanted to go home. They thought she might have set off walking, or hitch-hiked. So they went back. I still haven't heard off them. I don't know what to do, Luke.'

The tears finally came. Derek was a slight figure who tried to make up for his fragile figure with bravado and strong language. At twenty-two, he was still so young, and Lucas would always think of him as a kid brother. Lucas put an arm

THE WILDE DIARIES

around him and Derek hugged him.

'Don't worry mate. We'll find her.' Lucas said.

He just hoped he'd done a better job of convincing Derek than he had himself.

***

Lucas and Derek went their separate ways, Derek promising to call him as soon as he heard anything. Lucas drove back to the house, trying to piece together everything he could recall from the night previous. Embarrassment ate away at him in huge bites. And he felt sorry for Mandy. She was a good soul. He just hoped that when she did turn up, that Derek would be able to sort things out. An apology from Lucas Wilde would help that.

The drive out had helped him. Getting away from the house for a bit so he could clear his head. The mess from the night previous would be waiting for him when he got back but clearing that up first point of business meant he could pretend it never happened. Of course for that to happen he'd need a glazier from the Yellow Pages.

He pulled into the drive planning the clean-up operation and was met by an unwelcome sight.

'The fucking nerve.'

Standing on the bottom step of the house large as life was Malcolm. That sorry-for-himself victim look plastered all over his marked face. Maybe Jack Mayberry was right. Maybe this guy was a leech. Band manager Johnny stood up from the step when he saw Lucas.

'What's this? Safety in fucking numbers?' Lucas muttered to himself as he pulled up beside Johnny's car. He got out and slammed his door shut. 'What the fuck do you want?'

'I came to see if you'd calmed down,' Malcolm replied. His tone was normal. They'd had enough run-ins in the past for Mal to know that it would all blow over, given enough time. Only this was different. It was drunken nonsense they'd fallen out over before. Mal had never betrayed Lucas like this in the past. 'I got bored waiting. We nearly climbed through the window.' He smiled.

'I thought you were looking for Mandy?' Lucas answered shortly, ignoring Mal's defusing attempt at humour.

Johnny stepped forward, 'Sally took Dizzy back home and they're going to look for her. She'll turn up. Daft kid.'

'So you haven't calmed down?' Mal asked, his tone snappy liked he'd been wronged.

Lucas leapt forward and grabbed Mal by the shirt, shoving him against the wall.

'Jesus, Luke!' Johnny shouted.

He stepped towards them before Lucas shouted. 'Fucking stay out of this, John. Mal knows what he's done.'

Malcolm's face contorted, 'I haven't done anything for fuck's sake!'

'Don't fucking think you can worm your way out of this. I told you that in confidence you twat.'

His teeth were grinding and his whole body tense, he'd

THE WILDE DIARIES

lifted Malcolm off his feet.

'I fucking told you that wasn't me,' Mal yelled back.

He slapped his hands against Lucas' grip. Lucas stepped back and a tiny bell rang in the back of his mind. Something about the statement rang true. He couldn't say for sure what it was. Perhaps something in a dream. The red mist fell obfuscating the idea.

'You owe me a fucking apology.'

Mal's eyebrows rose and his face dropped in near-cartoonish surprise. 'I owe *you* an apology?! After that fucking show you put on last night?'

'Alright, Mal,' Johnny said in a that's-enough tone.

'No, John. He needs to hear this.'

Lucas quickly stepped forward, his nose almost touching Malcolm's. The colour and bravado fell from his bruised face. 'I don't need anything from you. Get the fuck off my driveway.' His eyes burned into Malcolm's and that's where he kept them as he said, 'Both of you.'

Mal gathered himself quickly. 'Don't worry. I'm going.'

Lucas stepped back and watched as Johnny and Mal got into Johnny's car.

He was already inside the house before they'd left the driveway. The moment the front door closed, the phone rang, shrill and sudden causing him to jump. Before he picked up he knew it was going to be Derek. For an awful moment he thought Derek was going to say that they'd found Mandy dead.

'Hello?'

'Hi, it's Des.'

The tone wasn't hysterical. In fact, it was oddly calm.

'Just calling with an update mate. She isn't at home and hasn't been back. Her mum's called the police, so they'll probably be round at some point. Just thought I'd let you know. You know...'

So he could tidy up. And hide the drugs.

'Okay mate. Thanks for calling.'

'All right.' Des sounded lost himself.

'Des?'

'Yes mate?'

'She'll turn up.'

'Yes mate.'

He hung up. Lucas said she'd turn up, but it felt empty. Wrong. He had felt that everything would be okay, but now the hangover was wearing off, he wasn't so sure.

When he saw the state of the room from the night before, the notion of Mandy turning up safe and well vanished completely. Glasses scattered. Sticky drink stains on the floor. And of course the smashed window. Lucas pulled the torn net curtain aside, leaned against the frame of the broken window and stared out at the curtains. There they were, clinging to the rail amongst shards of jagged glass as pristine as the day they were bought. No scorch marks. No blackened edges. But looking at them conjured up that smell of burning just the same.

THE WILDE DIARIES

***

The glaziers were already on their way. A twenty-four seven service whose usual waiting time shortened to as soon as possible when it turned out the guy he'd spoken to was a Soothsayer fan. The perks of fame. He turned back into the room and spied the Ouija board. It stared back from its place in the centre of the floor, challenging him; seemingly imbued with the same energy as the night before. Not an inanimate thing, but as alive as he was. 'More alive than Mandy,' he muttered. He froze. Where the fuck had that come from? Premonitions were never a skill he'd possessed before, and he'd never held any belief in the paranormal, something that had made whatever had happened the night before all the more scary.

Lucas started to clean the mess in the room, tidying the glasses and ferrying them into the kitchen, swapping them for a cloth to wipe up the booze that had formed in sticky patches on the floor. As he went back down the corridor he was struck by the feeling that something was wrong. Something had changed. When he went back into the room, he expected the glasses would be back where he'd picked them up from. Or the pictures on the walls would all be on the floor. Or the few bits of furniture that were in there would be strewn across the floor, smashed to matchwood. He paused outside the door.

It was closed.

Just a breeze. A breeze that came in from the window you smashed. Get a grip of yourself, for fuck's sake.

MARC W SHAKO

He grabbed the handle and pushed the door open. He was almost disappointed to see everything as he'd left it – the Ouija board staring back at him defiantly from the centre of the room. If the pictures were all on the floor, or the small table smashed to pieces, it would at least go some way to explaining the unsettling things Des had talked about. As it was, it could only be put down to his own mental instability. Perfect, with the band meeting in a few days and him having to turn up with a handful of half-baked song ideas.

He quickly tidied the room but left the Ouija board exactly where he'd found it. If he didn't have to touch that thing, he wouldn't. He locked the room off, it would be fine as it was until the glazers got there. Now all he wanted to do was what he always wanted to do when he felt like this – play the guitar.

Recently, he hadn't been able to do anything, because the source of his misery and the remedy were one and the same. He shuffled across the hallway into the reception room, normally a brighter, airier room, if not for the setting sun. The first thing he lay his eyes on when entering was the reel to reel tape player atop the chest of drawers, the one he used to record any song ideas, though he supposed he wouldn't be needing that tonight. He flicked the dim lights on and picked up the battered acoustic, noting how dead it felt compared to the electricity he'd felt from the Ouija board the night previous.

It hadn't always been that way: until quite recently it held

THE WILDE DIARIES

that same liveliness that the Ouija board had, feeling alive in his hands. Exactly when the magic had gone he couldn't pin down, and maybe it was all in his mind, but it felt before like something was going to happen, the same way your hair stands on end before a storm. Back then, the guitar was his refuge. Whatever shit the world threw at him, he didn't care. That was the thing with music; when people went to the record shop, that's what they were buying. It wasn't the songs themselves, but what they represented. The only way to travel through time, transported to when the mood was carefree, the girl loved you (and you loved her), and friendships would always be that strong. That's what he felt in the studio before a take. It was that same chemistry they produced on stage that Mick McKenzie set out to capture in the studio - bottling lightning as he called it. It's what John Lennon felt before recording *Imagine*, or Bowie with *Life on Mars*, or the Stones with *Gimme Shelter*. *That's* what people were buying. Bottled lightning. But there hadn't been any lightning for a couple of months. Christ, there was nary a cloud in the sky.

Then something happened.

A melody. Gentle. Haunting.

He played on, not wanting to stop to record it, lest it vanished. The chords seemed to flow naturally, as if he weren't thinking of them, but they were somehow coming through him, from God alone knew where. *God, or...?* A nebulous melody formed in his head, gathering together the way the sun must have done billions of years ago, drawing together tighter, more compact, ready to burst into life.

Then, as quickly as it had come, it vanished.

He started over, repeating that same progression of chords, and at first it worked. It worked and sounded beautiful and melodious and haunting, until he approached the same point, and like a cloud in the form of a teapot or elephant that disappeared when you took your eyes off it, it was gone.

He cursed loudly wondering where this song had come from in the first place, then it hit him. All at once, everything came back. The dream, the empty street, the busker. And the song. The busker said he was the spirit who contacted him through...

Ice slid through his veins and Lucas jumped to his feet and propped the guitar in the corner. He bolted across the hallway and unlocked the door, desperately seeking the key to overcoming his writer's block - the Ouija board. He grabbed the planchette from the side of the room where it had ended up last night. Sitting on the floor cross-legged, he placed the planchette in the centre of the board. The wood felt like just that in his hands – wood. No electricity. No anticipation.

You're worrying too much. Over thinking. Focus.

He cleared his throat and addressed the empty room. 'Is there anybody there?'

He waited. In the hallway, the grandfather clock ticked a solemn beat, a metronome for a funeral march.

'Is there anyone there?' He said it louder this time. As if

THE WILDE DIARIES

the spirits were there, just hard of hearing. He couldn't give up, not now. The answer was too close. The solution to his creative constipation, months of worry and frustration, a lock to which the board, it seemed, was a key. But tonight there was no electricity, the same way there was none when he held his guitar. He turned off the electric lights and replaced their glow with candles, glancing at the ripped net curtain fluttering beside him in the night breeze.

'Is there anybody there?'

Now he wasn't asking, he was pleading. Like a man with a rope around his neck talking into a phone, waiting for the Samaritan on the other end to answer. Now he was relieved he wasn't waiting for the Samaritans; he would have kicked the bucket by now.

After a fruitless hour he was interrupted by the knock of the glaziers. They'd had time to pick up cameras on their way to his place and he smiled for photos and signed singles and albums. While they worked, he drank. Neat bourbon. Something to numb the weird he was feeling. Hoping that by the time the glaziers left, he'd be drunk enough to pass out.

But sleep was hard to come by. Since the window had been fixed, hours of tossing and turning followed, getting his legs tangled in the bedsheet, glancing at the green lights of the digital alarm. Thoughts rushing through his mind. Thoughts of Mandy. Thoughts of Derek, and Malcolm and Sally. Thoughts of the busker, and his dream. But mostly, the thoughts were of the song. That next missing chord change, the name of an old acquaintance that lingers on the tip of your tongue, but never stepping forward. The elusive melody that just escaped him and got further away the more he focused.

And when he did finally drift off, the sleep was shallow and haunted. Dark dreams, of shadows and secrets, all saturated in evil. A dream that he couldn't remember when he awoke, scary and threatening, but the moment he drifted back into that shallow slumber, it continued as if he'd never awoken. Until finally, the sleep wasn't haunted. Wasn't shallow. It was deep and pleasant.

That was when, for the second time, he met the busker.

***

Golden grass swayed in the field and although Lucas had never been in this field before, he knew exactly where it was. He would have known even if he wasn't staring at the gnarled, twisted tree that marked the halfway point between his house and the town – The Ship Inn to be exact. And even the reason he'd been drawn to this nondescript part of the area was clear. From the area of that twisted tree, some two hundred yards ahead, floated the gentle sound of an acoustic guitar. And he knew, as he drew closer, that it was a melody he would know. From the shade of the tree he saw a man's knee, and the head of a guitar.

He moved around in the shade of the tree slowly, not wanting to disturb the playing, not wanting to interrupt the

THE WILDE DIARIES

song. And as he heard the song now, with the smell of the blossom and the gentle, constant drone of bees searching therein, he knew he wasn't afraid to interrupt because it would stop him filling the gaps in his memory of the tune, because here in this place there were no gaps; he knew the song complete.

The Busker's smile beamed from below the brim of his hat. His playing was effortless. Masterful. With even the most complex sections tripping from his fingertips. Lucas was reminded of the line of a man playing so easily it was like ringing a bell. When the final chorus came around Lucas sang along, and the busker finally looked up and smiled.

The song finished and although it was the same length as before Lucas got the feeling that it had ended much too soon.

'I can't remember it,' Lucas said.

The busker smiled, 'You will.'

It was hard for Lucas not to sound like a man asking for lent money to be paid back, 'When?'

'When the time is right,' the busker replied, his voice perfectly relaxed. 'You really need to apologise.'

'Apologise? To who?'

'Who have you upset?'

Lucas squirmed. He wasn't one for apologising. He was used to receiving apologies.

'Come on, who?' The Busker cajoled.

'Derek. But I've already apologised to him.'

'Nobody else?'

'I told the manager to fuck off today. And Mal. But Mal...'

'What?' The busker was playing again, not looking at Lucas. 'What did Malcolm do?'

'He embarrassed me.'

The busker tut-tutted and shook his head. 'We both know that's not true.'

Lucas thought and his mind went back to the previous meeting with the busker. In town, at the war memorial. The warmth of the sun and the flapping bunting overhead. That was where he'd realised that the message on the Ouija board wasn't Malcolm betraying him. It was the busker trying to get his attention.

'There it is.' The busker smiled.

The busker looked up above Lucas's head and his own eyes followed naturally. Tied around the branch was a long green silk scarf. It flapped in the breeze like a slow motion replay of a wild fire hose. The more Lucas stared the more it seemed that video replay was in reverse. The scarf was Mandy's. Lucas stared at it, his heart filling with an overwhelming despondency.

'So sad,' the busker said.

Lucas nodded, his head cricked back at a strange angle. 'Can I ask you something?'

There was no reply.

He looked back down and saw the busker was gone – his guitar resting against the tree where he'd sat. Lucas ambled over and picked up the guitar, before sitting in the exact spot

THE WILDE DIARIES

from where the busker had vanished. The wind rustled the leaves of the tree and a kaleidoscope of sunlight shapes cast through to the ground around him. He gazed back up at the scarf, still winding its odd, hypnotic dance. Looking back at the guitar he placed his fingers on the fretboard forming the shape of the first chord of the new song and strummed.

'Lucas?'

The voice came from above. From the scarf. It was Mandy.

He looked up to see her feet twitching in mid-air. Her fingers clawing at the scarf as she pulled with both hands, scratching the skin on her throat.

'Lucas.'

Now the words restricted to a gag, her eyes bulging and bloodshot from her red face. Lucas froze, pressing back against the rough bark of the tree. She was wearing the same clothes from the party: that same pink sweater clinging tightly to her pert breasts. Lucas stared at the firm nipples poking through the thin material.

He felt a presence beside him, looming over him, angry. And from this direction he heard another voice, this one clear and angry. It too was Mandy.

'Lucas!'

MARC W SHAKO

3rd *September 1977*

He awoke with a start, again gasping for air, his throat sore as if he'd been choking – or more precisely, as if he'd been choked. For a second he sat rubbing at his throat, then he stopped.

The song. He remembered it. All of it. He bolted downstairs, not bothering to let daylight into that dark upstairs hallway. His guitar was waiting for him in the reception room. This time he paused to set the reel to reel onto record, before plonking himself on the stool, and now, like it had before so many times in the past, the guitar felt alive.

The tape reels span atop the machine at unerringly different speeds, the atmosphere now as it was before they'd held the séance. He strummed the first chord to check Old Faithful was in tune.

'Never in doubt.' He smiled to himself, before counting in.

This time, the song flowed from him as it had the Busker. In his mind he used a capital B when he spoke about the Busker. It felt wrong not to.

He forged ahead, playing with abandon, undeterred by the idea the next section of road around the bend could be missing. Each chord change was smooth, his voice never straining, even at the higher notes. It sounded as good now as when the Busker played it, that niggling doubt that the next line would be woolly nowhere in his mind. He was back.

THE WILDE DIARIES

Here comes the chorus. Got it?

Got it.

The chorus came flowing like a river, unstoppable, and exactly as haunting as when he'd heard it before. At that moment, the happy sunlight cascading through the windows vanished and a chill descended upon him. He played on but his focus was interrupted, his attention drawn to the door.

The outside world was closed from him, but as he stared at the door, a sound came from the other side. A faint scratching. Theoretically, he could stop playing now. Stop and investigate. He had the main part of the song down. There was a middle eight coming, but now he had the rest of the song, it would be straightforward to figure that out – there were only so many chord combinations that would go with what he already had.

But he didn't want to stop. He wanted that middle eight on tape. He wanted the whole song down, no matter how rough a version it was, no matter what could be heard in the background. If he got the whole thing on tape there would be something to work with. Capturing this song had already proven to be like hunting with a net to catch smoke. It had proved elusive enough over the past couple of days. This feeling had evaded him for weeks – maybe months.

Now the scratching was loud. While he'd been thinking about pausing, it had developed into a ragged scraping sound. The darkness that had fallen outside was not just a cloud eclipsing the sun, but it seemed a gathering storm: large drops of rain pelted the window.

The middle eight is here. What do we do?

Keep going for fuck's sake. Don't stop now, you'll lose it.

Time slowed as he strummed the last chord of the chorus and his fingers formed the first chord of the middle eight, and as they touched the fretboard the scraping sound coming from the door stopped. The door and window exploded inward.

Lucas screamed, leaping up to his feet. The storm had blown the window in, but it was what stood in the doorway that scared him.

The Busker.

From his dreams and into real life. His footsteps clumped from the wooden floor as he marched to the reel to reel, his gait stilted and unnatural. His long coat flapped in the wind and Lucas watched in slow motion as he dragged the tape player to the edge of the drawers before slamming it to the floor. The tape whirled and chewed and snarled and Lucas felt a heartache like the loss of a loved one.

Like Mandy?

'No!'

The Busker turned to him, eyes blazing. He strode over to Lucas in what felt like an impossibly short number of steps, grabbing him and lifting him with one arm.

'Wait,' Lucas choked. 'You said I could have it!'

'We didn't shake on it.'

The Busker turned and now Lucas was staring at the

THE WILDE DIARIES

ragged maw of the broken window at the other end of the room; glass shards protruding like rows of shark's teeth. The Busker hurled him towards it. The distance between him and the window was huge, but the moment the Busker let go, he knew he would reach. The Busker was strong, and he flew ever closer to that jagged glassy death, huge hailstones pouring in from outside forming a polka dot pattern beneath the window. His throat was on course for the biggest shard, he was dropping. Dropping, just at the worst angle, unable to reach out in time to save himself. The curtains fluttered and as he got closer he saw the weave pattern of the fabric. He was awaiting the feeling of warm liquid spilling down his neck and the coppery taste of death. His hands slapped against the cold stone of the wall either side of the window, his body dropping until he felt the sharp point pressing against the skin of his throat, ready to burst through...

He bolted upright in bed, soaked in sweat, awoken by the shrill ring of the telephone. His whole body felt cold and he reached up to his throat. His head was still in that cloudy place where cold fingers reached out to you; a nightmare reaching out from the realm of sleep and into the land of the woken. Another dream, and once again, one he couldn't remember. And though the bedroom looked exactly the same as it had in his dream, the feeling was different. There was no urge to rush downstairs. No urge to grab his guitar and start recording. It was all gone. Not even the ringing telephone could hurry him.

MARC W SHAKO

In the short space of time since the Ouija board and the fight, his writer's block and the circumstances had finally taken over his mood. It was strange to him that he hadn't noticed it before. There was no feeling at all now. Just a numbness. Without the ability to create, he was nothing. The parquet flooring was cold underfoot as he staggered into the hallway. From the top of the stairs he could see the phone, with its curly cord and rotary dial, sitting on top of the small corner table by the door. Ringing shrilly as if to hurry him. But he didn't hurry. Not many people had the number for this phone. Because the house was a purchase to take him away from outside distractions, the only ones who had the number were band people. The other thing stopping him answering the phone was the expectation of bad news. The dark dreams he'd been having were to do with her, he was sure.

There was something else too. A song. Yes. In the dreams. As he stumbled downstairs he couldn't be sure if the song was real, or just his subconscious fucking around with him. Either way, he didn't appreciate what was going on. The happiest day of his life was when he discovered that he was born to make music. When he performed the first song he'd ever written and his cousin Susie responded to it. More than that, she'd actually *cried*. And she wasn't the crying kind. Now that the powers he'd been given had gone, it was worse than the time before he wrote. Back then, he went through life with his eyes closed to the possibility. He had no idea of what he

THE WILDE DIARIES

was capable of. Now, there was a sense of loss. Fucking writer's block. Shit, if it came down to it he'd sell his grandmother to overcome it.

'That's not true,' he said aloud. Things had a way of becoming real if you wanted them hard enough. 'Not you, Gran, sorry.' He paused unsure he should verbalise the next thought, for the same reason he'd spoken out to protect his grandmother. Then he said it anyway.

'I'd sell my soul.'

The phone stopped ringing.

Lucas Wilde turned around and went back to bed.

5th September 1977

Two days passed before he got out of bed again. In that time he recalled that the song from the dreams was a real thing, and an original at that. He'd also remembered the strange man who performed it. The Busker. The Busker had told him that for ownership of the song to change hands, they needed to shake on it. He was hoping that the Busker would reappear in his dreams, so they could strike an official deal. That seemed important for some reason. But there were no dreams. No nightmares either. Nothing about Mandy.

The police came and went. He told them about the argument, not mentioning the Ouija board. He just wrote it off as drunken oversensitivity from all sides. There were many witnesses to Mandy leaving and him staying, and the police were fine with that. Since then he went back to bed, the only time he'd left was to go to the toilet, but from there he just ambled back into bed; climbed back between the sheets and slept, hoping to dream. The phone was ringing constantly. If he could motivate himself to get out of bed he'd do it only to unplug the wire. 'If' could sometimes be the biggest of words.

6th September 1977

He ventured downstairs to the kitchen on the third day. The phone rang as he walked past, like it was watching him. He told it to 'Fuck off' and carried on into the kitchen to make a sandwich. It stopped ringing and started again, he ignored it still, making tea. The tea was no good. White specks of fat floated around the top. He cursed and poured it away. The sandwich wasn't much better. Stale bread. Old Cheddar cheese. He ate it in the kitchen before heading back upstairs, using the silence of the telephone as a marker for when to exit the kitchen.

When his foot planted on the bottom step, the phone rang behind him. Now he stopped.

Maybe if I answer it, they'll leave me alone. Maybe it's nothing to do with Mandy. Or maybe she's been found. Just ran away like a silly child. It's probably just to confirm the band meeting next

THE WILDE DIARIES

Monday. I'll postpone. Buy myself another week. If I've still got nothing then, I'll throw the scraps that I do have to Mayberry. Let him figure something out, he's so fucking eager.

He turned and picked up the phone. He put the receiver to his ear without speaking.

'Hello?' a nervous voice crackled from the other end of the line. It was Malcolm. Probably calling to plead his innocence again about last week. Lucas said nothing.

'Lucas, it's Mal. Are you there?

He stood in silence, he wanted to say something, but he wasn't sure what.

'Lucas, I was hoping I could come round. We need to talk.'

It wasn't about Mandy. That was a relief. No, it was Malcolm wanting to talk about Malcolm. Perhaps Mayberry was right. Maybe Mal and Sally were on the take, riding his coattails to get whatever they could from him. The thought was an ugly one, and not something he could truly bring himself to believe.

Without a word he replaced the receiver, trailed upstairs and climbed back into bed.

7th September 1977

Hunger finally drove him out of bed. He drove into town and visited the little café where Carol the waitress had a knack for guessing your order before you could tell her. From his table in the window the red public phone box stared back at him all through his breakfast. He wasn't sure what had brought it on, perhaps the alcoholic's moment of clarity, but he felt he should call Johnny and apologise. Mal probably deserved a phone call too. He was still angry at him, but there was a nagging feeling that Mal was telling the truth. There was no betrayal. The wound was still raw though, having his weakness publicly exposed. But if there was no betrayal, didn't it mean accepting that there was someone reaching out to him through the Ouija board?

The waitress left one pound of his change in twenty pence pieces instead of a single coin. He snatched them up and crossed the road to the phone booth. He called Johnny first.

'Hello.'

'Lucas?'

Johnny sounded bright at the realisation it was Lucas. Ever the peacekeeper, Johnny would have been eager to put the latest kerfuffle behind them.

'Alright mate. I just wanted to apologise about the other day. You were just trying to make sure we didn't kill each other, as always. I shouldn't have spoken to you like that.'

'Oh, forget all that shite. But you should call Mal.'

Lucas said nothing. It came as no surprise that Johnny should still play peacemaker.

'He swears up and down that it wasn't him fucking

around... you there Luke?'

Lucas bowed his head and accepted that, at some point, it had to be done. 'Yeah. I'll call him.'

'Do it now.'

'All right. Cheers mate.'

The phone clicked and the line went dead. He grabbed another twenty pence piece to call Mal. As he dialled the number into the rotary, something stirred inside. With each number something was taking shape.

A melody.

A chord.

Lyrics.

The phone started ringing and suddenly it was there. The missing chord. The final piece of the puzzle. He had the whole song.

Malcolm answered, voice coloured by a hint of desperation. 'Hello? Hello?'

The voice shouted through the swinging receiver as the door to the phone box eased shut.

***

Lucas ignored the speed limits all the way home. He belted the song out at the top of his voice as he careened around corners. The house stood out on the horizon, and only now did he notice how it appeared imposing and ominous. Before, it impressed him; now it observed him. Scrutinised him, the way a snake sizes up potential prey. The car rumbled and shook, and Lucas whipped his head back to the road. He'd drifted off the smooth surface and two wheels now bounced along the grass verge. He yanked the wheel to get the car back on the road. Sweat formed across his entire body at once. He started the song again from the beginning, louder than before.

By the time he'd got to the middle eight he was pulling into the drive. He bolted from the car, not bothering to close the door or turn off the engine. From the road, the car wouldn't be seen and the house was too remote for a potential thief to just be passing by. In all honesty, he didn't care. To get this song down would pay for a thousand cars.

You're not singing, Luke.

He entered the shadow of the house and shuddered, before starting the song over again. As he bound into the house and the drawing room where the reel to reel and acoustic called home, he wasn't sure he could remember it all.

Go in. Hit record. Grab the guitar. And PLAY.

He stopped dead.

'Fuck!'

The reel to reel player. He was sure he'd left a tape in there, ready to record. It sat empty. He grabbed a new tape from the drawer, hands shaking as he loaded it into the player. The tape snagged and wouldn't feed through the mechanism. It twisted and curled like an earthworm.

'Come on, for fuck's sake!...'

Finally it was in place. He wound it forward to make sure it was in place.

THE WILDE DIARIES

'Yes!'

He wound it back to the start.

You're not singing...

He hit record and snatched up the acoustic. Before he was on the stool he was strumming the opening chord. The words were there in his head awaiting their cue.

The cue came and the words tumbled out, and Lucas smiled as he sang. But as the chorus approached, the smile faded.

What's the first line? Shit. Fucking think, you moron. Come on...

He strummed the first chord of the chorus but before he did, he knew it was wrong.

'Fuck!' He screamed.

He played the chords leading up to the chorus again, hoping to trigger something. Every chord he tried sounded wrong.

'For fuck's sake it *must* be one of you! How can you all be wrong?'

He stood quickly, slamming the guitar back into place in its stand. The tape was next for his wrath. It squealed as he grabbed it from the machine and tossed it across the room. The opposite side still dragging the snarled tape through the mechanism. This recording session was over.

***

It was dark by the time he remembered that the car was still running in the driveway. Clutching the half empty bottle of

Bell's whiskey, he staggered outside to turn the engine off and lock up. The night had a chill in the air, but he barely felt it, thanks to the booze. The thought of calling Malcolm and apologising for their altercation the other night couldn't have been further from his mind.

The night followed the same familiar pattern as every other that week so far.

He went into the room where the Ouija board sat, unmoved from the night of the séance (the glaziers, it seemed, had just worked around it), desperately tried to contact the strange Busker from his dreams, without success, and drank until he fell asleep. The sleep was never in the same room as the Ouija board. As soon as contact failed, he left the room and locked the door. The atmosphere in there was heavy. Despite the failed attempts at contact, the room always had a presence to it. The feeling you were being watched. He'd either go back to his guitar and play the old songs or stumble up to bed. Tonight he stumbled up to bed, one thought on his mind: how soon until I see the Busker?

He wouldn't have to wait long.

***

The loft was empty, apart from an old wooden school desk which sat in the middle. The attic space was split into two rooms, separated by a narrow hallway. The room he was in was the one on the left. It was odd because the last time he was in here there was a bed. And a window. Now there was

THE WILDE DIARIES

just a desk and no real light source, though the room was not dark. Footsteps echoed from behind him, the sound of a heavy-soled shoe clumping off wood floor. He didn't need to turn to see who it was.

'You know why we're here, Lucas?' That same old man's voice coming from a young man's mouth.

Lucas nodded.

'Good. Let's not waste any time then.'

He appeared at Lucas' side and slipped a piece of paper on the desk. The word 'Contract' at the top, a few paragraphs of text, and at the bottom of the page was a block of tiny writing. It reminded him of the recording contract he'd signed with Giddy-Up records.

Lucas looked up to see the Busker, and the light source, directly behind him, rendering him a large silhouette.

'What do I sign it with?'

The Busker pointed back to the desk and when Lucas looked back, there was a large white quill lying across the page. The weight of the quill surprised him, heavier even than the pen he'd used to sign the original Giddy-Up contract. He dipped it into the inkwell. Between the final paragraph and the block of small print he scrawled the first 'L' onto the page in crimson and stopped.

'Red ink?'

The Busker laughed. 'You do want the song?'

'I do.'

He nodded at the contract with his head, 'So sign.'

The contract, he thought, was just for the song. But it felt like so much more. Most contracts represented binding. This one, to Lucas at least, represented freedom. Freedom from the inability to finish a song. Freedom from the insomnia that came with it. Freedom from the heavy drinking he'd been using as a crutch. He also thought about the dreams he'd been having at the lavish parties with the people he admired - people who all knew who he was. This song would elevate him to their level. That's why this felt like so much more than gaining a song. This was a hatch in the glass ceiling.

Yes. That's all it is. Don't worry. Just sign.

Lucas scrawled the rest of his autograph. He stared at the page and felt a wave of nausea rise up from his stomach.

'Congratulations Lucas,' said the Busker, holding out a hand. There was a moment's hesitation, just as there was with signing. He paused, but now a voice spoke to him. It was his own voice.

You've already signed. You didn't read the small print. It's too late now. You might as well do it.

He reached out a hand, and as they made contact, he woke up.

8th September 1977

Burning sunshine woke Lucas abruptly. A strange feeling lingered from his dream, though, as usual, he couldn't recall

THE WILDE DIARIES

the details. Despite the glorious sunshine, Lucas felt sad, empty. Bereft. He couldn't shake the feeling of loss; nor could he place it. He sometimes had feelings of sadness before he came down with a cold, but this wasn't that. It was different, but if he was forced to say how, he'd struggle. He'd never really known anyone who'd passed so he couldn't equate it to that, but wondered if this feeling could be similar.

He sighed deeply and uncontrollably as he raised himself upright, surprised he couldn't feel the effects of the previous night's drinking. He didn't feel hungover, nor hungry, nor thirsty. He simply didn't feel.

It was when he was tottering downstairs, wondering what to do in place of breakfast when it hit him. Hard like a wave. He recognised it instantly as inspiration. It would only be when he reflected back later that he would realise that it wasn't accompanied with the usual excitement. There was no buzz. The feeling itself was detached: alone. In his recording room, he grabbed his acoustic. Now it vibrated. Clutching the neck he closed the door to the outside world and hit record on the reel to reel. The reels jumped into life and whirred gently as he crossed back to his playing position.

Did I put the tape in there?

He perched himself atop the stool, now taking his time to settle before he played. There was now no need for hurry or haste. It was as if he'd played the song a hundred times. It was his and he knew it was there waiting for him. He strummed the first chord and the guitar sang. Again, it would only be when he looked back that he realised he felt no urgency. No excitement. No joy. That gentle warmth of giddiness that came with these moments before was absent. But it had no negative effect on the playing. It was measured, precise, and powerful. Like the emotions were there but coming from another place.

Lucas launched into the vocal and it sounded rich and warm. Not like he'd just woken up. Like he was in the middle of a set; perfectly warmed up. The lyrics soared and flowed into the first chorus, the chord changes now coming easily. The second verse followed. Natural. Easy. The moment at the end of the second chorus where the middle eight neared, he didn't hesitate. Now he was imbued with a certainty that when he got there, the chords and lyrics would be waiting for him. Before he knew it, the final chorus was upon him. He had no recollection of playing the last verse. The chorus finished and he repeated it once, just because it felt right.

The final chord faded to silence and he stood. The reels on the tape were spinning, and on them was what Lucas felt was his best song yet. A real classic. Something that people would listen to in years, just like people still listened to The Beatles now. He'd give it the working title *Greater Than Me* from the refrain. He calmly walked over to the player and pressed the stop button.

Now in the silence of the room, the air felt different. Heavy.

It felt like a dream. There was a fear that the door would

THE WILDE DIARIES

come flying inward to reveal a man in a long black coat and wide brimmed hat. Before he had time to process this, he heard a faint sound. A gentle scratching. Like a small animal trying to get in from the hallway.

The phone burst into life. The ringing made him jump and he placed a hand on the door handle. In the heavy silence between the rings he listened. The scratching had stopped. He opened the door expecting to see the man from his dream, but the hallway was empty.

He stepped into the hallway and strode towards the phone. Now he was ready to talk. He was ready to listen to Mal. Maybe he wasn't full of shit after all. Perhaps it had been the Ouija board all along. Now he had a song to prove it. And if it wasn't Mal on the phone, he could happily tell Jack Mayberry or Johnny that they could have their band meeting. The third album was going to launch them through the glass ceiling and into the stratosphere. Into superstardom. This was it. The big time awaited. His writer's block was a thing of the past, and album number three was about to be born. He snatched up the receiver on the fifth ring.

'Hello,' he said. A statement, not a question. He was back.

A sniff came from the other end of the line, then silence.

'Hello? Jack? Hello? Is that you fucking around, Mal?'

When the reply came the voice was empty and robotic. 'Luke, it's Des.'

Lucas didn't hear whatever came next. He didn't need to, he just knew it. Whether this was the reason for the sadness he'd woken up with, or that was something else, he couldn't say for sure. But the reason Derek Boyd had called him this morning was to bear bad news. Mandy was dead.

GREATER THAN ME

12th October 2015

I closed the second diary and placed it beside me on the bed. My first thought was to go straight into diary #3, such was my desperation to know what happened to them, but more than that, I wanted to hear that song. *Greater Than Me*.

I couldn't think straight. Tired and itchy and irritable from the night before, I stepped into a hot shower. Clouds of steam rose and I tried to get the image of Mandy hanging from my mind. The picture so clear it was almost as if Lucas' dream had been my own. There was a photo of Lucas, Derek and Mandy stuck in the back of the diary. Mandy was wearing what she wore in Lucas' dream. Tight jeans that grew into impossibly large flares, and that pink sweater that left nothing to the imagination. In my mind's eye the image of her bulging eyes and hand reaching out for help played out over and over, her feet kicking out for a floor that wasn't there. In the photo Derek looked deliriously happy, a man fully aware that the fame that music had brought came with certain advantages;

here was a man batting far above his average. But Lucas looked like he belonged in a different picture entirely. His smile was empty. A mask. The eyes tired and lost. He had the look of a man close to the end of his rope.

I shuddered at the turn of phrase my mind reached for, turned off the water and as I dried, my mind wouldn't leave one thought, like a needle stuck in a broken record, and the thought was this: If Lucas Wilde had written two of the best albums I'd ever heard, exactly how good was the song the man himself dubbed the best he'd ever written?

Thoughts of people and diaries and friends and houses all evaporated.

I had to hear that song.

I crossed to the lumpy armchair and grabbed my laptop from my duffel bag. The song might be an old one, but that didn't mean a version of it couldn't have found its way onto the Internet. I sat on the bed, laptop before me, typing furiously. The Ship had Wi-Fi but the signal was weaker than the house wine I'd drunk with dinner.

It was no surprise that *Greater Than Me* had been recorded by a number of artists. Probably different songs completely, after all, music was littered with examples of different songs that shared the same name: Three different songs entitled *The Power of Love* charted in 1985, by Frankie Goes to Hollywood, Huey Lewis and Jennifer Rush; The Beatles and Primal Scream (amongst others) recorded songs called *Come Together*; and, lest we forget, *For Whom the Bell*

THE WILDE DIARIES

Tolls, recorded by Metallica in 1985, and the Bee Gees in 1993.

The strange thing about *Greater Than Me* was that Lucas Wilde was not one of the artists listed. The top six results in the search were all videos by some young starlet Zach Fox. An androgynous, doe-eyed twenty something with cheek bones that you could cut yourself on, probably someone who held pride of place on many a teenage girl's bedroom wall. I was pretty far from the target demographic Zach Fox catered for, and I was tempted to watch the video from a private window that wouldn't show up in my search history.

The video was overproduced: lots of slow-motion and close-ups of those doe-eyes and cheekbones. The song was a genuine surprise. Like the video it was overproduced, but well-written. Incredibly well-written. Melodic and beautiful. To be fair to Zach he could play an acoustic guitar with a little panache, too. It wasn't the case of here's a pretty singer, let's write him some songs. Here was a musician. As the song drew to an end, I fully expected the dramatic key change. The bane of modern, lazy songwriting. Not all key changes are bad but these days it was a signal that the writer has run out of ideas, and not something a real tunesmith like Lucas Wilde would ever contemplate, even at the height of his block-driven dry spell. I was waiting for the token key change in *Greater Than Me* and it never came. With the song still playing in another window (one that, now I'd heard the song, I didn't mind appearing in my browsing history), I opened up another search: information for Zach Fox's version. By the time the last, haunting chorus faded out, I was sold. The song was so good, I wouldn't have been shocked to find out it *had* been written by Lucas Wilde.

I scrolled down.

Written by Zach Fox.

'Jesus, cheekbones can write, too.'

All well and good, but a blind alley. I still hadn't heard Lucas Wilde's song. Then I was hit by inspiration. The tape on the reel to reel at Seth's... I scrambled around in the box for the key to the house and grabbed my car keys.

***

The drive over to the house was a short one. The area was so flat that two items stood out on the journey. The house, and the tree. In the short time that had passed it looked like the police were finished with the house, the only sign of them ever being there the blue and white tape crisscrossing the old front door. Proof once and for all that Seth really was dead.

For a second, it struck me as strange. The finality of it. But that wasn't dominating my thoughts. I should have felt bad about it, but there was no feeling of guilt either. If I had to say, I'd say that was by design. Whose?

His. The Busker's.

I peered at the door atop the stone steps and shuddered as I stared at the police tape. That blue and white tape would have represented nothing of any issue to Seth. The rules were made for him to break them. Seth was a man built to suffer

THE WILDE DIARIES

for his art. A small problem like police tape was nothing, after all, we're talking about a guy who bought a house because he thought it would make for a better book. For me, the blue and white tape was a different kettle of fish altogether. Dealing with authority figures was always a struggle. I had few dealings with the police, so I wasn't the kind of person who'd argue with them. The fact was, I wasn't built to break boundaries. If I ever did anything wrong, I got caught. Straight away. No warnings, no close calls, no you-were-luckies. Caught. Bang to rights. And if I was in a situation, I couldn't talk my way out of it. Not like Seth could.

I stared at that tape for what must have been five minutes, holding that key in my hand until it was slick with sweat and I could smell the metal. I stood staring with the box beside me (I wasn't leaving that anywhere), and it felt like it was daring me to go inside. Maybe it was the idea of not leaving Seth's work unfinished that compelled me to go in. Maybe it was the fact that I had a real mystery on my hands, and the answers lay on the other side of that big, old, wooden door. Maybe it was both of those things. One thing I can say for certain, that the idea of Lucas Wilde's unreleased album and the money I could make from it definitely had something to do with it. If I'm being honest, maybe that had *everything* to do with it.

When I placed a hand on the door, it gently swung open. Not even locked. I checked over both shoulders, expecting the police to jump out and arrest me. For what? I wasn't breaking in. Entering, yes. I wasn't sure that they would leave the place unlocked, which set me further on edge.

'Find the tape player and get out.'

The dim foyer stared back at me, at once tempting and challenging me to enter. I crept inside. On the inside the house looked a little different. Not because it was different, just in the same way nowhere looks identical the second time around. The way your mind readjusts to the angles and distances and light. You never saw a place the same way on the second look. But now, even in the midday sun, the hallway was just as gloomy as that first night, despite pale sunlight filtering in through the semi-circle of stained glass above the door. It felt as though Seth were still here. That at any second one of those doors would open, and he would shamble out. Drawn, haunted face staring with those empty eyes, brain tissue oozing from the hole where his right temple used to be.

I gently closed the front door behind me, noticing the small corner table at the bottom of the stairs with a landline telephone, in exactly the same place Lucas kept his, and the grandfather clock Lucas had mentioned in the corner opposite. It was strange I hadn't noticed it before, but then again, the last time I was here I had other things on my mind. It ticked away with an empty, dry sound: something else I hadn't noticed before. The hallway now seemed wider. The door at the bottom of the stairs stood open, and it became at once clear that this was the room where Lucas had held the

THE WILDE DIARIES

séance. Just peering into that room set me on edge and I could imagine the smell of burning from the fictional fire. Opposite the front door was the kitchen. Through the doorway, the end of a thick-topped table was visible, a table that I imagined extended the full length of the room, all the way up to one of those old farmhouse bread ovens. I could confirm that later, now all I wanted was to find the reel to reel.

Both doors on the left were closed, the one leading to Lucas' 'recording room' criss-crossed with more blue and white police tape. I picked up the box and stood before the door. In my head the door was swinging open to reveal the rug, the armchair; then slowly swinging further to expose the drawers, the reel to reel, and finally, just before losing the last of its momentum, Seth's foot, and the gun. I shook the thought from my head and snatched the police tape down, twisting the doorknob, hoping against all hope that the door wasn't locked. However afraid I was to go inside, I wanted so badly to hear the tape. It opened. Again it swung to reveal the rug and the armchair. I stood frozen as it swung further, again revealing the drawers. It slowed and there was a gap where the reel to reel had been. The police had taken it. I'd seen them do it on the first night, from the front seat of my car, when the box now in my arms was stashed away in the foot well behind my seat. The door stopped. I stepped into the room, again noting that the first time it had felt smaller. There was no Seth, no gun, and no reel to reel. A clean-up crew had already done their work. If it weren't for the dark patch on the floor, it would almost have been as if Seth had never existed at all.

In the silence I stood, wondering how I might find a way to listen to the tapes, when I heard a dull thud. From upstairs. I turned my head to get a better angle, and it was unmistakable. Tramping the floorboards above me was the clumping of boots. There was somebody else here.

What if it was the police? I wasn't supposed to be here, whether it was my house or not. What would happen if they found me here? Could they arrest me? But what for? It's my house. I haven't broken in. Impeding a police investigation? They've taken everything they need. Think for fuck's sake. Think. What would Seth do? As I stood panicking, there was another sound above me.

I decided to go upstairs.

***

I stood at the foot of the U-shaped staircase, peering up to the landing halfway, craning my neck in a vain attempt to glimpse the upper floor. The sounds had stopped and now it struck me that I'd never seen the upstairs of the house. I was supposed to stay here, before Seth—

Another thud sounded.

I froze. My heart jumped before settling into a new, faster rhythm.

I eased up to that landing, treading carefully close to the wall, hoping to avoid a creak that would give me away. Still

THE WILDE DIARIES

hugging the wall, I crossed the short landing to the bottom of the next flight of stairs and peered through the wooden railings, into the upstairs hallway. The wall facing me was home to three doors, God knew how many more doors hid around those corners. Silence again filled the house, broken only by the dry tick of the grandfather clock. The footsteps were consigned to history, but they had been there. Four or five, as clear as the clunking tick echoing in the hallway now. The stairway was wide enough for two to walk up, side by side. If there was somebody upstairs, they would have to pass me to get out.

The polished wood of the handrail was smooth to the touch and I placed a reluctant foot on the first step. I made my way up, slowly and surely, the whole time my eyes glued to that definite stone corner, waiting for someone to appear. For an awful moment I thought that could be Seth.

When I got to the top, I was standing on a short hallway, the only light from the window over the stairs. A shelf sat beneath the window, and I imagined that once flowers and plants sat on top, making it appear welcoming and warm. Now it was empty. Bereft of welcome and one more sign of the emptiness of this place. But it wasn't empty, no matter how it looked. Facing me were a total of six doors, and another narrow staircase fading up into darkness. The hallway was carpeted and the boots sounded like they had come from a bare wooden floor. Somebody was in one of the rooms.

'Hello?' I tried my best to sound authoritative. 'Who's

there?'

I waited, but the only sound was the hollow ticking of the clock drifting up from downstairs. I went on, sure that the footsteps would have come from one of the first at the opposite side of the house from where I had been, which meant a room at the bottom of that dark attic stairway.

The door to my left was my inkling. I reached out with my right hand and kept the space to my left in my line of sight, in case somebody came from the hallway behind and tried to make a dash for it downstairs. My heart thudded in my chest as I stood before the door. A thousand possibilities played out in my head about who could be on the other side of the door.

A policeman...

A thief...

A dead writer...

A busker.

I grabbed the doorknob, shocked at how cold it was, and turned. The door swung open, showing the bare wooden floor inside. I burst in, hoping to surprise whoever was in there, questioning why I hadn't bothered to grab some sort of weapon on my way up here.

The opening door revealed a collection of Seth's musical gear. A black Fender Stratocaster with white trim leaning against a Marshall amplifier. A beautiful Washburn acoustic lovingly placed in a stand. And a pile of books, the top one sheet music for *Dark Side of the Moon*. But it was clear by the

THE WILDE DIARIES

layer of dust that covered everything and the motes that sparkled in the beam of sunlight dissecting the room that this room had been long abandoned. Seth had given up on his music, just as Lucas had. Just as I started to wonder if I'd imagined the footsteps completely, I glanced in the corner. Moments before the view was obscured by the open door. Now I saw a figure in my peripheral vision. A dark shape, bouncing, moving erratically.

Just as my horror was peaking, the figure started to turn. I turned too. And we both screamed.

***

It was Edie, in headphones, dancing to a song on another reel to reel tape player.

'Oh for fuck's sake!'

We both laughed and she placed a hand on her chest and drew a deep breath. She looked a little tired, and a little sad, oh-so-slightly vulnerable. It was then everything came flooding back. Rushing at me through time. The feelings I still carried for her.

I wanted to be the one to comfort her. The feeling was overwhelming, much stronger than any doubt I'd carried that she had cheated on me with David all those years ago. The intervening twenty years hit me at once; a mixture of bad relationship choices, one-night stands and real potential partners who were kind and caring and loving and beautiful, but unable to hold a torch to Edie. At that moment if she'd told me that she had cheated on me with David, I think I could have forgiven her. Then again, I was probably better off not knowing.

'You scared the shit out of me, you twat,' she said, still smiling as she pulled the headphones carefully off her head.

She ruffled a hand through her adorably untidy hair and it settled into a resemblance of the style she wore the other night, shorter than the old days, a frame for her porcelain doll features.

'What are you doing here?' she asked.

'I might ask you the same thing,' I hoped my tone came off as jokingly as I intended.

She smiled again, 'I just wanted to come back. For one last look around. I still can't believe he's gone.'

I could only nod. The right words always did evade me at times like these. That's where David was better. Charismatic. Probably how he was able to steal her from me.

'You?'

'Sorry?'

'Why did you come back?'

'Oh, right.'

I thought about lying. About saying I wanted to be closer to Seth too, but she would have seen right through it. I wanted to tell her about the diaries that Seth had given me. I wanted to share this news with someone. Anyone would have done, but better that it was Edie.

'Where's David?'

THE WILDE DIARIES

She turned away and started to absent-mindedly rearrange the headphones and tapes into some semblance of order, not to tidy things, but to avoid the question. He'd done something wrong. Something that she didn't like. For a second a tiny bomb of warmth exploded in my heart. I was happy. Not because she was sad, but because he'd let her down.

'He had to leave. For a few days. Business.'

'Now?'

She froze for a moment before continuing her fidgeting. 'The timing is terrible. He apologised of course. But there's a crisis at the magazine and they need him, apparently.'

The magazine. The creatively named Politics Fortnightly. The name was crap, but the magazine was not. Still selling well in print (although readership was falling) and one of the most popular online politics pages in the country. Impartiality was the one thing they had over most of the others in the field. Actual journalistic integrity. We had worked there together, straight out of uni. It was when that first promotion was coming up, it was between me and him. And just as he'd been doing with me and Edie, he was sowing seeds of doubt about me at work. If it was on writing alone, I had a chance. But the politics? The office politics - I never had a prayer. He was a ruthless bastard. Got the promotion. Stole Edie. I was left with a nervous breakdown and move back home. Where I've been since.

It was typical of him to go now. That bastard. Leaves her

just after her brother dies. Like there's no-one else at the magazine who could deal with it. Self-important prick.

'Oh. I'm sure it must be important,' I said, trying to comfort her after my earlier insensitivity.

She stopped tidying and glanced at me, her pale blue eyes filling with tears. If I had to guess I'd say it looked like she wanted to share something with me. It was only there for a second, then it was gone. She dabbed at her eyes with a sleeve and then smiled at me, 'You still haven't told me why you're here.'

With David out of the way, and her feeling shitty, it felt like it might be the best time to share. 'I'm looking for something. A song.'

'If it's a song you're after you should listen to this,' she thumbed over her shoulder at the reel to reel.

'What is it?'

'Just a little song called Greater Than Me.'

My heart skipped. 'That's what I'm looking for.'

What she said next made my hair stand on end.

'Only it's not Zach Fox's version.' She frowned, 'Hang on... How did you know to look for it?'

'Long story, I'll explain later. So you've heard of Zach Fox?'

She rolled her eyes and giggled, 'You're such an old fart, Joel.'

I shrugged and smiled back at her.

She stood back and pressed play on the reel to reel.

THE WILDE DIARIES

'Listen to this.'

I'd never heard him speak before, but Lucas Wilde talked as he sang. It wasn't like listening to the unintelligible drone of Ozzy Osbourne and being blown away by the unrecognisable singing voice. This was the same softly spoken voice that could at once move you with its fragility then surprise you with its power. I suppose with everything I'd just learned, what happened next should have been obvious; the song that came out of the speakers, raw and unpolished and beautiful, was the same one I'd heard earlier. The song I'd heard performed by Zach Fox. The Lucas Wilde version that floated out of the speakers was a demo. Poor overall sound quality; a gentle hiss of white noise; distant, echoing vocals struggling for centre stage against the ring of the guitar; but incredibly moving. A haunting version of Greater Than Me by the original artist. Lucas Wilde strumming on Old Faithful. As I listened I was struck by the idea that we, Edie and I, were of a handful of people to hear it. That rare moment in time where something is created, birthed, from nothing.

While it was undoubtedly a beautiful moment, it wasn't lost on me that my money troubles could well be over. Not because of the demo tape recorded by someone with cult status in the music industry; the number of people interested in Soothsayer in 2015 numbered probably in the low thousands. The ship for making money on this as a bootleg had sailed about twenty years ago. But because Zach Fox had recorded it, the game had changed. Not only had he recorded it, according to the pages I'd read on the web, he'd also gone so far as to take credit for it. Which meant one thing: Plagiarism.

Never in the world of art has a word been so dirty. The number of out-of-court settlements in the music industry are evidence of such a fact. Zach Fox would not like this to become public knowledge. On the contrary. He'd like nothing more than for this to remain exactly as it was now: a dirty little secret. And it could.

But it was going to cost him.

***

'But you can't prove that Zach Fox didn't record it,' Edie said sitting on the stool by the baby grand piano, 'originally, I mean.'

I sat on the black leather bar stool where Seth probably did his acoustic playing and pointed to the reel to reel.

'That is recorded on a technology from Lucas Wilde's day, and there's no mistaking that voice. That can only be Lucas,' I replied, trying to contain my excitement at this new turn. 'The only thing I'm not sure about is how Zach Fox got his hands on it.'

Revelation dawned across her face. 'Holy shit.'

'What?'

'Didn't Seth tell you?'

I shrugged, as if to show it was obvious he hadn't.

'The last owner of the place, before Seth bought it.'

THE WILDE DIARIES

'Well I know it was a musician, but...'

It finally hit me. Seth told me the name but at the time I didn't recognise it. Of course, I knew what Edie was going to say before she said it.

'It was Zach Fox.'

I needed to think. And I really wanted to be somewhere else. It felt weird being in the place knowing that my friend had taken his life here just a few hours before. I was sure Edie felt the same.

'Are you hungry?'

'Starving,' Edie replied. 'I haven't eaten since we got here.'

'There's a nice place in town. The waitress guesses what you order before you can tell her. Let's go.'

***

The café was half full when we arrived, the unoccupied tables home to dirty dishes left over from the lunchtime rush. We sat ourselves at one of them, by the window, looking into the street. Carol came along in that graceful way of hers and cleared the dirty dessert dishes and said she'd be back in a couple of minutes to take our order (or tell us our order, if my last visit was anything to go by). I nodded and as she moved away she revealed something on the wall behind her. It couldn't have been there before, I would have noticed it. A photo taken outside the café – it was Carol, in her twenties, beaming a huge smile. Time had treated her well, but back then she was a real stunner. Knock-your-socks-off pretty with an hourglass figure. The man beside her had an arm draped around her shoulder. That man was Lucas Wilde.

The photo was signed. "All the best, Carol. Best brekkie in Britain! Lots of love, Lucas Wilde."

How the hell hadn't I seen it before?

'Steak pie, chips and veg. And for the lady... Ooh quiche with salad. The quiche is lovely.' I turned to see Carol smiling beside me.

'Yes. That sounds great.'

'And two coffees. Strong, black, two sugars in each. Are you okay my love? You look a bit... lost.'

Edie nodded, 'I'll be fine. I think it's just been too long since I had anything to eat.'

She waved the order and winked, 'I'll get this for you.' She turned and floated back into the kitchen.

'Are you okay to do this now?' I asked Edie.

'I need the distraction,' she smiled.

As we sat and waited, then ate, the other customers left around us, and Carol quickly manoeuvred herself around the tables, clearing them and resetting them as she went. She never asked if my food was okay, because she already knew it was, just smiled at me once between shuttle runs to the kitchen. As we ate we talked about how Zach had ripped off Lucas. My mind kept going to the diaries. I wanted to tell Edie, but every time I tried, I backed out.

We were re-connecting on a deeper level and it felt like

THE WILDE DIARIES

more than her wanting company because David had left town, but I was also conscious about the money I could get from Zach. I would have to share it with Edie and she'd pose the question about cutting David in. That was not something I was interested in. I stared at the photo of Carol and Lucas. Trying to figure out when it was taken. He didn't have the haunted look like he did in the photo with Derek and Mandy. Maybe this was just after he arrived. Full of the optimism granted by a fresh start.

Carol reappeared to clear our plates. She smiled. She nodded at the photo, 'You look too young to be a fan of his.'

'Born too late, mum always said. I like anything from that era.'

'I'd have thought he'd have been closer to your age.' She nodded at the wall behind me before disappearing into the back.

I turned as she vanished and saw another framed photo of her with another man. This man was about the same age as Lucas in the first picture, but she was older, closer to how she looked now. This photo was around five or ten years old, but that same beaming grin was planted on her face. This picture too had an inscription. The man in the more recent picture was all doe eyes and cheekbones.

"Thanks for the fry-ups, Carol. You're number one! All the best, Zach Fox."

***

A public place is an uncomfortable option when it comes to ideal locations for extortion. That's why we left and went back to my room at The Ship. There, I logged into my Twitter account. I hadn't checked it for a week. I had no new messages and one new follower. That made me up to four hundred and sixty-one followers. But my profile was not the reason we were here.

I couldn't speak for Edie, but I was a little uncomfortable being alone with her in the hotel room. She was a married woman. One I had a past with. One I'd liked to have had a future with, if we're being truthful. She seemed fine with it and made herself comfortable on the bed with her own Twitter feed.

'What are we looking for?' Edie asked.

'Anything that suggests he ripped off Lucas Wilde.'

'You don't think he'd flaunt it on here do you?'

'Let's just look and see.'

Zach Fox's Twitter feed made for interesting reading. His profile had over 30 million followers. I became follower 33,105,042. His account started back not long after the platform had launched. His first tweet came on 22nd March 2008. A generic message with a link to one of his first catchy, but bland efforts - Love Thing. It had 21k retweets and 47k likes. Hard to imagine they were all there from the start and much more likely it was fans scrolling through his history and boosting his back-catalogue. As I read down a lot of the original posts were about random thoughts and links to songs.

THE WILDE DIARIES

Reading through from past to present, it became clear that the author of the tweets was the same person, and I had the feeling that they were written by Fox himself; he'd stayed in control of the account and not palmed it off to a lackey. And credit where it's due, the songs were real earworms. Usually based around the theme of love, trust and betrayal, the songs were three minutes of catchy hooks and lyrics above and beyond the cheese and cliché of the charts. The tweets went on like this for a couple of years. Then it changed. A black hole where post history should exist.

'Edie?'

Edie was scrolling and searching lost in her own world. Her reply came absently, 'Yeah.'

'When did Zach Fox release Greater Than Me?'

***

The black hole in Zach's Twitter feed coincided with the time he'd no doubt found and then ripped off what Lucas Wilde referred to as his best song yet. Edie sat upright on the bed, phone in one hand, glass of wine - her third - in the other. The sun had set and the conversation had turned from what we expected Zach Fox to do (I wasn't sure, perhaps threaten legal action; Edie was convinced he'd cough up anything to keep his dirty little secret), to Seth.

'Has it sunk in yet?' she asked.

I shook my head. 'Not really, it was so weird seeing him, and then...'

'How was he? When you saw him?'

At once his gaunt haunted figure came to mind. Thin, emaciated, exhausted. I looked at her, checking if she really wanted to know, hoping more than anything to see that seed of doubt in her eye that would free me from the obligation. It wasn't there. 'He didn't look good. He was drawn. He looked like he had something heavy on his mind.'

'Did you think he could—'

'No. Not for a second.' I looked away now, embarrassed that I had been the one with him when it happened. 'If I thought for a moment that he would...' It seemed a thought neither of us could complete.

'I know. Seth was never the most forthcoming when it came to his feelings. He was hard to read, even for me. I just wish he'd said something.'

Her eyes filled with tears, and more than ever I wanted to hold her. To comfort her. But I couldn't do it. It wouldn't have been right, to do that in the hotel room. David should have been here to offer her comfort. It seems my masking of my discomfort was poor.

'I'm sorry,' she said.

'No, God no, don't apologise.'

'It's just that David should be here to...'

She broke down crying and I finally stepped up and offered her a shoulder, somewhere to dispense of tears. My heart rate elevated as I held her and it was hard for me not to think of our past together, however inappropriate that might

THE WILDE DIARIES

have been.

'He should be here,' her voiced sounded small. 'I think he's having an affair.'

'What? No, I... I don't know what to say.'

I felt sorry for her but I couldn't help the bitterness that came with it. Before I could complete the idea, Edie voiced it for me.

'You wouldn't have left me like that.'

It was now I realised that she had stopped crying. Her voice was low and scratchy but the tears had already stopped. Her hand rested on my chest and I wondered if she had felt my heart rate quicken. She peered up at me and our eyes met and I saw in them a tiredness. She was tired of the uncertainty. Tired of wondering where he was when he said he was working late. Wondering who the late phone calls were from. The text messages. It was all there, written in her face, and for that same moment she saw in my face that I would never do any of those things. I was something else. A different kind of security.

Her eyes closed and she leaned in ever so slightly. At the moment our lips touched, a sound broke the silence. A *ping!* like a bell. A message. She pulled away and my first thought was that the message was David. Divine intervention to stop her infidelity. She wanted an excuse not to cheat. She stopped and looked over. But the message wasn't on her phone. It wasn't from David. It was on my laptop.

It was from Zach Fox.

MARC W SHAKO
13th October 2015

Edie and I had spent hours chatting away into the night just like old times and this interruption had taken three hours to come through. I had a new follower using the handle @Gr**terTh*nY**. I followed back. Within seconds, my inbox had a message from my new follower.

'What does it say?' Edie asked excitedly. The moment between us had certainly passed, like leaf on a stream, gone to somewhere new, never to return.

'It says, "@Gr**terTh*nY**: 'Who the fuck is this?'"'

This brought an excited chirp from Edie. 'What are you going to reply?'

Given confidence from the wine I'd drunk, and pissed off at his interruption, I spoke as I typed. 'Who it says on the account. Who the fuck are you?'

Edie was positively giddy. 'Oh my God. I like this Joel! Where has he been?!'

I smiled and stuck out my tongue, she smiled back, glint back in her eye. Maybe the moment hadn't passed after all. I held her gaze and felt something bloom inside me, then I got another message.

'What did he say?'

'He says "Why are you trolling Zach?" Fuck's sake. It's him isn't it? Pretending to be a lackey.'

'Definitely.' She smiled.

Again, I read my message as I typed. 'If you were Zach, you would know.'

THE WILDE DIARIES

After fifteen more minutes of nothing, I had another new follower. @F*xyZ*ch*r**. And a message. I ignored it and went in with a question.

@J**lBr*w*rB**ks: 'That really you, or a minion?'
@F*xyZ*ch*r**: 'Me. Tell me what you want.'

I started to type out the word money, but changed my mind when I got to the 'e'.

@J**lBr*w*rB**ks: 'For now, answers. How do I call you?'
@F*xyZ*ch*r**: 'What?! Fuck you! Ask here!'
@J**lBr*w*rB**ks: 'We both know that there's already enough for me to get you into a lot of trouble. That's why you're here. If I were you, I'd be nice to me. So... How do I call you?'

There was a short pause, maybe I'd overplayed my hand, but I didn't think so. Edie looked at me and I saw that she thought I had.

My inbox flashed.

It was his Skype contact information.

I called him. We spoke. He told me everything.

MARC W SHAKO
Zach's Story

I'd been number one in twelve countries, and my last song *Baby it's You* had just peaked at number eight in the Billboard chart. I'd cracked America. I was part of a dying breed in pop who wrote, performed and sang my own music. That's not to say that the people you see in the charts aren't talented. No doubt they are. There are better singers than me. There are better guitar players than me. There are better songwriters than me. But people that can do all three? Not so many.

Not that I was an overnight success. I'd worked my arse off to get where I was back then. I started busking, playing a lot of Beatles, Stones and Soothsayer songs. I'd even throw in a composition of my own. That developed to playing at friends' parties, where I'd get people telling me they really liked my songs, so I started playing small local venues; the kind where you can hear the abuse from the audience loud and clear. That's where I developed my stage act. The humour. It all came from that. But it was years before it started paying off.

Then one night, it was a case of right place, right time. I'd got a few thousand followers on my YouTube channel, then out of nowhere, in a few months, I was up to a few hundred thousand. At the time I thought it was organic, that's a laugh. Anyway, the official story is a producer had seen his kid (daughter, I think) watching my videos. He liked what he saw enough to come to a gig. I'd only got the gig because a friend's band had dropped out; the singer Steve had got laryngitis.

THE WILDE DIARIES

Funny how things work out. Anyway, I went as the support and the second I'd finished *Love Hurts* this guy jumped on stage. There and then he offered me a record deal. Promotion, the lot. I'd 'made it'. My YouTube channel had a million subscribers by the end of the next month. That is the official story.

What really happened is I got a message, on YouTube. We exchanged details, and next thing I know, I've got five days of studio time paid for. And I don't mean some dank local studio. The mixing desk looked like something from the Starship Enterprise. All expenses paid too. Food, drinks, weed, hotel, the lot.

I got back home and mum told me that someone had paid her mortgage off. I put the new stuff online and things are snowballing there, but I didn't hear anything else from my donor for a few months. Not until some small time local label offered me an album deal. Before I could agree, I got a message. Don't take that deal, take this ten grand from me, and enough studio time to finish your album, again, all expenses paid. I thought it was too good to be true, but I called the hotel and studio, they said it was all paid in advance, with the option to extend if need be. So that was that. But it was after I finished recording, in my last night at the hotel I realised what an opportunity this was.

***

'Mr Fox.'

MARC W SHAKO

The shout came from across the hotel lobby. Businessmen and tourists all milled about, some checking in, some riffling through leaflets of tourist attractions. The shout must be for someone else, nobody knows me here. I carried on, lightly bouncing on the thick carpet, guitar case in hand, head fuzzy from the afternoon of drinking and smoking. I could almost feel the soft cloud of bed underneath me. I'd empty the mini bar tonight and rent something exotic from the TV and check out in the morning. Maybe my donor had arranged travel back home, maybe I was to pay for it myself. No matter. I still had most of the ten grand. I'd only spent five hundred on clothes on what my donor said was my day off from recording. A light hand tapped my shoulder.

'Mr Fox?'

I turned. It was one of the reception staff. A little older than me. In good shape. Her tits making the buttons on her blouse earn their keep.

'This is for you.'

She handed me a note. I was semi-stoned and half drunk and in the shock of it all I can't even remember if I spoke to her before she was gone.

The handwriting on the note was from my donor. He said his name was Tony, but I thought it might be fake.

'Congrats on finishing the album. Tonight, we celebrate. The car will pick you up at eight.'

Beats the minibar and porn rentals.

I slept for a couple of hours, showered and hoovered a

THE WILDE DIARIES

line to pick me up. By the time I hit reception, the car was already waiting for me. A black stretch. The doorman opened the door for me and I climbed in.

'Zach, meet Brandy.'

That's all Tony said. I'd never met him in person. He was small. Cockney. Well dressed, one gold ring on his hand. Younger than I expected. Brandy smiled. She managed to look stunning and cheap at once. A tiny bit of cleavage peaking out and the figure-hugging dress somewhere between too short and classy, a tantalising glimpse at what was out of sight atop those near-endless legs.

Brandy moved from beside Tony and sat next to me, handing me a glass of champagne before gently placing her hand on my thigh.

'Congratulations, Zach. I hear the studio are impressed with the album. Are you pleased with the outcome?'

Brandy's fingernails tickled above my knee as she stroked.

'Yeah it sounds great. Thanks.'

Tony raised his glass and Brandy did the same. We clinked.

'Just the beginning. You are about to have a night you'll never forget. Driver,' he said, voice raised. 'To the restaurant.'

The restaurant was packed. Waiters dressed in suits and bow ties. The sort of place you have to book months in advance. Only they were falling over themselves when Tony walked in. 'Mr Smith' this and 'Mr Smith' that. They'll do that for me one day. They put us on a table right in the middle, explaining to some mid-life crisis and his daughter/girlfriend there had been a mix up. He wasn't happy, but he moved.

Tony was excited, going on about the future. Brandy was rubbing my cock all through dinner. I wasn't that hungry anyway. Not for food. Tony paid after, said the car would take us to the club and that we should have a good night.

It was dark as the car pulled up to the club, the stretch pulling the eyes of the line with it as it stopped outside. I didn't know the place, but the clientele looked classy. The driver opened the door for us and I set off for the back of the line, but Brandy pulled me by the hand and led me to the VIP entrance, gold dress hugging her hourglass shape, dark hair swaying.

'You'll never have to queue again,' she said, smiling. 'We're with Tony,' she told the doorman.

He was a brute, but at the mention of Tony's name, he became a pussycat. The music rose as we descended into the club. The carpets were thicker than the ones at the hotel. No club in my hometown would dare put anything this nice on the floor. Inside, the room was black, white lights flashing over the chequerboard dancefloor, ornate mirrors on every wall. We crossed the floor and Brandy was leading us for the VIP area.

'Don't worry,' she smiled, reading my face.

A bouncer bigger than the one outside opened the door for us. Inside was quieter, but the place was jumping. Hot

THE WILDE DIARIES

young things dancing about, waiters shuttling drinks from the bar to the tables. I glanced across the room and my eyes landed straight on [musician - name redacted]. Could it be him? This is the sort of place I imagine he'd hang out. He didn't look out of place.

'Fucking hell, there's [musician].'

Brandy just smiled. She must come here all the time. See folks like him all the time.

Before we could take our table, I got another tap on the shoulder. Just like in the hotel, I was struck dumb. I turned and it was a girl. She leaned in and whispered into my ear. I glanced over her shoulder at Brandy, seeing if she'd react. There was just another smile.

The blonde spoke.

'[Musician] says would you like to join us?'

I glanced over at him, surrounded by women, wearing tinted shades, shirt opened halfway, and he was smiling, waving us over. We followed the blond, who was taller and leggier than Brandy, to his table.

He stood and offered his hand. 'Tony said you'd be coming. Have a seat.'

We sat, and I was trying my best to play it cool.

'We're drinking bourbon. Want one?'

'Sure,' I nodded.

He waved a hand and a waiter appeared like a genie summoned by magic word.

[Musician] leaned in and said, 'I've heard a few of your

songs, Zach. Do you write your own?'

'Yeah. Yes. Yes I do.'

'Really good stuff.'

That was it. We were talking about songs that influenced us and our favourite solos and classic albums and drinking and smoking and snorting. We danced with the girls and took selfies and partied all night, having a wild time.

Next thing I know it's morning and I'm alone, awake, struggling to get my bearings. It's the hotel. I'm naked. The bed sheets are ruffled. Someone has been in bed with me. Brandy. I jump up, hit by a dizzying wave as I stagger over to the safe. I've got two grand in there. Have I been drugged? Why would Tony give me money and then rob it back? He wouldn't. The safe is locked, and when I open it, every penny is accounted for.

I span around, too quickly, and saw a note on the bedside.

'Thanks for a wonderful evening. Brandy X.'

Okay. Cool. I fished my phone from my jeans and there's a message. It's not from Brandy. It's from [musician]. Bits start to come back to me. Have I made a cunt of myself? Fucking hell. I've said or done something. I was wasted. High as fuck. *Tony will be fuming.* I ran to the bathroom and threw up. I got back and opened the message.

'Fucking hell. Rough as fuck. Great night though. Next time you're in town, give me a shout.'

***

THE WILDE DIARIES

That was that. I packed up and went home. Quit my day job. The day after, I got a message from Tony. He wanted to meet. He was in my neck of the woods. A car came and picked me up and we had dinner. He said [musician] loved me. I signed a contract with Tony that night. Before we went our separate ways, Tony said to me that things are different for me now. I thought he meant with the contract. He meant the partying.

'The people in our world are private. No more selfies.'

The pictures from my phone from the other night had all disappeared. The next time I was at the studio, I reached out to [musician]. We partied again. But it was on another level. He introduced me to [actor - name redacted]. They introduced me to another drug. I wasn't going to do it at first. That was the best high I've ever had. The people, the surroundings, the high. And every time, these parties are getting wilder and wilder.

That's when I met [celebrity - name redacted]. That's the thing no one can prepare you for. The first time you appear in the papers it's all set up. You stumble out of a club with the latest hottie on your arm, and *Bang!* That's it. Goodbye old life. People want to know who you are. They want to know *everything*. That's the thing with the Internet. It's so easy to find out who someone is and everything about them. Why someone would want to know half of that shit is beyond me, but my good luck story kind of took off. Fate or whatever.

***

MARC W SHAKO

After *Two Good to be True* I was tired of the attention. I was only two albums into my career but you crave something your whole life and realise it's not all it's cracked up to be; you just want to be able to go to the shop for a bottle of milk; or down the local for a pint, and you realise that that part of life – that part of you – is dead.

I wanted somewhere to get away from it all. I remembered reading that Lucas Wilde had done something similar when he was at a similar point in his career, and I got thinking, where did he live? He was a huge influence on me. Like most of the best ones in the business he died way too young. The old showbiz adage about leaving them wanting more was never truer. Look at all of the iconic musicians in the 27 club: Jim Morrison, Janis, Jimi, and of course Lucas. It didn't take me long to find out about the house. I'd just signed a new contract with a huge advance, maybe investing it in property wasn't such a bad idea. I just had to hope that the house was empty.

I heard that it had had a few owners since Lucas, but none of them had stayed for too long. That was probably why the place was available at such a knock-down price. I snapped it up and gave myself a short break. I'd been touring pretty much two years straight, and that hadn't left me much time for writing. The plan was to hole up at the house, middle of nowhere, no distractions, and knock out enough songs for a new album. Maybe even a double-album, really take the piss. But it didn't work out that way.

THE WILDE DIARIES

The house had this magnetism when I approached it: that way you can see it from miles away and it looks like it's calling you in. I fell in love with it (probably easier for me to do because Lucas had once walked the same rooms). But then I started hearing things. Little things, but enough to unsettle me. Footsteps upstairs. Creeping at first. But not always. Once it was stomping. A door would creak, even if I had all the windows closed. Those kinds of things would distract me, just as I was getting going. And I'd have to stop. It happened every time I got into any sort of rhythm, like the house didn't want me to write. Soon it developed into writer's block. I'd just signed a contract for three albums and here I was I couldn't finish a fucking single song. I started going for walks to clear my head, or exploring the house. That's when things changed.

I don't know how I'd missed it before, but I found an old box in the attic. Just sitting there in the middle of the floor. Just an old box. Plain, taped up the sides. Anyway, I open it up and fucking jackpot. Tapes and diaries. Left by Lucas.

At first I thought I'd stumbled upon a bit of rock history. (Well, I had.) I expected it to be bootlegs or rough copies or something. My first thought was that I had some kind of Soothsayer Anthology on my hands. Outtakes, demos, that kind of thing. It was a huge deal for me, like I said, I worshipped Lucas. When I played it, I realised that it was way more than that. It was new stuff. Obviously Lucas died before they did a third album. As the last surviving member, Jack Mayberry had gone on to a half decent solo career, but he'd never recorded the songs – and they were good songs, fucking dynamite. So I did a bit of research. They were unreleased. I was the only one who knew about them.

I thought it was impossible, so I'd record bits of them, snippets of chords or whatever, and put them online as teasers, waiting for the moment someone would pull me up: "I know that one!" or "That's so-and-so by this-or-that band!" But they never did. The longer it went on, the more attractive the idea became of nicking them. It wouldn't be the first time somebody nicked a song. Fuck me, some people got very successful careers out of it. I was still struggling to finish a new song of my own. So I did it. I sat, worked out the chords, and recorded *Greater Than Me*. I sent it to my manager and he was over the moon.

'Best thing you've ever written!'

I felt sick. Not only had I stolen it, but he thought it was 'my' best. At that point there was no way back. I had to keep the secret. I deleted my social media history that had anything to do with the house or the songs. I recorded my own versions of the songs and if I'm being honest, I didn't even read the diaries that Lucas had left. I couldn't bring myself to do it. I shoved everything back into that box and hid it back away in the attic. That was that. Or so I thought.

That's when the dreams started.

***

Dreams. Zach had dreams, just like Lucas had.

THE WILDE DIARIES

'What dreams?' I asked.

'Listen, while I'd love to chat all day, I've got a tour to get ready for.'

He motioned towards the camera, reaching for the lid of the laptop to close it down.

'Not so fast,' I said, completely unsure it would have any affect. He stopped. 'I'm not done.'

'I have to go.'

'I'm not stopping you. But we talk again. Tomorrow. Then you'll find out how to stop the world knowing about your dirty little secret.'

A look of disgust washed over his face, and I expected one to wash through me, too. But it didn't. I felt great. Alive. He was going to pay whatever it took to keep me quiet.

I closed my own laptop and looked over at Edie. She'd been out of shot for the whole conversation, just listening. There was a look in her eye that I hadn't seen for a long time.

'What happens now?' she asked.

As far as Fox went, I'd have to be careful, ask for too much and there's no reason for him to keep going. He's better off outing himself, then I'm fucked.

'It's time to find out how much Zach Fox is worth.'

'Right now?'

She was staring at me, eyes smouldering, moving slowly, seductively around the bed, until she was standing over me, my face in her hand.

'It can wait.' I replied.

MARC W SHAKO

***

Edie reappeared from the bathroom, naked skin aglow from the warm lamp light. She crawled back into bed and hugged her cold skin against me for warmth. We lay silently, enjoying the moment. My mind wandered as I stared into the slight crack that ran from the wall like a river on an old map.

'I have to ask something.'

'Sounds serious,' Edie said, her voice coloured with the hint of a smile.

'Are you... you know, on the pill, or something.'

'On the pill or something?' she asked, stifling a laugh.

I frowned and looked over at her. 'What?'

She finally giggled aloud. 'The time for that question was about two hours ago.'

'I got carried away.' I was trying not to sound defensive but succeeded only in making her laugh louder. 'Okay. Taking the piss.'

Her laughter subsided, 'To answer your question, no.'

'No?'

I wriggled my arm from underneath her and sat up. She did the same, bedsheet dropping, just covering her breasts.

'I wouldn't worry about it.'

'Wouldn't worry?'

'The truth is, we've been putting it off, having a baby I mean, but neither of us are getting any younger. We've been trying. David and me. For about a year and a half. We decided that careers... my career, could go on hold. My decision. I just didn't want to wait any longer and honestly, I thought it would just happen like that,' she clicked her fingers. 'It hasn't worked out like that. Not even a close call. I haven't even been late.'

'Seriously?'

'You sound surprised.'

'Sorry, it's just... I just thought that you two... well, you seem like the perfect couple.'

She barked a bitter, ugly laugh. There was no music in this one, and for a second, I got the shivers.

'There's a lot that goes on behind closed doors. People put on their best faces, but it's all for show. Like wearing a mask.'

Kept in a jar behind the door.

'What?'

'Nothing.'

'Anyway, I don't want to talk about him.'

The twinkle was back, and even now I knew the answer to the protection question, we made love again.

***

The morning was dull and grey and distant thunder rumbled just loud enough to wake me. Edie was in the shower, and my first thought was to join her, but no sooner had the thought dawned on me than the gentle white noise of running water stopped. Plan scuppered, I reverted to type, and reached for my phone. My usual habits were checking the news (sports first - typical bloke), then social media.

This morning I wouldn't get as far as social media.

The sports news was normal enough, United scraping another nauseating last-gasp win, gossip pages reporting transfer stories 90% of which would come to nothing when the window finally re-opened. A mid-order batting collapse from England and impending defeat against Pakistan.

As Edie brushed her teeth, I read the world news which could have come from any year in the past thirty; problems in the Middle East, concerns over voting patterns in elections, controversial politicians' comments. Then, my eyes were drawn to the most popular stories on the site. There, at number three, sandwiched between yet another stabbing in London, and a celebrity wedding announcement between two people I'd honestly never heard of, was a story about music which normally, I'd have skipped right past. But not today.

'Edie?'

The sound of brushing teeth stopped.

'You have to come and see this.'

Her head popped around the door, droplets of water clinging to her bare shoulder from her wet hair. 'What is it?'

'Come and see.'

She grabbed a towel and wrapped it around herself and emerged from billowing steam into the bedroom. The headline said some pop starlet had announced the postponement of his forthcoming UK tour, leaving fans in the video in tears. The singer in question was Zach Fox.

THE WILDE DIARIES

I messaged him through every avenue open to me, needing to find out what was going on. My biggest fear being he'd folded. Decided to throw the towel in. Sick at the thought of giving up whatever for free to someone trying to blackmail him. That's probably how I would have felt.

'I've overplayed my hand.'

Edie had a look of shock like someone had slapped her. 'What? No way is he going to just give up everything because you're asking him for money. You've seen how long he's been at this. That is not something you walk away from. He's accustomed to a certain lifestyle, he can't just go back to living like Joe Soap, man on the street.'

'So what now?'

'You still haven't answered my question,' she replied.

'Which was?'

'How you knew to look for the tape. The Lucas Wilde version of Greater Than Me.'

'Right.'

There it was. The elephant in the room. Well, not the elephant itself, but the ringmaster leading the pachyderms out before the crowd. It led to a thorny thought. All of the signs were showing that Edie and David were more than going through a patch. She was thinking of leaving him. Was I suddenly a viable option? Getting along was never a problem, we had always been close, but something she'd said about becoming accustomed to a certain lifestyle... I wasn't able to provide that. Not without the blackmail money that we hadn't yet got from Zach. But would she really leave David? He'd been away one night and we'd slept together. I felt like shit. Not because of David, fuck him. But it felt like I was taking advantage, my friend still not in the ground.

'Heard anything from David?'

'I don't want to talk about him.'

'When is he due back?'

She fell silent. It was clear she was thinking about a difficult conversation she'd have to have when he did get back. Was this just a fling to pass the time? That would be a very Edie thing to do.

'Soon. I'll have to leave straight away in the morning.'

'In the morning?'

'Yes,' her face brightened a little. 'In case he comes back early. Until then, we'll have to think about something to do to pass the time.'

She lay down and loosened the knot in her towel, pulling me down beside her. Just at the moment we were about to kiss, she spoke. 'You can start by answering that question,' she said, with a cheeky smile.

I told her as much as I could about the diaries, not mentioning Seth's talk of sacrifices and symbolism. I'm not sure why, but I never mentioned Seth's notes on the memory stick. Protecting myself instinctively, perhaps. From what? I couldn't say. I just felt that Seth's notes had as much value as the diaries themselves. When I finished, she said:

'Jesus, no wonder he's cancelled his tour. You really have

THE WILDE DIARIES

got him by the short and curlies, haven't you?'

I shrugged a little. 'That's not all though.'

Her eyes brightened, and I leaned in for a long, sweet kiss. She didn't resist.

'Was that what you wanted to show me?' she smiled.

'No,' I smiled back.

'Well, go on! The suspense is killing me!'

'There's another diary.'

LUCAS WILDE'S DIARY #3

8th September 1977

Lucas shivered in the dim hallway; hand barely able to grip the phone receiver. 'Are you sure?'

The question all he could muster from his shock at the news that Mandy was dead. He thought Derek had put the phone down at the other end and was about to check this when he spoke.

'I've got to go,' was all he said.

The phone clicked to a dead line and left Lucas standing in that gloomy, cool hallway. He should be celebrating. On the reel to reel in the next room was the best song he'd ever written, but now he felt nothing. Numb. In the back of his mind, or maybe in his heart, he knew before he picked up the phone that Mandy was dead. All he could see was Derek standing by the war memorial in town, telling him what he'd said on the night of the séance. How shocked he'd been by his awful demeanour, let alone the words he'd used.

Lucas staggered into the kitchen. He heard the clock

ticking but didn't look at it. He didn't want to know if it was 'too early' to drink. He grabbed a bottle of bourbon and a heavy bottomed tumbler and turned back for the door, stopping. Three doors stared back at him: the one leading to the room where they held the seance; his recording room; and the study.

The room where they had the séance was out of bounds. The window had been fixed, and the sticky patches of alcohol removed from the floor, but *it* was still in there (the feeling so bad now he couldn't bring himself to even think the words 'Ouija board'). He'd remove it at some point, despite being unsure that was to blame for the strange feeling in the room, the feeling of being studied by unseen eyes. The door to the recording room was open, inviting him, but all he could think of was the dream and the scratching. There had been a man in the dream too. A dangerous, malevolent man. Lucas felt this sinister figure was somehow connected with the song he'd just recorded, and he didn't want to sit in that room, staring at the reel to reel, being constantly reminded of him and the dream.

He opted for the study. He opened the door and stepped in. The heavy curtains were still drawn from whenever it was he'd last been in here, keeping the warmth of the sun from the musty, cool air. He set bourbon and glass on the small table by the fireplace and opened the window a crack. This wasn't the most welcoming of rooms, but it would do. If he went upstairs he'd just end up sleeping and he didn't want that. But why?

THE WILDE DIARIES

It wasn't because he'd only just got up. Only been awake for an hour after God knew how much sleep. No, there was something else. And like most things that had been happening to him these days, the man from the dream was somehow connected. The man was a singer. He played too. A busker. If he went to sleep, *he*'d be there. That was bad, how?

Mandy.

He had something to do with Mandy's death.

He didn't know how the pieces fit together. If they fit together. But there was something to it. He jumped to his feet and moved to the door to close it, sure that when he got there, a boot would appear and block it. He slammed the door closed and turned, the bottle of bourbon calling him. He patted his jeans pockets and was relieved to find his lighter and smokes.

By the time he'd got halfway down the bottle and halfway through his cigarettes, he'd put a lot of it together.

The busker *The Busker* had appeared to Lucas in his dreams, though he couldn't say how many times. It was the Busker who'd played the song. The song he'd recorded earlier. He had given the song to Lucas. And somehow, because of that, Mandy was dead? That couldn't be right.

But it is.

Now he wanted to meet him again. Confront him. Find out what he'd done. It was all well and good giving him the song, but if that was the price, he could forget it.

That was Lucas' first thought and it lasted for less than a

second.

He didn't want to meet the Busker to confront him. There was no wanting to challenge him about what had happened to Mandy. He wanted to thank him. Thank him for the song and ask for more. It should have disgusted him, but it didn't. There were glass ceilings to shatter and music worlds to be dominated. He wanted to dominate them. And with the Busker's help, he would.

***

Lucas stood in the room, eyes gazing into the Ouija board. They came into focus and the blurred letters took shape. He couldn't say how long he'd been there, staring. He'd taken the time to draw the cold and the darkness outside (the curtains hung back in place free of charge, courtesy of the window repairmen - the perks of fame.) All he could say is that the ominous dread that hung heavy in the room the last time he'd been in here was now gone, just when he needed it the most. He knew that if he tried the board now nothing would come of it, but still, try he did. He sat cross legged and set his glass beside him.

'Come on,' he whispered, more to himself than the board.

He shook his hands loose and placed a solitary finger lightly on the planchette, instantly disappointed by the lack of energy.

'Come on,' he repeated. Louder this time, pleading with

THE WILDE DIARIES

the board and its masters on the other side.

'Are you there?'

Nothing.

'Is somebody, anybody, there?'

He nudged the planchette, just to check it wasn't snagged with the grain of the wood. It slid, the pointer moving from the middle of the board up to the letter G. He dragged it back to the empty space above the row of numbers and tried again.

'We need... I need to talk to you. It's important.'

The air felt light. Just normal air in a normal room. No magic. No electricity. No energy.

'Fine. Fuck it.'

Lucas jumped to his feet.

'And fuck you,' he said sounding like a spoiled teenager as he kicked the board across the room. The board only slid a few feet against the friction of the carpet, but the planchette hit the far wall. He left. Not stopping to get his glass. It had been a strange day, the huge positive of the song (which mustered little in the way of emotion) and the gutting shock of the news about Mandy. That was enough for one day. Now it was time to sleep.

But sleep was hard to come by. Gusts of wind blew hard whenever it neared, and when he did finally drop off, he was immediately awoken by the images of his nightmares. Mandy, reaching out for him with the delicate fingers of one hand, the other clawing at the scarf wound tightly around her throat. Her eyes wide staring pleadingly for his help as her feet swung wildly below her, tiptoes pointing down, like a ballet dancer, searching for the ground.

If it wasn't Mandy, it was *him*. Standing in the doorway to his bedroom. A black shape cut out of the light. When he snapped awake, the door to the bedroom was closed, as he'd left it. This went on all night, until the sky started to lighten outside. It was then, and only then, that he fell into a deep sleep.

9th September 1977

It was already late by the time Lucas woke. The effects of the bourbon weighed heavy on him, his head dull and sore, stomach churning. Good job, food in the house was scarce. He gingerly raised his head to see the digital alarm clock, green figures glowing noon. The floor felt cold and refreshing as his feet touched it, a feeling he wished he could replicate across his whole body. For a moment the hangover fog left him unsure why he'd decided to drink so much in the first place, then he remembered. It hadn't been a dream, it was real. Mandy was dead.

He stood slowly and went to the en-suite to piss, the frosted window obscuring the grey skies beyond. He perched himself on the edge of his bath while he brushed his teeth, trying to arrange thoughts of the strange man from his dream.

THE WILDE DIARIES

Today was not a day for moping.

He already had one new song for the album. Today was time to finish what he already had half-written, hangover or no. In the past he'd found that a hangover had given him some interesting ideas. The cloudy feeling like the evil twin of being high. They were always half thoughts. Never free-flowing like the magic carpet high from marijuana, but still, he'd be able to get something down.

In the recording room, he set the reel to reel to replay the new song, hoping to kick-start his day. He grabbed his acoustic and played along. The chord changes were all in the right places, though he struggled to recall all of the words, but it felt more like he hadn't played the song for a long time, rather than learning it anew. Once it had finished, he pulled a notebook out and started to play one of his unfinished numbers. He got to the same place and tried to add a not-so-obvious chord, but nothing seemed to fit. The go-to chord of A-minor was the only thing that felt right.

'Give it five minutes,' he sighed to himself.

He stumbled for the kitchen. Maybe a glass of water would help, if only to take his mind off how thirsty he was. On the way, he glanced into the Ouija room. The board sat in the middle of the carpet. Was that where he'd left it? He stood over the board, unfinished glass of bourbon carefully placed in the top left corner and the planchette pointing to the word 'No'.

'No,' he read aloud. 'That'd be about right.'

He reached down and grabbed the glass, the idea being to finish the booze, but the smell persuaded him otherwise. He nudged the board with a petulant kick and the planchette slid to the number 2.

He poured the remnants of last night's drink down the sink, swilled out the glass and filled it with water. Before he could drink there was a knock at the front door.

He skulked back into the recording room and peaked through the window, hoping to catch sight of who had dropped by unannounced. The caller knocked again. Without moving the net curtain he leaned around.

'What does he want?'

Lucas turned and saw the reel to reel. Before he answered the door, he snatched the tape down. He didn't want the third degree about the new stuff, it wasn't ready. The tape safely tucked away in a cannister, Lucas went to the door.

'Alright, Jack?' he did his best to sound surprised.

Jack's face dropped a little at the sight of Lucas.

'I'm fine mate. Are you okay?'

'Yeah. Great. Well. Yeah. Okay...'

The two men stood looking at each other for an uncomfortable second.

'Come in, come in.' Lucas stood back and Jack entered, heading straight for the recording room, as was usual.

'No.' Lucas cringed at the sound of desperation in his own voice.

Jack stopped and turned.

THE WILDE DIARIES

'Let's go in here,' he said, gesturing to the room with the Ouija board.

He let Jack go in first and remembered the Ouija board was sitting in the middle of the room. Any hopes of him moving it before Jack saw it were quickly vanquished.

'What's this?' Jack said, his tone a strange brew of mocking and genuine interest.

'Oh that,' Lucas tried to sound casual but wasn't sure he'd succeeded. 'It's nothing. Just fucking around really.'

He bent to pick it up and noticed the planchette pointing at the number 1.

'Sit down,' he said pointing vaguely in the direction of the seats as he stuffed the Ouija board under the chest of drawers.

'Want a drink?'

'No I'm alright.'

Lucas tried his best to pretend everything was fine, but Jack's uncomfortable demeanour suggested that he knew all was not well.

'You all right then?' Lucas tried to shift focus away from himself.

'Yeah. Bit worried about Degsy to be honest.'

Degsy was Jack's name for Derek. He'd called him that from day one. Derek seemed to like it. Lucas had tried calling him that himself, but the word felt strange coming from his mouth.

'Right. Shame about Mandy.'

'I'm still in shock to be honest.' Jack Mayberry looked genuinely saddened by the loss and it made him feel bad for not being so badly affected by it himself. The only thoughts he'd had were guilt that his strange friend had something to do with it, and even that was overshadowed by the concern that he'd never see the answer to his writer's block again. It had barely registered how Derek might be feeling.

'That's why I came to see you. You don't look very good mate.'

'I'm okay. Just not sleeping well. That's all.'

'You don't have to put a brave face on it, Luke. It's okay to grieve.'

Where had this guy come from? Where was the competitive, argumentative, arrogant twat he'd known all this time? He wondered if it was niceties because Jack knew that he, Lucas Wilde, was his Golden Ticket. But he did seem genuinely concerned. It was throwing him off.

'I'll be alright mate. Honestly.'

Jack's features clouded over. 'Have you been eating?'

Lucas shook his head. 'Drinking mostly.' His eyes drifted to the carpet where he could make out the outline of a drink stain. From the seance. He shuddered and quickly looked back up. 'But it's not serious. I've got a grip on it.'

He tried changing tack.

'Wait till you hear the new songs.'

Songs. Plural. Adding pressure to himself.

Good work.

THE WILDE DIARIES

'Yeah?' Jack's face brightened a little. 'Look forward to it. The band meeting's been put back hasn't it.'

'Till after the funeral, yeah.'

Gives me more time to write.

'I just hope Degsy's going to be okay...' Jack tailed off and looked like he wasn't sure he should carry on, before doing exactly that. 'Do you think you could give him a ring? Just for a chat. A shoulder. I know it would mean a lot.'

Lucas nodded. 'Yeah. I'll call him later.'

Jack stood, and Lucas followed suit.

'I'd best be off. Just wanted to make sure you were okay, with you not answering the phone.'

'Yeah. I took it off the hook. Wasn't ready to talk.'

About the songs. Because there weren't any...

They moved into the hallway and Lucas opened the door.

'Remember to give Des a ring.'

'I will,' he nodded.

He waved Jack off as he pulled from the driveway in the British Racing Green Mini Cooper of his. It was a relief to watch him drive away, though he couldn't say why.

It's because of the song. The new song. My song.

Lucas closed the door and locked it.

'Shut up,' he mumbled to himself.

***

Lucas closed the door behind Mayberry and headed straight

back to the room they'd just left. Something was happening with the Ouija board. The planchette had moved. From the number two, to number one. It seemed to be counting down.

'To what?'

The cool metal of the door knob gently vibrated in his hand and it was then he wondered if he'd closed the door. A chill passed through him. Whatever had been missing before was certainly here now. The door swung open and the heaviness hit him at once. *He* was there. Unseen, but there was no doubting his energy filled the room, just as it had the night of the seance.

Getting back into that room had been all he wanted, but now, watching that door swing slowly open, he had doubts. He'd have done anything to meet with the Busker before Mayberry had shown up, but that energy in the room had the place packed with malevolence. Just as he looked into the room, so it looked back at him. The door came to rest, and Lucas was about to step inside when he stopped. The Ouija board he'd just kicked under the drawers now sat in the middle of the room.

Without stepping forward, he leaned and grabbed the door handle and slammed the door shut, twisting the key as he did. Just as he was about to walk away, he slid the key from the lock and into his shirt pocket. He would have left the house altogether, but for some nagging feeling that if he did, he'd be away from the one place he had always met the busker. So he just drank. Watched the telly, but there was

THE WILDE DIARIES

nothing on. Only show jumping. After an hour of that he changed channels, but that wasn't much better. One boring programme was followed by the next which was worse. That got him through to the football results, not that he was overly interested. Liverpool had won again, which he hoped might have cheered Derek up a bit. Probably not. After all Mandy was

Dead. Say it.

not around anymore.

So all the while he'd drunk and played and read and drunk until it was time for bed. But of course sleep never came. Bedtime for him now was Christmas Eve and he was a kid, waiting excitedly for the gift he'd be given by the strange man. Minutes turning to hours of trying and failing, trying and failing to sleep, all the time his failure writ large by the luminous green lights of the alarm clock. So, he'd come back downstairs and dug his stash of dope out from the kitchen drawer and got high.

Lucas stared at the reel to reel like it was some sort of puzzle. The fog of dope and booze that he'd greedily consumed since Mayberry had left had his head swimming, Jack's genuine concern for his wellbeing leaving him confused. Was it that? He was so high, that he was now standing before the reel to reel, unsure of if he'd loaded the tape right. Maybe that was it. He shrugged and hit play.

There was silence as he turned and flopped into the chair. Then a note faded in. A decaying note gaining in strength and volume until it coalesced into the attack strike of a loud strum. He'd loaded the tape backwards. On it went, his voice garbling the words as he reversed his way through the chorus again before starting the final verse. The decay and attack of the notes and muttering gibberish of the lyrics together forming a creeping, crawling, sinister sound, which from nowhere was joined by something else. Something different.

Between the chant of the lyrics another voice could be heard. Low.

A whisper.

A wave of goosebumps rose on his arm. The hairs reached for the ceiling and waved like rushes by a river. He pushed his rubbery, stoned body up from the settee and lurched for the player.

Now more voices joined, and as he hit the stop button, he would have struggled to say all of the voices were human.

With a loud *click!* the room fell silent. He rubbed the goosebumps from his arm. It had been enough to knock him semi-sober as he hurriedly changed the reel around, desperately wanting to drown the dreadful silence with something. The reels squealed backwards through a rewind and he leaned in to see if he could make out any of the strange artifacts from the chaos he'd just heard. There might have been something. About halfway.

His stomach lurched. What *was* that? Had he really heard anything? Another loud click made him recoil. The tape was

THE WILDE DIARIES

back at the beginning. He jabbed the play button and waited for the music to start. On the tape, the reassuring sounds came of him settling into the seat and strumming an open G chord to make sure Old Faithful was in tune. She was. She always was.

Sure that no more horror was going to spill from the speakers he slumped back into his chair and lit a fresh joint, eager to replace the buzz that the tape had just killed. He sang along with the tape, not forgetting a single word. By the time the song finished, he'd completely forgotten about the strange sounds when he heard the song backwards. Buzz restored, he picked up his guitar and played. Mostly the new song. Some of the old ones. He even squeezed another verse out of one of the unfinished tunes.

It was after 4am when he decided it was time to try sleeping again. He turned everything off and his foggy head floated into the hallway. His eyes were drawn to the crack of light coming from the gap in the seance room door.

Didn't I close that?

He glanced at the lock to see the key sitting there and shrugged. He stumbled across to the room and peered inside the door. There was no one inside. Just the Ouija board.

Does he want me to contact him?

He drifted into the room and his light head floated high above the board. His eyes strained to focus on the planchette. When they did, he saw that the pointer was on the number zero.

'Countdown,' he muttered, before turning back from the room and closing the door.

As he tottered to bed, his feet barely touching the stairs, he wondered with a touch of sadness whether he'd ever see the Busker again.

He needn't have worried.

***

A high yellow sun beamed bright light across the lush green landscape and into Lucas's eyes. He shielded them with a hand and surveyed the countryside around him. It would have looked like the fields surrounding the house, if not for the lack of hedgerows; the road stretched to the horizon in all four directions from the point he stood, the house nowhere in sight. Fluffy white clouds drifted on a gentle breeze that swayed the grass and carried the smell of dry dirt through the air. He waited, hoping for something more, but nothing came, just more of that same dull, arid air. A bee droned idly by but instead of the sound fading it grew louder, until Lucas realised that it was no longer the bee he could hear.

He turned in the direction of the noise and saw a van moving slowly towards him from the north. A hairy-legged tarantula, joints coloured with bright orange, crept by in his shadow and went on across the road until it was obscured by the faded red van. The van jerked to a halt a few yards ahead. Lucas waited for somebody to get out (and he hoped it was Him) but nothing happened. The engine hummed, idling at

THE WILDE DIARIES

the crossroads, before the pitch gently rose as the truck eased away. As it did, it revealed a figure sitting atop the rock at the corner opposite.

A figure in a long black overcoat and fedora hat. He was playing a guitar. He was playing *Greater Than Me*. Lucas wandered over, but the figure never looked up, narrow, pointed chin visible beneath the wide brim of the hat.

'Hi.'

The Busker's lips curled into a grin at the corners. 'Lucas.' The final *S* coming in a hiss.

He stopped playing and finally looked up.

The grin developed into a full on smile, revealing teeth that were crooked and stained. 'How's that songwriting going?'

'Very funny.'

He started up again, playing a lazy, slowed down version of *Greater*.

'I've got something for you to listen to. If you like.'

'Wait.'

He stopped playing and froze for a second, the smile nowhere to be seen. His head seemed to lift in slow-motion and Lucas wasn't sure he wanted to see the rest of his face. In fact, he was sure that when the face did appear, it wouldn't be one he recognised. Or worse. It would be someone else's completely.

Like Mandy's?

Before he knew what was happening the awful moment had gone and the Busker stared at him. 'Go on...'

Lucas felt his mouth dry instantly and the breeze that blew now chilled him.

'Mandy.'

The Busker went back to playing. 'What about her?'

'So you know who I mean?'

'Of course.' That smile again. 'Sweet girl with the even sweeter sweater-bunnies.'

'Did you...'

The Busker was looking at him again. His expression was blank, his gaze challenging.

'Did you kill her?'

'Now why the fuck would I do something like that?'

The tone was as blank as the expression on his face. Not hurt by the accusation. Flat calm. The Busker carried on playing and asked, 'How did you know where they'd find her?'

This question confused Lucas. He didn't know where they'd found her. But the dream at the tree. It was so clear. So vivid.

'And besides,' The Busker asked, 'would it make a difference if I did?'

Lucas stared at his feet to see the tarantula creeping slowly away. Both men knew the answer.

'Hey!' The Busker's smoky voice shouted.

Lucas peered up.

'Don't worry. It'll all work out. In the meantime...' He looked down and hit the D string to tune the G on his guitar. 'Listen to this.'

THE WILDE DIARIES

Before Lucas could object

Not that you would object, right Luke? You both know the Mandy conversation is well and truly over

his strange new friend had launched into a song. Fast. Punchy. Lucas stepped back and listened, his mind going through every song he'd heard, trying to find a match. The search came back: no results found.

The hair on his arms stood in spite of the warm sun as lively verse turned into singalong chorus. Alive on its own, his foot tapped along. This was as infectious as anything he'd written. Even the really early stuff.

The Busker looked up and straight into his eyes. Looking through him as he played.

'You want it?'

Lucas nodded. Once. Small. Subtle. But the Busker would have known if he hadn't said a word.

The bee droned by again and this time the engine noise rose louder than before.

The Busker played harder as the chorus came along. Lucas turned to see the faded red van tearing along the road, tyres worn, one door grey and unpainted, speeding in the same direction it had come from before. But now there was another noise. The faint drone of another engine. He turned to see a familiar car coming along the road intersecting the first.

Whose car is that?

Behind him, the Busker was playing with such intensity

it sounded like two, three, a dozen guitars all at once. But Lucas couldn't turn away from the unfolding horror. The van and the car were fifty yards apart, but Lucas knew if one of them didn't slow, they'd surely arrive at the crossroads at exactly the same time.

Sadness swelled in him. Not for the driver of the larger vehicle. He'd probably be fine. But the car—

Whose car?

Its occupants were surely doomed.

The chorus started another loop behind him and the Busker's raucous vocals were barely audible above the grinding metal. Engines screaming. Horns blaring. Tyres screeching.

Twenty yards apart.

The Busker reached the final chord and just at the moment he strummed Lucas recognised the car.

'Oh no.'

That was the moment the bonnet crumpled on impact.

10th September 1977

Lucas burst into the land of the awakened and leapt from his bed. His heart thudded in his chest, he guessed the result of some hideous nightmare. What that nightmare was about, he couldn't say, and at that moment, didn't care. It had almost certainly contained his strange friend, that much he'd worked

THE WILDE DIARIES

out by the song currently going around in his head. And while he was sure that he wouldn't forget the song, he ran to his guitar all the same.

This latest song was faster than the first - what Dizzy would refer to as a 'stomper'. But the lyrics weren't throwaway, on the contrary. What separated this tune from other happy fare was the complexity of the lyrics. Not merely rhyming couplets - there were rhymes within the lines of the verse. At once the kind of song they as a band could open with, and the kind of song the fans would be singing on the way home from the show.

A fresh tape was loaded into the reel to reel and those reels were spinning, ready to accept the latest classic. The air crackled with static energy as Lucas wielded the pick, ready to strike. And just as the split second came where it seemed that the moment would be gone forever - and that moment teetered on the edge of the precipice of being lost forever like a forgotten dream - that was when he struck. *Bam!* Like a boxer toying with an exhausted opponent, Lucas railed against the trembling strings. Every scrap of frustration he'd bottled up in the past few weeks surged from him in a torrent of unbridled energy, a wild horse galloping headlong for the horizon yearning to explore what lay beyond. Every note, every word, all pouring from him - through him - like water from a burst dam. The previous line already forgotten as the next spewed forth, rising, building into something huge, like a tidal wave, until finally, it was finished.

MARC W SHAKO

Lucas stood breathless in the centre of the room, heart thumping in time to a beat that had now fallen silent. He stood there for a minute, motionless, just catching his breath, veins surging with adrenaline that made his hands tremble. On light feet he crossed the room to the reel to reel.

He hit the stop button and stared at the tape like it was the Mona Lisa. This song was better than the first. His mind was already arranging the rest of the as yet unwritten album around them. Between them. Bookends that would elevate the songs sandwiched between almost to their level. That was the illusion. Two songs into the writing and album number three was already a classic.

***

The rest of the day flew by. He spent a frenzied two hours tidying the house, buoyed by the energy of the new song - and something else. Something more. A welcome return to his old self. Now his steps felt lighter, the burden of writer's block lifted from his shoulders. Even those momentary glimpses of Mandy, eyes bulging, lips blue, feet desperately kicking out for the promise of a foothold, couldn't bring him down. He even got his appetite back. Which was a problem (or at least it would have been on another day) because the cupboards in the house were as bare as the day he'd moved in.

He dressed for the outside world and headed into town. He would visit the butcher, the grocer, the bakery. He would re-stock the fridge and cupboards (but not before he'd treated

THE WILDE DIARIES

himself to a decent meal at the café).

Despite the hustle and bustle of the street outside, the café was quiet, typical for midweek, and Carol was delighted to see him. She told him his order and when it came out the portion was twice the usual size. Carol said he looked too thin. The only other customer in the place didn't seem to mind this favouritism. She was slightly older than him and didn't look like a fan (although it was hard to tell sometimes), but it was obvious to Lucas that she found him attractive. The way she'd retouched her hair to ensure perfection when he entered. The way her eyes had lit up when he saw her and smiled. The way he noticed her eyeing him constantly in his peripheral vision. All of these things happened to him a lot. Who knew, maybe after he'd finished here he'd invite her back to the house.

As he placed the final forkful of food in his mouth, something changed. The light happy feeling of the morning faded, like a cloud had crossed the sun. With that same creeping dread where his dreams inexorably putrefied into nightmares, there was a lingering sense of déjà vu, and for no reason he could explain, his eyes were drawn to the window.

Across the road, two men were talking. They were alone. Lucas scanned the street trying to grasp where everyone else had gone. The two men were lost in conversation, old friends perhaps, themselves oblivious to the change in the surroundings. A car sped past, obscuring the view and when the two men reappeared at the other side, they were no longer in conversation. They were standing side by side, staring at him.

'You finished there?'

He fought with everything he had not to scream. His heart leapt and he turned to see Carol scoop up his plate.

'Sorry, love, did I give you a scare?'

Lucas turned back to the window and outside, shoppers milled by and the two men were still chatting, like they had never been doing anything but. He turned back to Carol and forced a smile from his numb, tingling lips.

'That was lovely thanks. Just the job.' His own voice sounded strange to him, like he was hearing it from outside himself.

She smiled back. Only the smile never reached her eyes. Like she knew this was a nightmare. Like something was going on, but she couldn't give the game away.

'Just the bill?' she asked, a polite gesture considering she already knew the answer. She went into the back and Lucas again noticed that the other woman was still eyeing him, while getting ready to leave. He offered a polite, wan smile, hoping to connect with someone in the real world, anything to shake off the nightmarish pause in reality. It was a relief when, as she stood and put on her jacket, she smiled back.

But it didn't last.

Behind him, he got the feeling there was someone staring. He didn't want to turn around, but much in the same way he would in a dream, he turned anyway. Once again, the feeling that he was trapped in a nightmare descended around

THE WILDE DIARIES

him like a cold cloak. Silence reigned and it was almost as if time around him had stopped. He felt his throat tighten and his heartbeat increase, and instantly his eyes were drawn to the two men. Only now he recognised one.

Tall. In a black fedora and long black coat. The men said their goodbyes and the Busker turned, walking away with a stilted, rigid gait. Lucas expected him to turn towards him, revealing some horrible, ghastly void where his face should be, but he didn't. He turned away.

The silence was shattered by a deathly wail.

Lucas turned to see the woman on the floor. Her eyes were wide and wild. Filled with a frenzy that convinced him she was on the verge of madness. It was anyone's guess if she could make it back.

Her feet kicked out as she scrambled backwards, away from the window. She backed against the cake display, still scrambling, feet still kicking against chairs.

Lucas turned back to the street and both men were gone.

Carol rushed in.

'What happened?!'

Lucas couldn't speak. Couldn't move. He was frozen in horror at the sight of the woman's sanity unravelling before his eyes.

Carol crouched and held the woman close. The woman's eyes were still wild, staring at the window. Carol held her head into her chest and stroked her hair, desperately trying to calm her, realising for herself that this woman was on the brink of insanity.

The cook came from the kitchen to see what was going on.

'Get a glass of water!' Carol shouted.

The cook was frozen.

'Paul!'

He snapped awake and nodded before vanishing into the back.

Lucas was numb with fear as he edged towards the woman, her eyes still wild with terror. It felt like an out of body experience as he neared her, tears streaming down her cheeks as she gasped for air in staggering, haltering breaths. Carol tried in vain to console her and Lucas was sure that the poor woman had gone insane.

Paul bumbled from the kitchen with a glass of water and silently passed it to Carol. He edged back instinctively like the madness was contagious.

Carol tried to give the woman a drink but her head was shaking from side to side, whatever shreds of her remaining sanity rejecting what she'd witnessed. She started muttering. It sounded like a mantra. Repeating the same thing over and over. Carol looked up at Lucas who just shook his head, signalling that he couldn't make out what she was saying. He hoped that Carol would also read it as confirmation he didn't know what had triggered this chaos.

The mantra became slightly louder at Carol's prompting and four words started to take shape. Lucas felt his skin crawl

THE WILDE DIARIES

as his subconscious came to a conclusion his conscious mind was yet to reach.

'Say it again, love,' Carol was whispering.

'He didn't have feet. He didn't have feet.'

He didn't have feet. He didn't have feet.

Carol frowned and looked up at Lucas before turning back to the woman.

'He didn't have any feet? You mean like a ghost? Who do you mean?' Carol asked.

Lucas knew who she meant. He knew where this was going. His subconscious knew how this story ended.

'He didn't have feet.' The woman carried on shaking her head as she repeated, her wild eyes desperate.

Like Mandy's.

Her mind was reaching for sanity just as Mandy's feet were reaching for a foothold. She opened her mouth to speak: Lucas knew what she was going to say and the floor fell away beneath him.

'He didn't have feet.'

He didn't have FEET.

HE DIDN'T HAVE FEET.

The words came in a harrowing cry that Lucas would forever hear when he was at his most vulnerable.

'His feet. His fucking feet... They were hooves.'

***

Lucas would never be sure if he paid for the food at the café.

MARC W SHAKO

On the way home he almost lost control of the car on three separate occasions: one because of the speed at which he was driving; the other two because he almost left the road – too busy staring in the rear view mirror, utterly convinced he was being chased by the devil. He was supposed to be heading for refuge, but as his house appeared on the horizon, it had changed. The allure it once held was now something else. The black windows seemed to be staring in a sinister gaze. He tried to shut it from his mind. There was nowhere else to go.

Once back home, he barricaded himself in, locking the front door and dragging the long dresser from the recording room and placing it across. He yanked the phone cord from the wall and bolted upstairs to his bedroom, sure all the while he was being pursued. He locked the bedroom door behind him, eyes searching for something to block this one too. The chest of drawers was just low enough for him to be able to lock the door over them. There he stayed, fighting sleep for two days. He was sure that if the man from his dreams could get to him in the real world, then attacking him in his sleep would be no challenge. He sat on the edge of the bed, holding the poker he'd grabbed from the study for protection. The atmosphere hummed, charged and ominous, leaving him waiting for the scratching sound from behind the chest of drawers. There he sat for two days, listening intently, staring at the door. On the second night, the supply of coke was gone from the nightstand and fighting sleep was his biggest challenge. Now the poker served another function: that of

THE WILDE DIARIES

makeshift alarm. Every time a wave of exhaustion passed over him, swaying his heavy head and dragging his eyelids lower, the poker would clatter to the floor and force him awake with a start. And it worked.

For a while.

Eventually the cocktail of no sleep and the after effects of the drugs hit him hard, and the next time he heard the clang of metal on wood floor, he watched in horror as it sank into the floor, as if it had landed on thick goop, swallowed and absorbed into the morass. A crippling vulnerability crept through him. He'd lost his only protection. He'd thought of finding out where to buy a gun. But that didn't help him now.

'Why didn't you? Why?'

He had no gun. No poker. No protection. His vulnerability circled his mind, gaining strength each time until he felt like the crackling, electric air itself could hurt him. And when he was at his lowest, when he was sure that even the most innocuous of things was a threat, that was when it happened.

A noise, from the en-suite bathroom. The sound of bottles falling from the windowsill. Like the window was being opened. The sound of an intruder gaining entry. The door gently swung open. Frozen in place, he could only stare as the door opened into the bathroom, revealing the curtain flapping lazily in the breeze. More than anything he wanted to peer around the corner and see if there was anyone in there. Then, another sound, from his left. From the door leading to the hallway.

The key in the lock on the inside of the door turned. It rotated slowly until there was a click. It fell from the lock and landed on top of the drawers. A loud *BANG!* sent the chest of drawers flying across the room and slamming into the wall opposite. It exploded on impact but still he was frozen, eyes glued to the door, all the while his mind screaming

GET UP! GET UP! GET UP!

But he couldn't. All he could do was sit there and watch as the door to the hallway swung open and he was sure that when it did, *he'd* be standing there, filling the doorway with his hideous silhouette.

But the doorway was empty.

There was a tapping from behind.

Gentle.

Light.

Too faint to be recognisable.

Finally, the grip of fear was released, and flight took over. He raced from the room and into the hallway. There was a second, louder tap behind him in the bedroom. It sounded like a branch tapping on glass. He didn't look back. Instead he bolted for the stairs. For the front door. Escape. He hit the landing halfway down the U-shaped staircase expecting to see The Busker standing between him and the front door. What he saw was worse.

'No!'

The dresser stood between him and quick egress. Now he

THE WILDE DIARIES

was certain the Busker was behind him. A scream of terror escaped, and another tap came. From the bedroom again. Even though he was now downstairs the tap was louder. He ignored it and grabbed the drawers that blocked his escape. The same moment he felt the cold wood against his hands a loud *THUD THUD THUD THUD* rattled the front door. He screamed and backed away.

The tapping on the window upstairs. It was rhythmic. Almost identical intervals between the loud, single taps. It somehow meant escape.

Luke?

A voice on the other side of the door. Not from *Him*.

A familiar, friendly voice.

He froze, staring at the front door as another sound rose behind him. On the wooden staircase. Slow. Deliberate. Closing in with ominous inevitability.

CLUMP!

CLUMP!

CLUMP!

The sound a hard-soled shoe might make.

Or a hoof.

He was frozen, staring at the front door, too terrified to move.

THUD THUD THUD THUD

again the door rattled.

And again behind him

CLUMP!

MARC W SHAKO

CLUMP!

Clump.

The last one gripped his heart with an icy hand. It was no longer the sound of footsteps on bare wood. It was the dulled sound of footfall on carpet. He was downstairs. He was just feet away.

LUCAS!

'Jack?'

The muffled voice of his friend. He was on the other side of the front door. It should have given him comfort, like help was at hand, but it wasn't so. He was outside, and against this enemy, Jack would be as powerless as he was. Instead he felt lost and alone. He wanted to see Jack more than anything, but he felt he was slipping away. Like he may be trapped in this nightmare forever.

Clump!

Clump!

Clump!

His mind was focused, waiting for the key that would unlock this horror and free him. The tap on glass. He couldn't say how or why, but the tapping was his way out of this. But still he waited. The presence behind him loomed sinister. Evil. He knew that it was almost upon him and if it got to him, that would be that. One thought now formed and solidified from the nebulous horror. This was a dream. If he didn't wake up, he'd be trapped here forever.

As he stared frozen in place at his own shadow on the

THE WILDE DIARIES

front door another grew from the top of it. Grew and kept going. Tall, with a fedora, now blacker than ever. And against his shoulder, he felt a weight. A hand lightly placed.

Come on Jack if you've ever felt anything for me please help me now oh God I beg you we'll do whatever you want put three minute solos on every damn song...

TAP!

11th September 1977

Lucas opened his eyes, heart gripped by the nightmare. He sat up quickly, wondering what had woken him. A pebble tapped from the window and a sound came that gave him some comfort.

'Luke? Are you in there?'

Jack Mayberry's voice from outside.

He surveyed the room. Everything was as he'd left it. Bathroom door closed. Drawers flush against the locked door. Key in the lock. Poker on the floor beside the bed. His feet were still on the floor. He'd just fallen back into the soft welcoming bed when exhaustion had finally overtaken him.

'Lucas!'

The room felt light and airy. No heaviness. No presence other than his own. Another pebble tapped off the window. He crossed to the window and opened it. Jack Mayberry stood outside dressed top to toe in black.

'Aren't you ready? I've been calling you.'

'Ready?'

Shit. The funeral.

'Give me a minute. I was in the shower.'

He ran into the bathroom (relieved to see the window closed), stripped, jumped into the running water and out again, just long enough to wet his hair and cover his lie, grabbed a towel and headed back into the bedroom. He slid the heavy drawers back from the door but they stopped. The uneven floor pushed against the feet at the other side.

'Fuck's sake.'

He ran around to the other side and lifted, dragging them away from the door. The moment they were clear, there came a creak as the bedroom door swung gently open.

***

They arrived in Jack's car in silence. Not much in the way of conversation had passed between them on the journey. Jack had asked about the time it had taken for Lucas to open the door. It was impossible that he hadn't heard the commotion of Lucas removing the dresser from outside. He asked about it, but Lucas just lied, saying that he wanted to try a new layout with the furniture. Then he asked how come he wasn't ready (luckily, he'd come early so they could have a drink before they left). Lucas left him with a bottle while he rushed back upstairs and got ready.

The day was bright and warm for the time of year and

THE WILDE DIARIES

most of the people waiting outside for the service to start had removed their extra outer layers. The couple he'd (correctly) guessed as the parents stared at him balefully as they pulled up; Lucas wondered who'd told them about what he'd said to Mandy before her disappearance. It wasn't Des. It just wasn't his style. Fucking Sally. Her and Malcolm had opened their big mouths. He didn't want to say anything to Jack - he could do without the I-told-you-so look (or worse, the speech). It was a surprise to him that Derek wasn't angrier at him. He was too sweet. Too trusting. Loyal to a fault. He deserved better from Lucas, and from now on, that's what he'd get.

They got out of the car and Lucas was struck by the strange atmosphere that the people there would rather be somewhere else. Not out of disrespect to Mandy but more because it was a bad situation that they would rather avoid. This meant it was final. At least, that's how he felt. But for him there was another feeling.

'Degsy's over there,' Jack pointed, breaking Lucas from his contemplation.

Derek was standing close to the entrance to the chapel, but far enough from Mandy's mum and dad for Lucas to feel comfortable joining him. His face was red and puffy from crying.

'Alright mate?'

Derek looked up and brightened a little when he saw him. He threw his arms around Lucas and started to cry again into his shoulder.

'I can't believe she's gone.'

This was his first funeral and no one had told him what to expect. Or how to behave. Everyone else here was sad. Sad because they'd lost someone they cared about. Someone they loved. He might have felt that way himself, if things hadn't been so fucking weird. At least the cloud of threat wasn't hanging over him. It was just a normal day. Or at least, it would have been, without the funeral. No, he was sad, but more than that he was distracted. Despite the fear and the strangeness all he wanted to know was if the Busker had any more songs for him. Derek's sobbing brought his focus back.

'It'll be all right, Des, mate.'

He swapped places with Jack and passed his condolences to the girl next to Derek. He couldn't remember her name, but she was Mandy's friend. Lucas knew he'd slept with her at some point in the past, before Derek and Mandy had got together.

'You don't remember me, do you?'

'How could I forget?' He looked into her eyes intensely, hoping she wouldn't press him for her name.

She smiled a little before turning to greet another new arrival and Lucas was left staring at his shoes, trying to avoid eye contact with the parents. He wandered away a little, further from the parents and borrowed a cigarette from a group of older men smoking. Jack joined them, getting his attention by gently nudging his arm.

'You seen who's here?'

THE WILDE DIARIES

He looked up and saw Jack gesturing to the parents. A tall girl with long dark hair was hugging Mandy's mum.

'Is that—'

'Shelley Hart,' Jack finished.

Lucas never heard him. His mind was firing, trying to figure out the connection between Shelley and Mandy.

'How does *she* know Mandy?' Jack whispered.

'I have no idea.'

A strange hush fell over the small gathering and everyone turned towards the front. He couldn't see through the crowds but the rising sobs told him that it was the hearse arriving. The group of smokers put out their cigarettes as one and moved closer to the crowd. Jack and Lucas followed, Lucas unable to stop his eyes focusing on Shelley's hourglass figure. Beyond her, his eyes fixed on the hearse at it meandered up the long, winding driveway.

Six men he didn't recognise carried Mandy's coffin inside and the crowd turned and followed. Shelley turned too and Lucas saw the side of her face as she made her way into the chapel. He couldn't say what it was but he noticed her face change, like an idea had come to her, and at that moment, she turned at looked at him. Three years of relationship flew at him in a second, and he got the shock of his life when she offered a polite smile. No hard feelings.

A mix of odd silence was punctuated by sniffles from the front row inside. He just stared at the coffin. A low murmuring started in the front row and he realised it was

Mandy's dad; he was sobbing.

The eulogy started and the vicar's voice was low and soothing. Hypnotic. It hadn't dawned on him before but now Lucas realised exactly how tired he was. He didn't know how long he'd slept in the grip of his latest nightmare. It could have been a few hours, it could have been a couple of days. But it was low quality sleep. However long it was, it felt now like he hadn't slept at all and the more that voice droned on, the closer he drifted to unconsciousness.

He focussed on the words: Mandy's horse riding; Mandy's pet rabbit; Mandy's job at the hairdressers; Mandy's firm tits inside that tight pink sweater.

Jesus Lucas wake up!

The job at the hairdressers. Was that how she knew Shelley? He opened his eyes wide, trying to break the hypnotic spell of the soothing voice luring him like some Pied Piper into the land of the sleeping. The hairdressers was close to the correct answer, but not quite it. He sat there trying to recall from where Mandy and Shelley knew one another, and a soothing feeling washed over him. Like he was in a different place entirely. Warm, comfortable.

A sharp dig came at his side and he opened his eyes to see more than a few eyes staring. It was Jack's elbow.

'You were asleep,' Jack whispered in harsh tones.

He surveyed the surroundings as one by one the heads turned back to the front. The curtains drew across the coffin and Mandy's mother let out a sharp, distressed wail.

THE WILDE DIARIES

Lucas was barely fighting sleep and couldn't wait to get out of here. He wasn't sure if he'd fallen asleep again because next thing he knew, everyone stood. They started filing out to the strains of Amazing Grace, and Lucas saw in the next room, between him and the patch of bright light outside that meant escape, there was a chair with a bronze metal plate. Coins clattered against the metal as he realised in horror that he had no money.

'Fuck.'

It came out louder than he expected and the old woman in front turned around, frowning.

'Now what?' Jack asked in a much lower voice in a tone that suggested he'd cut the sentence short before adding "for fuck's sake".

'The collection. I haven't got any money.'

'For fuck's sake.'

Maybe he'd been saving it.

He reached into a pocket and pulled out a one pound note. Lucas took it.

A soft voice came from behind him. 'Hi.'

He turned round to see Shelley. She slipped a piece of paper into his hand.

'Oh no it's okay, I've got—'

'My number,' was all she said before giving that polite, gentle smile and turning to the front.

Pound note safely dispatched, his body decompressed thinking the ordeal was over and he could get out of here.

Then he turned and saw through the crowd that there was one more obstacle. He had to give his condolences to Derek. And Mandy's parents.

The queue in front of him dwindled until he was stood facing Derek, thinking of something to say. Derek just hugged him tightly and he returned the gesture, whispering in his ear, 'I'm sorry mate.'

He moved on, but there were no hugs here. Just the stony faces of Mandy's mum and dad.

'I just wanted to say—'

Was all he managed before his face was warmed by a loud, high-pitched slap which burned his cheek and caused all eyes to turn to him.

'You've already said enough, I think,' Mandy's father replied before hugging his sobbing wife.

Lucas sat in silence, the side of his face still burning as Jack drove him home. They'd been on the road for twenty minutes and neither had spoken.

'That was fun,' Jack said, glancing at Lucas.

Lucas smiled. 'Fuck off.'

Jack started giggling, then laughing aloud. Lucas couldn't help himself. It was the first time he could remember laughing since the night they'd come off stage, after upstaging Burning Bridge. The rest of the journey they chatted about the old days and the tour where they both felt something big was building.

As they pulled onto the gravel driveway, Lucas felt a lot

THE WILDE DIARIES

better than he had for a long time, in spite of the funeral.

'You coming in for a drink?' he asked Jack.

They were getting along better now than they had in years. Just two friends rather than rival Alpha band members fighting for supremacy. He was sure that Jack felt it too.

'No.'

'Oh.'

Maybe not.

'I can't mate. Promised Denise I'd get back. That's why I'm driving. Wanted to tell you earlier but it didn't seem right, at a funeral. She's pregnant.'

'Oh. Wow.'

'It won't affect the band. We've already talked about it.'

'No, mate, that's... just a bit shocked. I didn't know you were trying.'

'For a bit now.'

'Well congratulations, man,' he smiled.

'Thanks mate. We'll have to celebrate. Maybe when we get the band back together. Next week.'

The rest of the band had already spoken about when they'd get back. Without him.

'Next week.' He nodded. 'Wait till you hear the songs I've got.'

'Can't wait. See you soon mate. Get some rest.'

He nodded and got out. Jack lifted one hand from the wheel in a wave as he reversed and turned to leave. Lucas could hear his bed calling. He needed sleep and he got it. And with the sleep, came dreams.

12*th* September 1977

Lucas awoke with the sun and felt refreshed. He'd fallen asleep not long after returning home from the funeral, relieved to find the house without a trace of that dreadful atmosphere he'd experienced in his dream, and slept through until morning. The sky was a deep red and shepherds all around would be cursing their luck. He couldn't recall if he'd dreamt or not, but nonetheless felt drawn towards his guitar. There was a song in him.

He wasn't sure how to feel about the development of a new song. The likelihood was that once again, he'd dreamt and not remembered it. There was genuinely nothing. He'd remembered snippets of previous dreams, even if he couldn't recall the whole thing. Now it was like the Busker had something on him. The Busker. Taunting him like the sober friend teasing a massively hungover drinking buddy about his abhorrent behaviour while under the influence. He didn't care for the feeling. Not one jot.

The feeling started to evaporate as soon as he set foot in the recording room and was instantly replaced by the feeling of excitement as he pulled out a fresh tape. The new tape whirred on the reel to reel as he strummed the open G on Old Faithful from his place atop the bar stool. It was, as always,

THE WILDE DIARIES

perfectly in tune.

The tune unfolded as he played. The lines coming to him one at a time like he was making it up as he went along.

Only I'm not the one making it up, am I?

This new song was melancholic and beautiful. It would make a nice change of pace to the album after the opening. As he strummed and played images flashed into his mind. Images he guessed were from the dream that had brought him to this song.

The song came to a natural end and he sat as the final chord resounded and faded. It was another classic. All of the best albums he heard rarely had more than three classic songs on them. It was the classic songs that elevated the rest of the album to classic status. That was what he had now. Three classics. If he could write the rest to fit the mood that was it: A classic album. A classic album to follow one of the strongest debuts and an outstanding follow-up. One that would launch them to the top and with the right album, they'd be mentioned in the same breath as The Beatles and Dylan.

This should have been the best of times.

It was not.

DIRTY SECRETS

14th October 2015

I closed the diary and turned to Edie. A thick, black darkness had fallen outside while we were lost in Lucas Wilde's memories. What I saw in her chalky face reflected my own feelings. Not glee that there were two more songs, songs that likely Zach had also stolen, but fear. That creeping horror at the idea that the man from Lucas's nightmares had cropped up in real life. We sat in silence for a while trying to understand the implications of what we'd just read.

'Maybe it was the other way around: he saw him in real life first and he just slipped into his subconscious,' I offered hopefully.

Edie didn't look convinced. She agreed anyway. 'Yes. Yes, it must be that.' She stayed silent for a moment and then asked, 'So what happens now?'

'Lucas mentioned two more songs. What are the chances Golden Boy ripped those off too?'

The frown melted from Edie a little and her motions

became less rigid, more natural. 'High, I'd say. But where are they?'

'They'll be at the house somewhere I'd have thought,' I replied.

I just hoped that Edie hadn't seen the shudder pass through me at the thought of going back.

As we neared the house, even in the darkness of the countryside, it felt as though the old place was watching you. *Expecting* you. We stood outside, peering up at the empty black windows, sensing that they weren't quite as empty as they appeared.

'You don't have to do this. You can wait out here.'

'Fuck that. I'm not staying out here on my own. Besides, I want to hear these songs.'

'About that,' I started. The next part of the sentence was going to come out clumsily however I phrased it, so rather than hesitate for too long, I continued, 'This... These songs, what we're doing. I'd rather—'

'David didn't find out,' Edie finished.

'Right. I don't mean to sound rude, it's just...'

Edie's expression didn't change. 'Don't worry. I get it. I think. And considering our "research" earlier, I'd prefer he didn't know either.'

An embarrassed smile gently turned the corners of her mouth and I nodded.

'Shall we?'

'Let's go.'

THE WILDE DIARIES

After reading the second diary, entering the house felt very different, but after the third... It had been bad enough knowing that Seth had taken his life here (I still expected to see him exit one of the rooms and stagger into the hallway), but knowing now about the recordings on top of the séance as well, it was as if the place were a time bomb, and we were just waiting for it to go off. The electric lights were dim too, like the place was cast in shadow. I didn't mention it to Edie, but I could almost sense the presence of the strange Busker here.

'Okay,' I said, 'I'll try the recording room, you look upstairs.'

'Fuck off!' Edie shouted.

I laughed.

'You twat!' she said hitting me on the arm as she did.

'You wait here,' I said and pushed the door to the recording room open.

It swung gently and I recalled the blood stains from my previous visit. There was no need for Edie to see such a graphic reminder of her dead brother. I waited for the door to stop before stepping inside. The dresser Lucas had once dragged into the hallway to block the front door, the one which was home to the reel to reel player was still there. Zach Fox hadn't changed much of the furnishings in the place, and it certainly was no priority for Seth.

'Don't you think it's weird?' Edie asked from the doorway.

'What's that?' I said as I made for the bottom drawer

Lucas mentioned keeping his tapes in.

'Well, young modern guy like Zach not changing any of the furniture. You'd think he'd want to put his own stamp on the place. It's like a museum.'

'He does kind of worship Lucas. Maybe he wanted a museum,' I replied, absent-mindedly rifling through the contents.

'I suppose,' she replied. 'Any joy?'

I slid the drawer closed. 'Nothing.'

'Try the others, then we'll check elsewhere.'

I opened and shut the other drawers, fruitlessly searching for more evidence of Zach Fox's plagiarism. As I did, my mind drifted to Edie. Now I wasn't so sure she was going to leave David. This felt less serious, more like a bit of fun for her, holiday from a life that hasn't quite panned out as expected, but a life that she'd go back to all the same. I couldn't pretend to be happy about that, but I had to play it cool. It felt like the moment it stopped being fun was the moment things ended. It unsettled me a little how well she was coping with Seth's suicide. It was hard for me, and I barely saw the man. She was his sister, but they'd always had an odd relationship. People grieve in their own way. Maybe I was being used as a coping mechanism.

The drawers were devoid of anything that could be considered evidence of plagiarism, but just as I started to feel that this trip would be fruitless, a piercing scream echoed in from the hall.

THE WILDE DIARIES

I rushed into the hallway to find Edie backed against the wall, eyes wide, finger pointing at the door to the room where some forty years earlier, they'd held the séance.

She barked a harsh whisper. 'It's just opened on its own.'

I gestured for her to stay behind me and crept towards the room. The door was wide open revealing the contents of the room within. The furniture pressed against the walls surrounding the rug where the group had made first contact with the strange character from Lucas Wilde's dreams. I reached the doorway and stopped. My skin crawled and ice cold crept down my back.

'Edie. Come and see this.'

'What is it?'

I replied without taking my eyes from the centre of that rug.

'Come and look.'

It took a few seconds for Edie's warmth to touch my back. As soon as it did, she gasped. 'Did you put that there?'

'I think there's two.'

'Fine, did you put them there?'

'You've been with me the whole time.'

'I mean before.'

Entering the room slowly as if approaching a wounded animal, I replied softly, 'Why would I?'

In the middle of the rug where a Ouija board sat some forty years before were two square boxes. Each one big enough to hold a reel to reel tape. I expected to find them empty. A tease from whatever darkness possessed this place. But I was wrong. As I reached down for them, I expected the door to the room to slam shut. Or the window to explode inward. Or to turn around and find Edie gone, replaced by the tall figure of a man in a hat and long black coat. Something. But nothing happened. I can't say I was disappointed.

The boxes had the tapes for the second and third song written by the Busker. Once upstairs by the reel to reel player in Seth's music room, Edie was quickly able to confirm that each had been stolen by Zach Fox, and each could be found on the same album as Greater Than Me. I actually recognised the third. It had been playing everywhere the summer it was released.

But it was stolen.

The time had come to turn up the heat on Zach Fox.

***

By one o'clock the next afternoon, Zach Fox was sitting opposite me and Edie in the room where Lucas Wilde had first made contact with the Busker. David was still away dealing with the crisis at the magazine. He'd barely called in the time he was away either. Once a day. Not asking how she was doing. Totally focused on himself. "I can't say too much," he'd say, "but this looks good for me". Typical ruthless David.

Zach had come because the message I'd sent had told him that if he wasn't here by noon, I was plastering his dirty little secret all over social media. A panicked call came at half

THE WILDE DIARIES

past eleven saying he'd be late. When he finally arrived I barely recognised him. He looked awful. Like a man who hadn't slept. A man who been up all night crying. Whatever had happened, it had been enough for him to cancel his tour.

Edie and I had barely slept either. We'd gone back to my room at The Ship and formulated a plan, then we made love. What it lacked in duration it made up for in intensity and afterwards we'd both slept soundly until sunrise. She'd got up early and gone back to the Travelodge outside the city to make funeral arrangements. When David didn't show she called and said she'd be here. It was nice knowing I had her to myself for at least one more day.

Zach sipped at the tea before placing the cup back down with a trembling hand.

'Why did you cancel the tour? Because of this?' I asked.

'No,' Zach laughed bitterly. 'Not because of this.'

He appeared as if he was about to burst out crying. Or throw up. 'Because a friend of mine, someone who worked on the crew, is dead.'

'I'm sorry,' Edie said.

Zach's voiced filled with scepticism. 'Are you really?'

Dead. A crew member. On the eve of the tour. Seth's words about sacrifices rushed back at me, my subconscious telling me this was significant. No such thing as bad publicity, isn't that what they say? The tour was sold out, though. There again, his name was at number three in the trending news stories. People who didn't know who he was yesterday might today.

But it's crazy. Who would do that?

I put it aside and broke into the discussion before it got too heated. 'Listen, Zach. Let's cut the shit.'

'Let's. Tell me what you want and let me get the fuck out of here.'

'Before we tell you what we want, I want you to tell me how you got the songs.'

Any sorrow Zach felt for his friend vanished in that moment. 'It's money you're after, right?'

'That's right.' I said.

'Let me tell you, you don't have the first idea of what you're fucking around with here. There are forces at work...'

'The Ouija board?'

His voice rose, 'The Busker.'

Silence fell throughout the room and the only sound was the dry empty ticking of the clock in the hallway.

'Why don't you explain it to me?'

Zach nodded, and retold the story of how Lucas Wilde's songs had ended in his hands.

***

Zach sipped his tea and placed it on the table beside him, not speaking for a while, replaying the events he'd just relayed to us over in his mind. Finding the tapes. Researching their originality and checking and triple-checking if they'd been released anywhere. Then the dreams of the Busker started. It

THE WILDE DIARIES

had brought him fame and fortune, but looking at him now, I sensed a regret. I sensed that however much material wealth he had, he'd go back to the times before in a heartbeat. Finally, he spoke.

'I did what the Busker told me: I made an album. Took the songs he'd given to Lucas and used them as cornerstones to a classic album that would sell millions. It was so popular that it even caused CD sales to spike, at a time when numbers were in decline. Everybody wanted it. It was the most downloaded album of the decade and I read somewhere that the album was in one-in-six houses in Britain. I became a household name. All before my twenty-fifth birthday.

'I used the fragments of other songs I already had and tweaked them into a similar style to the others, before sending a demo of the whole thing to my manager. He was delighted. I was not.

'I felt like a fraud. Like I'd sold my soul. But the songs, damn it, the songs. They were so fucking good. I poured everything I had into that album. Writing, polishing, tweaking. That's probably what hurt the most. As much as I worked on those other songs, however good I made them, they weren't a patch on the ones Lucas had written. They were so strong. Timeless, almost. They're so original, but the first time you hear them, it's like meeting an old friend.'

He paused again, his eyes staring out of the window, and I could see a reckoning going on. He was wondering whether or not he should divulge certain parts of his story, calculating if they would give us too much over him. His eyes came back into focus and with a defeated sigh, he continued.

'That was another thing. I felt like I was losing my mind. I found these tapes with songs written by my musical hero, but when I did I started having dreams about him.'

'About Lucas?' Edie asked.

'About the Busker. He told me that he wrote them, and the worst part was, I believed him – with absolutely no evidence. For the same reason anyone believes anyone, I suppose. Because I wanted to.

'The dreams with him were getting worse. At first the dreams came about once a week. I'd be dreaming something normal (whatever normal is, for a dream), I don't know, I'm in a supermarket, or on a beach, or in the shower, next minute, *he's* there. A shadow crossing between the aisles, and I go looking for him, but he's gone. Or he's the guy playing guitar sitting under a palm tree. Or I get out of the shower and on the white tiles of the floor there's a trail of muddy prints that just stop dead in the middle of the room.'

He didn't say "footprints" or "boot prints", just "prints". That was all he needed to say. A shudder passed through all three of them.

'Then the dreams took a darker turn. There was always this sinister edge, just bubbling beneath the surface, and you could feel it coming, just something in that ordinary setting went wrong; someone at the beach starts drowning; an old lady falls at the supermarket. I remember this one dream, it

THE WILDE DIARIES

started normally enough, I was at the pictures with a girl, Jenny. I knew her but I hadn't seen her for years. Really pretty. Great body. Nothing romantic ever happened between us, she friend-zoned me before I got famous, but I remember always liking her. Anyway, we're in the foyer, tickets in hand, buying popcorn – even though neither of us like it – from this pimply kid. The kid knew me, was a big fan and said lots of really nice things about me in front of Jenny, asked for an autograph, and she's warming to me nicely. Things are going great.

'We go into the screening and it's half-full. So we take our seats while the trailers are on and Jenny whispers, asking me what it's like being recognised everywhere I go.

'I jokingly tell her that it's fine because I know everyone, and she giggles. I'm certain that it's going to happen between us. Then I glance up at the screen, and it's an aftershave commercial, in a fancy house. And there's a famous actress that I used to go out with, and Jenny asks if I know her, which is a bit awkward, so I lie. Then, next thing, I see this figure. Totally out of place.'

Zach swallowed hard.

'It's Him. This clean, white house, black and white chequered floor, then this guy with a long black coat and a fedora. And he turns, looking back over his shoulder, and smiles. He's looking at me, and no one else. And I get this urge to tell Jenny that I know him, even though it's nothing that impressive.'

His eyes were watering now, his voice wavering.

'So I turn to tell Jenny that I know him. And when I turn, it isn't Jenny. It's *Him*. Sitting next to me. Looking right at me, smiling.

'That was one of the early ones. They got worse. They went from being creepy to being ultra-violent. People dying or screaming in agony, being tortured or attacked. Explosions. Fights. Executions. We're just talking and all of this crazy shit is going on in the background. In the end I stopped sleeping. I'd take whatever the fuck I could get my hands on just to stay awake. I would stay awake for days, but the second I nodded off, there he was. That smile. Teeth too big one minute, like Mr. Hyde in that old black and white flick, then straight and clean the next.

'Obviously, not sleeping did me no good. I was awful to be around, and worse than that, I had an album to record and my voice sounded like shit. I'd be blaming everyone else for my problems, sacking people left, right and centre. People who had been with me from the beginning. I felt like shit. I'd want to drink, but that made me tired, so I'd dream and then wake up and take a shitload of whatever to stay awake to avoid the violence and killings and torture. It wasn't too long before it all got too much. I passed out from exhaustion in a recording session and woke up in rehab.'

'And that's when your Twitter feed went dark.' I said.

Zach nodded. 'I was there for a few weeks. In the beginning it was a nightmare. I'd act out and they'd sedate me.

THE WILDE DIARIES

Sedate me. Me, who was trying everything I could to stay awake. I'd be at his mercy for hours on end. Gradually the dreams got less violent, maybe because I was fighting sleep less, who knows. When I was finally getting to grips with the dreams, my biggest concern became the lie I was living. My manager wanted to get me well and out of there so I could start recording. All I could think about was the box. The box with the tapes and the diaries. A couple of friends had keys to the house (Steve, my manager, included). If one of them found that box and looked inside, I didn't know what they'd do. I was under the impression that Steve would hide it and say nothing, after all, he stood to make a fortune off the album too. But just that feeling of being caught in a lie, that was enough to keep me awake at night.

'I wasn't even sure why I kept the box. Nostalgia, maybe. If the lie did come out I'd have the diaries and tapes to sell. So I wouldn't be totally ruined. Maybe that was it. But the longer I spent in rehab, the stronger the idea was that I needed to get rid of any evidence. Proof of my plagiarism. Then the only ones who'd know were me and my imaginary Busker friend.

'That's what happened next. I got out of rehab. The dreams had tapered off again, back down to once a week, and they were back to the odd glimpses of the Busker showing up in random places. I didn't need to stay awake to avoid them, they just became something that happened to me. My aunt's got high cholesterol and the doctor told her that on its own it wasn't life-threatening, but she'd have to take pills every day for the rest of her life. I equated it to that. The Busker was my high cholesterol.

'I went straight to the house and found the box. It hadn't been touched. Or at least, if it had, whoever found it made it look like it hadn't. I took it into the back yard and threw it into the fire pit. I opened the canisters so that the fire could get in, and I torched the lot. All of the evidence of what I'd done, up in smoke, until you showed up. I finished the album and that was that. No more dreams. No more worries. No more Busker.'

Zach turned to look straight at me.

'Or so I thought. I saw him again a week before you messaged me. The only thing was, I was awake...'

***

All the while as Zach spoke I felt myself instinctively moving closer to Edie for comfort. The retelling of what had happened explained Zach's obvious unease. Not just because his friend was dead. Not because we were blackmailing him. No. Because he was back *here*. At the house. Revisiting the scene of his crime and facing his abuser all in one go.

His fear was palpable and for a moment I felt bad for him and thought about backing out of the whole thing. It only took a glance at Edie to see she felt the same.

The ticking of the clock seemed to be growing in volume until Zach spoke.

'That's what you're fucking with. You want money? Take

THE WILDE DIARIES

it. Fuck it, take all of it if you like, but just know that it won't be your money. It'll be *His*.'

'You said you saw him. Outside of a dream...' I started.

Zach sighed. Heavy, tired. He really didn't want to think about it, that much was clear, but he also knew that he wasn't holding any cards. All he could do was try to scare us off with ghost stories.

'Things had been going okay. Everything was fine. No dreams, not bad ones at least. No issues with the booze or drugs. I was feeling good about myself. I moved out of here a couple of years ago. A few months back some writer or other bought it. At least, that's what I heard. That you?'

I shook my head, avoiding eye contact with Edie. 'A friend.'

'Oh. Anyway, I was clear of it. All the weirdness, the dreams, the house and its strange noises and things going missing and all of its bullshit. Normality. Just getting ready for the tour. I haven't toured since rehab. Every show is a sell-out. The Great British Public have missed me.'

He smiled but it wasn't real. His eyes twinkled with mania and for a moment I wondered if that was what the woman in the café looked like.

'I was out for a walk, just chilling. I like to walk around the town I'm going to play before a show. The way the tours are nowadays, I don't always get chance. It's usually a case of there not being enough time, one day here, back on the bus (or plane if I'm doing America), and onto the next place. No time for sightseeing, which is a fucker because now I've 'made it', I get to play in some awesome places. The other thing is the fans. In the beginning I had the time to walk around but the other thing was, nobody bothered me. They didn't give a shit who I was. It's funny. Back then, I'd be delighted if one person stopped me for an autograph. I'd be floating the rest of the day. Now I'm happy if nobody recognises me. Weird how things change.

'Anyway, I was out walking, and to avoid the crowds I went somewhere quiet. There was a wood behind the park. It's weird, when I was a kid, so we're talking the nineties, my dad would take us, me and my brother, out for walks in the woods near our house. We wouldn't see a lot of people, but there would always be someone else there. Not now. Go to the woods now and it's empty. You can walk for hours and not see another soul. Too many scary stories I think. Nothing bad's ever happened. Not to me. For somebody to hurt you they have to turn up first. Anyway, it's getting late, and the sun is setting somewhere and I'm thinking about turning back, and you know how a smell triggers something? I smelt burning. And as soon as I did, I was back in one of the old dreams. It felt so wrong being there.

'I was just about to turn around, when a few hundred yards ahead, I thought I saw movement out of the corner of my eye. I looked up and it was him. I know what you're thinking: How can you tell from a couple hundred yards? But I could tell. It was him. The way he moved. He just stepped

THE WILDE DIARIES

out from behind a tree and stood staring at me.

'I bolted. The trees rushed by me. The floor of the forest felt exactly the same as it did in the dream too. Soft. Spongy. But I glanced down and sure enough I saw the same knotted tree roots wait to snag my foot and break my ankles. I must have run for ten minutes or so, not realising how far into the woods I was. But you know what the worst part was? When I was running, and the trees started to thin out and I could see my way out, I expected him to emerge from the trees. I expected one of those feet to stick out and step into the path.

'So what happened?' Edie asked.

'I ran until I got back to the hotel, all the way expecting him to catch me, or step out in front of me. Either way, it felt like a warning. When I got back, I didn't even wait for the lift. I couldn't bear the thought of the doors opening and seeing him in there, waiting for me; or worse, for me to get in the empty lift and for him to step inside just as the doors closed. Fuck that. So I got to the room, opened the door, and checked that the room was empty before locking myself in. And I felt safe. Or safer. But I sensed in the back of my mind that I wasn't in the clear, like that moment you tell a lie and aren't sure if you're going to get away with it.

'Well, I didn't get away with it. The door was locked, and I was still out of breath, and so I slumped onto the bed and the second I did, the phone rang. It scared the shit out of me. The receptionist said it was my manager. The receptionist had transferred calls to me before that, but now her voice was different. Odd. I took the call and my manager sounded hollow, in shock.

'He said, "It's Chris." Chris is one of the roadies. But he's an old friend. I got him the job because I wanted to keep him around. He'd tried to kill himself. He came back yesterday and I asked him "Are you sure? Are you sure you're okay?" And I knew. I knew he was going to try it again and I did nothing. Steve was waiting for me as soon as I finished rehearsals last night. I knew that Chris was gone. He'd said he wasn't feeling well, gone back to his hotel room, took a red silk scarf that one of the back-up dancers wore, wrapped one end around the bedpost, and the other around his neck.'

The silence hung heavily again and I was going to speak, to say anything to break it, but before I got the chance, there was a knock at the front door.

***

My first thought upon hearing the knock was that Zach had set us up. Here was a man who, compared to me at least, had unlimited resources. It would be quite easy for him to contact a group of heavies and ask them to come to the house at a certain time. We were all frozen. That's when I realised. Zach had no idea who it was either.

Another bang followed. I stood, just as a silhouette appeared at the window. Cupping the light from his eyes with one hand.

'Hello? I know you're in there. I can see all of the cars.'

THE WILDE DIARIES

That's what the voice said. A voice I recognised at once.

Shit.

'It's David.' Edie replied, a hint of confusion and worry in her voice.

I opened the door and he stood there, hair perfect, drenched in cologne, gripping a bunch of roses.

'You're early,' Edie said over my shoulder. 'I wasn't expecting you till later.'

He stepped inside grinning, 'I have news.'

'I'll leave you to it,' I said and went back into the room with Zach.

Zach was standing, looking ready to go when I went back into the room. 'Sorry about that.'

'Just tell me what you want and let me get out of here.'

'Please,' I gestured to the settee and he sat once again.

I wanted to do more fishing on his previous story while Edie was gone. I'd ignored it before. Glossed over it in a moment of greed fuelled haste. But the thought of Seth's note about blackmail and silence and sacrifice and the death of Chris the roadie had my interest piqued.

'You said before the parties you were going to were getting wilder and wilder. Was it the new drug you mentioned?'

Zach's face changed. Like he'd said something he shouldn't have and thought he'd got away with it.

'Come on Zach. It's just us here now...'

He exhaled another heavy breath. 'How much do you

want?'

'No no. You tell me. Tell me about the drug and the price comes down.'

His eyes were weighing up whether or not to tell me. He was trying to guess how much I knew.

'I'd never heard of it. Everyone at the parties was doing it.'

'So everyone in the music biz is on it?'

'No. Not everyone. It's a handful of people.'

'Actors too?'

'Actors, sportsmen, politicians.'

'Where did it come from?'

'I didn't know. They had it.'

'And what did it do?'

'It was the most insane of highs. That's why the parties are private. You have no control. You'll do anything and not remember doing it.'

Blackmail.

'And that's why the parties were getting wilder?'

Zach's eyes washed over like he'd gone back somewhere. The colour slowly drained from his face and his eyes filled with tears.

'I think I've said all I want to say. Tell me how much you want.'

I'd got more than I expected from him. It was enough. I scribbled numbers onto a piece of paper as I spoke.

'I've been reading up. The music business has changed.

THE WILDE DIARIES

It's not all about sales now. Downloads. You barely make anything off those. Since mp3s came along your money is made from touring, so...'

I was interrupted by a delighted shriek from the hallway. Whatever David had said to Edie had left her delighted. My heart sank. Any thought of her leaving him vanished at that moment. It might be a sound that cost Zach Fox a lot of money.

'So to ask for a cut of the album sales wouldn't do it. In all honesty, the exposure from that album probably gave you a boost in the previous album sales. Ticket sales. Merchandise sales. I looked into how much you're worth.'

Giggling from the hallway now. I slid the paper across to him.

'I want twenty percent.'

Zach's eyes widened. 'Twenty percent of what?'

'Of everything. Your net worth.'

'I haven't got that kind of money!'

I stared at him emotionless. 'But you could get it. You have assets to sell. I don't have to have it all at once. I'm a reasonable man.'

'Reasonable! This will break me!'

'No,' I stopped him. 'Not sleeping in silk sheets. Buying Champagne that's not really Champagne. Getting hate mail instead of fan mail. Having to do your own grocery shopping. Being a nobody. *That* will break you.'

Zach couldn't even look at me. There was no hatred in

his face. Just resignation. Like a little boy with his hand caught in the cookie jar. He knew I was right. And even though I'd done less than he had to earn that money, he knew I was right. Losing all of the things he loved would break him.

I stood up. 'I'll give you twenty-four hours to think about it. We can sort out the details from there. And don't even think about the police. I can have you ruined before the night's over if needs be.'

Zach stood too. He looked like it was something he'd been waiting for, like there might be a hint of relief that living this lie was over. Whatever. I didn't care. He was going to pay up, and I was going to retire.

'I look forward to hearing from you,' I said opening the door.

He went silently into the hallway staring at the floor as he went. The chatter from the open kitchen door stopped and I glanced in there to see a bottle of Champagne and two glasses in front of a gobsmacked David.

Zach left and I went to the kitchen.

'Champagne? What are we celebrating?' I tried to hide my bitterness at David's good news.

'I've been at the magazine,' David replied, exuding smugness. 'There was a bit of a crisis. The owner was there.'

Edie chimed in, 'The editor was *not* handling things.'

My mind went back to my own time at the magazine. Wasn't that what they thought about me when I was passed over for promotion? David Thorne strikes again.

THE WILDE DIARIES

'Anyway, long story short, you're looking at the new editor in chief of Politics Fortnightly Magazine.'

'Well,' I said, eyes darting to Edie before settling back on David, 'let me get a glass for myself.'

'I'm sorry, but what was Zach Fox doing here?' David asked, voice high-pitched with intrigue.

'Edie didn't tell you?'

I paused mid-reach for the glass.

She'd better not have done.

'She didn't even say he was in there. Though I did wonder who the bright orange Lambo belonged too.'

Good. Very good. I brought my glass to the table and filled it to the top.

'We're just talking for now, but I might be doing a biography.'

'Jesus, he's only what, twelve?'

Edie replied, 'David! He's twenty-seven,' her tone coloured with a hint of admonishment.

'No, no. I mean. Well done,' David said, faking a smile. 'Good for you and all. It's just that they release bios and autobiographies before they can tie their own shoes these days, don't they.'

I fake-smiled back. 'It does seem that way I suppose. He does have some interesting stories though, right Edie?'

She just smiled, wanly.

'Listen, if you can make a quick buck, more power to you.'

I smiled, 'I think I can.'

Edie raised a glass, 'To success.'

We clinked glasses and I drained half of mine.

'Where's the little boys' room here, old chap?'

'Top of the stairs, straight in front of you.'

David went and we stood in silence until we heard the toilet door close.

'So David's landed the top job...'

I looked at Edie and I didn't like what I saw. She was going to stay with him.

'This is all happening so fast, Joel.'

'Not a word. Not a word about the songs or the diaries or any of it. Or I tell him. About us.'

Her mouth fell open. The last thing she expected from me was a show of strength in a moment of weakness. She said she needed time, but I'd been here before. I've seen how this story ends and the handsome guy with great hair always gets the girl. Especially if he's just got a promotion. She wouldn't want my dirty money, but that was fine. It just meant more for me.

The toilet flushed upstairs.

'Dry your eyes,' I said throwing a napkin to her.

'You're a bastard. You know that? I'd expect that from him, not you.'

'We both know how you're going to choose. I've just saved us both some time.'

The door opened, and Edie smiled widely, hiding her

THE WILDE DIARIES

sadness. 'So, a biography...'

All I could do now was to wait for them to go. Seeing them together like this in the moment of David's victory hurt. And I wanted to hurt them. But I had bigger fish to fry. I was just relieved that I'd kept Lucas Wilde's final diary to myself.

LUCAS WILDE'S DIARY #4

14th September 1977

Lucas surveyed his surroundings acutely aware that he was in the clutches of another dream. In it, he was also aware that it had been only three days since the last song he wrote, and therefore, he presumed, the last dream.

The auditorium where he sat may have been empty, but the buzz in the air suggested that it wouldn't remain that way for long. That same energy he felt before a show fizzed in the air, and a show here, in this place, well, that was the show to top them all. For Lucas, playing here would represent the pinnacle, the peak of fame and superstardom, after all, only the biggest acts sell out shows at the Royal Albert Hall. The picking of notes from a guitar drew Lucas' attention away from the high ceilings adorned with chandeliers and towards the stage. And the prickle of cold that touched him should have told him that it wasn't some sound engineer tuning up before the gig started in earnest. It was Him.

The Busker sat, head down focused on the guitar, hat

tilted at an angle thankfully obscuring his face. There was an aura around him the likes he'd seen only around the most famous. A charismatic magnetism only the best athletes, politicians and artists cast out. This was the elite. The other musicians he'd seen with this aura, he'd have gladly paid money just to look at, without hearing them play a single note.

Before Lucas could speak, the Busker started playing the last song he'd written, and he began to wonder how much of the Busker was him, and why the thought had never occurred to him earlier. The Busker played beautifully, and his voice echoed with wisdom thousands of years old. The moment where the gut-wrenching chord/melody change hit and the hairs on the back of his neck tingled, standing like a cobra mesmerised by this mystical snake charmer. The Busker cried out the chorus pleadingly and Lucas started to hear his own voice, coming from his tormentor's mouth.

Then it was over. Before Lucas could move the guitar was once again playing. This time something else. Something new.

His heart sped up with excitement. The new song unfolded before him, a sweeping epic, operatic in scope. Where the changes came Lucas felt a jarring shock at the sense of loss and longing for the part left behind, quickly replaced by the sense of adventure at the unknown unfolding before him, and an overwhelming excitement at what lay beyond the next line, the next verse. He wouldn't have been able to say how long the song went on for. All he knew was when it finished he was exhausted, but he wanted to hear it again. Every single second. The song was so long that recalling this when he woke up would be a minor miracle, but he also felt, *knew*, that if that was what the Busker wanted, that was exactly what would happen.

He left his seat and climbed the stairs to mount the stage.

The Busker spoke first. 'With this song, that makes four. You could finish what you've got yourself and make a pretty good album.'

He knew it was true, but still felt sad at what he implied. 'So that's it? That's all of the songs.'

'All of the ones for you. You take these, you won't need me anymore. After these, there will be no doors closed to you. You can do anything. Go anywhere.'

Lucas nodded. He understood. The dreams he'd had before the Busker showed, with him rubbing shoulders with the biggest names of them all, a place where he was their equal, that was where this path led. That's all he wanted.

'Of course,' the Busker smiled, 'there's a price.'

Lucas shivered and instinctively took half a step backwards. 'A price?'

'There's always a price.' His rotten teeth glistened in the spotlight.

Lucas searched his mind for what happened in the previous dream but came back with nothing, the only image he could summon up the signing of the contract in the loft.

'Are you going to kill someone again?'

'Again?'

'Mandy.'

'I've already told you that wasn't me.'

The words came out harsh and chastising. It made the skin of his scrotum tighten. He wanted to ask what this song would cost him, but was afraid, even in a dream; it felt like whatever happened here was binding. There were no loopholes here. This mattered. Whatever transpired now would echo in real life, he was certain of it. But still, he asked.

'What do I have to do?'

The Busker looked at him again and smiled. A sick twisted smile that reminded him somehow of rotten fish.

The Busker stood and walked away to the guitar stand and placed his acoustic down gently like a father handling a newborn. His feet clumped but Lucas didn't want to look down to see if the sound of the footsteps was boots or...

Don't. Don't say it.

The Busker turned and walked back, that stilted gait more uneven that before, and the long black coat swung open. Lucas' eyes were drawn down, and whatever was in his stomach in this dream curdled.

'You can't be serious.'

'What do you think would happen if you didn't do this?'

Before he could answer, his mind filled in the blanks.

He was scrambling downstairs and into the recording room. Not searching out his guitar, or even the reel to reel

THE WILDE DIARIES

player. No, he was searching out the tapes. He burst into the room gripped by panic. He slid on his knees to the bottom drawer and grabbed the first cannister. Hands shaking he loaded the tape into the reel to reel and hit play. The player whirred into life, but that was the only sound. No tuning, no talking, no song. The tape was blank. With a scream he threw it to the floor and grabbed the next tape. And the one after. The results were the same. He grabbed the guitar, but it felt heavy in his hands. There was no magic in it. No songs. No life. It was a dead weight.

Dead.

'NO! They're *my* fucking songs.'

The Busker just laughed at him. 'Not yet.'

Lucas looked down again and gagged. The bulge in the front of the Busker's stained trousers was bigger. He swallowed the vomit that rose up the back of his throat.

'No. There must be something else. Anything. Name it. Anything you want.'

'All in good time. For now, this.' This last word came out *thisss* in a reptilian hiss.

His stomach turned not just at the task in hand, but at the thought of losing the songs and going back to the mental block he had before.

'Oh God. Please. Please! There must be something else.'

The thought of never being able to finish another song stabbed at his gut. The thought of playing the same songs over and over to steadily diminishing crowds until there was nobody listening at all. He cried.

'You already know where that road ends, Lucas. So what's it going to be?'

He sobbed, 'But I've never...' His gaze fell back down to the swollen growth of the Busker's groin.

'You've *received* haven't you?'

'Yes.'

'So you know what you like?'

He nodded, his face burning, already alight with the deep sense of shame. 'Yes.'

'I can't hear you...'

'Yes. For fuck's sake, YES.'

'So you know what you like. That's what I want.'

He gagged again. Again he started crying. 'For how long?'

The Busker laughed. 'You'll know when I'm done.'

Lucas turned away and threw up between deep, wrenching sobs. 'I don't want to,' he blubbed.

'What?'

Lucas turned back to face the Busker but didn't - couldn't - look at him. 'Nothing.'

He edged closer to the Busker and his eyes fell again upon the huge swelling in the front of his trousers. He quickly looked away, 'Oh Jesus.' His mind tried to block out the thoughts and ideas about what exactly those stains were. As he got closer the smell quickly worsened. A thick stench the mixture of sweat and bad hygiene forced another gag as he fell to his knees on the hard wood of the stage before the

THE WILDE DIARIES

Busker. Hot tears fell down his face and a blooming sense of shame and self-loathing swelled in his heart. The Busker stood motionless, hands behind his back, tucking the long coat out of the way, giving Lucas a clear view.

'Do it!' a voice shouted.

Lucas turned and now the seats were no longer empty. The stalls were filled with a faceless crowd, all wearing masks. He recognised the voice. Someone familiar. Famous. An actor?

'Do it!' another voice cried.

'We all had to.'

The Busker cleared his throat. Lucas stared at the crowd for a moment, before turning back with a heavy sense of resignation.

With trembling hands, he reached up and unfastened the button on the Busker's trousers.

***

Lucas leapt from his bed, screaming, and burst into the bathroom. He slid for the toilet and grabbed it as his stomach wrenched, forcing a foul, stinking hot stream of viscous liquid into the bowl. For a second his eyes opened and saw the thick black ooze that hung in the water, and he threw up again. The vile stench of rotting made him gag and again he heaved, this time nothing but a fetid string of what he hoped was bile spilled from him. He flushed the toilet and fell to the cold tile of the bathroom floor and wept.

MARC W SHAKO

***

Lucas awoke shivering on the cold bathroom floor and retched into the toilet again. Nothing came out except for that same foul stench like sour sweat and rotten eggs, forcing a more violent attempt at vomiting. The vicious circle went on and on for minutes, each failed attempt at vomiting releasing that same nauseating stench until his abdomen ached and wailed in agony. Eventually it subsided and he crawled into bed and again started to cry. By the time he woke up it was already dark. There had been a fundamental shift in his world. There would always be a before and after. It would probably get better over time, or at least, that's what he tried to convince himself, but the strangest thing was, if he could wind back the clock and relive that same moment again, he wasn't convinced he'd choose differently.

What choice was there? It was that, or a life of ever-decreasing obscurity. That's no life at all.

He got up, dressed and ventured downstairs. The hallway felt dark and oppressive, like it was occupied before he got there. It sent a chill through him and it made him swallow hard, forcing a hand to his throat. His throat was sore but it felt less like a cold and more like bruising. He raised a hand to his mouth and gagged again. He slouched into the kitchen and opened the booze cupboard. If that solitary bottle of whiskey hadn't been there, he didn't know what he'd have done. He grabbed a heavy bottomed tumbler and filled it all the way up before swilling half of the glass down in one go. He burped

THE WILDE DIARIES

and the smell of whiskey mixed with the foulness emanated from his gut.

He drained the rest of the glass and slammed it on the counter. The clock was ticking before the booze hit home, he needed to start recording, and fast. He strode into the recording room and grabbed a fresh tape from the bottom drawer. The reel to reel whirred into life as he started to play. A new song. The fourth song.

The song soared into existence from his guitar, like the birth of a baby that would grow to become a legend. On it went building, growing, lulling, and climaxing into one of the greatest stories ever told. Lucas had remembered every note, every word, every change. This was the song that would elevate the whole album to classic status. A handful of the other songs finished in the same style and people would talk about this album forever.

By the time he shoved the guitar back into the stand, the buzz of the booze was starting to warm him. He lurched back into the kitchen and made himself a strong black coffee. Other snippets of his own unfinished songs went through his head as he waited for the coffee to cool. Drinking it still hurt, every time he swallowed it angered the bruise at the back of his throat, reminding him of what he'd had to do to get his reward from the Busker. As he stared into the cup, he hummed the tune to his favourite unfinished composition, and something happened. Something natural that he'd felt a hundred times before. The nebulous cloud of unfinished song coalesced into something whole. Not yet complete, but no longer shapeless. He rose and crossed the hallway into the recording room. This time, when he snatched up the guitar it thrummed in his hands, and when he strummed out the chords for the verse, there it was, waiting for him, like it had been there all along - the chorus. And it was a strong one, too.

Five minutes later, he hit the stop button and the reel to reel slowed to a halt, the fifth song for the new album recorded and ready to show to the band. Sure, the fifth wasn't at the same level as the other songs, but it was no weaker than anything on the first albums.

He stood in the hallway, listening to the ring tone from the receiver pressed against his ear.

'Come on, Johnny, answer.'

The caffeine kicked in and started to battle the alcohol in his system, and the elation of finishing two songs was fading, replaced by the feeling of not being alone. He instinctively turned and placed his back against the wall. The hallway was empty but for him and the buzz of the phone, even if it didn't feel like it.

'Hello?'

'Johnny.'

'Lucas?'

'I'm ready.'

'For what?' He sounded groggy. It sounded like Lucas had woken him up.

'I've got some songs ready. They'll knock your fucking

socks off mate.'

There was a stirring like Johnny had sat up. 'Really? That's great! I was starting to think you'd got writer's block or something with all the delays.'

'No fucking danger mate. My house, tomorrow. 8 o'clock. Invite the whole gang. Bring booze. And food.'

The was a slight pause.

'The *whole* gang?'

Lucas knew what he was getting at. Petty squabbles were beneath the newly invigorated Lucas Wilde. 'Yes. All of them. Malcolm and Sally too.'

'Brilliant. See you tomorrow.'

Johnny sounded relieved. Like the call had lifted a great weight from his shoulders. He'd had a weight lifted from his own, that was for sure. Album number three was taking shape. He was back.

15th September 1977

On the morning of the party, at around eleven, it started to rain, a downpour that wouldn't let up until the next day. Lucas' mood had improved slightly since the day before, doing his best to concentrate on the success that the new songs would bring and not on the pain that still came whenever he tried to swallow. His mind had protected him from the dreams and whatever had happened to him was already distant, like it had happened weeks ago, rather than a couple of nights.

He'd forced himself out of the house to buy food and drinks for the upcoming party. And he still wasn't sure if he was going to play the tapes or the acoustic to introduce the new songs, but he was leaning towards the tapes. That way he could gauge the others' response to the songs rather than worrying about the next line or next chord. He also thought it better to wait until everyone was nicely buzzed before he introduced them to the new material.

In town, he'd decided against going back into the café despite his hunger. After the last experience, he wasn't sure he could ever set foot in there again. His entire time in town was spent eyes constantly drawn over his shoulder, unable to shake the feeling he was being followed, watched.

Safely back at the house, he decided that the main party would take place in the recording room, and that the séance room would remain locked. The memories in there were too much for him, let alone what poor Des might feel. Everyone except Des had confirmed. Johnny was going to come with Mal and Sally. Jack was coming with "two plus ones, but one's for you", he'd cryptically said. And Dizzy's girlfriend was going to drive the two of them out there, Dizzy's main job being securing dope and talking Des into coming. Dizzy's girl Sadie would probably bring a friend whether or not Des came. Lucas just hoped she wasn't as talkative as Sadie. It would be great if someone else at the party got a chance to

THE WILDE DIARIES

speak.

He was more nervous about meeting Malcolm than he was Des. Des was always quiet and friendly. Whenever they'd had a disagreement about something, they could always talk it through, that was just Derek's laid back way. Mal was belligerent. Especially after a few beers. Lucas always thought that it was a bit of a show to let everyone know that he wouldn't be pushed around, and if he stood up to Lucas, the rest of them had no chance. It had got him this far, but Lucas was worried how much longer it could last, their relationship had strained to breaking point. Lucas had invited Mal and Sally tonight to extend an olive branch, but he was worried about how Mal would behave. If the olive branch was accepted then they could all move on to album number three like they always had: Together. Any shit from Malcolm tonight and that was it. Lucas was done with him. He felt bad for Sally. Sure she was a bossy cow, but that came from a place of wanting to protect Mal. They'd been together for so long now, it was hard to distinguish them as separate people. If Mal went down, he'd drag Sally with him.

There was no sunset that evening, the grey clouds just darkened until the sky was black, still pouring heavy rain. He turned lights on in the kitchen and hallway, left a light on upstairs so everyone could find their way to the toilet easily. The record player fired *Goats Head Soup* into the recording room and the only light in there was from a couple of lamps he had, just to get the mood right (there were no candles in the house). The small glass of whiskey he drank while he got ready calmed his nerves. He was surprised at just how normal the house felt. There was no heavy atmosphere. No feeling of being watched. No feeling of someone else being there. It was just a house. The Rolling Stones had only got as far as *100 Years Ago* before the doorbell rang.

***

In the hallway, the sound of rain was heavier. He wondered who had arrived first and decided it was probably Jack. It was usually Jack.

He was shocked to open the door to Sadie. How had she managed to get Dizzy ready early?

'Luke! Hello handsome, have you lost weight? You look thin. Too thin.'

'Hi Sadie. A bit yeah, come in,' he managed to mumble as Sadie burst past him.

Dizzy appeared, red eyed. 'Mate.' He said it like the word was heavy and he'd dragged it out.

'Mate.' He peered round the corner. 'No Des?'

'Just us. He's coming with Jack.'

'Oh. Right.'

Sadie had already made her way into the kitchen and uncorked the white wine she'd brought.

'Glasses?'

Lucas pointed to the cupboard over the sink before asking Dizzy, 'How is he? Des.'

THE WILDE DIARIES

'He's all right. He never says much, you know what he's like.'

'So this is the new pad.' Sadie asked, from the kitchen.

'This is it.'

'Let's have a tour then.'

This was Sadie's first visit to the house. She'd missed the party with the séance, Dizzy had come to that one alone. She came out with glasses of wine for herself and Dizzy and looked expectantly at Lucas.

'Er, yeah okay.'

He showed them the downstairs, omitting the room where they'd held the séance. Sadie wanted to see inside and even tried the handle, after Lucas had said it was out-of-bounds.

'I'm redecorating,' Lucas said, glancing sideways at Dizzy, who just shrugged.

'Let's go upstairs,' Dizzy offered.

They went upstairs (Sadie reluctantly) and Sadie asked loads of questions about the rooms and what he'd done to them, which wasn't much, and Dizzy just sipped wine and passed the joint he'd walked in with between himself and Lucas. Every time they exited a room, Lucas' eyes went straight to the narrow stairway that disappeared in darkness up to the attic. The thought of going up there gave him the creeps. Lucas was nicely buzzed and joking around with Sadie, mostly to distract her from the attic.

He was about to lead them back downstairs when Sadie

asked, 'Where do those stairs go?'

'Oh, that's just the loft. Nothing special,' Lucas replied, eyes already focused downstairs.

Just the room where I signed my soul away.

'We'd still like to see. I bet the views from up there are great.'

He felt his throat tightening.

'It's dark. I don't think the lights work, you won't see much.'

'Lucas, what are you hiding up there?' she teased. She was trying to make it sound playful, but Sadie was used to getting her own way.

'Come on, let's go down,' Dizzy said.

'I want to see,' Sadie replied.

Lucas was saved by a knock from downstairs.

'Help yourselves, I'll get the door.'

He left them, staring at the ominous dark stairway before he went.

***

Johnny smiled at him from the front step, water cascading off the roof behind. It was a relief to see Johnny. It was always a relief to see Johnny. Johnny was the father figure he needed, now he felt the wheels falling off his sanity. But there was something about this smile. Guilty. No, not quite. Something was wrong, but it wasn't his fault.

'Hello, Wilde thing,' a slurred voice came from behind.

THE WILDE DIARIES

Lucas had already stepped aside to let Johnny in from the rain when Sally came around the corner, propping up Malcolm.

'Sorry mate,' Johnny whispered as he came past.

'Hi Luke!' Sally planted a kiss on Lucas' cheek which he was sure had left bright red lipstick behind.

'Hi Luke!' Mal slurred, kissing the other cheek, the stink of booze lingering around him in an invisible fog.

'Let's go to the kitchen for refreshments,' Lucas said, shooing Mal and Sally in front of him.

He fired a glance over at Johnny.

Johnny whispered to him. 'They were like this when they picked me up. She's half as pissed as he is and she was driving. Fucking white-knuckle ride coming over here, it was.'

Mal propped himself against the counter and looked like he might fall asleep at any second. Trust him to come already pissed. He could see it now. Mal was going to annoy the shit out of everyone and ruin the vibe. Now it wouldn't be about the new songs, it was all going to be about Malcolm.

'You all right?'

Lucas turned to face Johnny, he was looking at him face clouded over with genuine concern. 'You look tired.'

I've bought a haunted fucking house, barely slept, barely eaten, sold my soul to get some new songs and sucked a foul smelling diseased dick and the one night I've set aside to celebrate getting over writer's block, fucking Malcolm's turned up arseholed and will make the whole night about him.

'I am a bit.'

Johnny smiled. 'Can't wait to hear the new songs.'

Lucas smiled back just as Dizzy and Sadie came downstairs.

'Johnny!' Sadie shouted. 'Doesn't he look thin? Too thin, right?'

Dizzy had lit up another joint and his eyes were half closed. When he landed on ground level from the stairs, he offered it to Lucas. Lucas grabbed it and took a deep drag, the smoke burning his bruised throat, making him cough.

'Wheyyy! Lucas can't take it!' Malcolm jeered.

'Don't fucking give him any of this,' Lucas said handing the joint back to Dizzy. 'And fuck off, Mal,' he shouted, hoping to make it clear that it wasn't friendly.

The Rolling Stones were now singing about Angie, so he headed into the recording room ready to turn the record over. The soreness in his throat had returned and from nowhere, just for a second, the faint whiff of sour sweat rose. He gagged, but just as quickly as the smell came it was gone. He flipped the record on the turntable as Johnny ambled in with two glasses.

'You okay?' he asked, thrusting a glass at Lucas.

'Fucking Mal,' was all he said.

There had been too many times to count in the past where Johnny had been mediator, stepping in and saving Mal (and Sally) from the chop. Johnny was less a manager and more like a dad to a bunch of wild kids.

THE WILDE DIARIES

'Just say the word and he's done.'

Lucas, it seemed, wasn't the only one tired of Mal's schtick. But hearing it come from someone else made him feel bad, mostly for Sally who was too loyal to cut Malcolm loose. Ballast.

He nodded, 'We'll just see how tonight goes, John, yeah.'

'Try to relax mate. You've obviously been overdoing it. Unwind and have a good night.'

He nodded.

There was a crash from the kitchen. At least two glasses had broken. Maybe a bottle too. Lucas rounded on the door ready to explode when there was a banging sound from the front door.

Johnny clapped him on the shoulder, 'You get the door. I'll see to him.'

Lucas drew in a deep breath, trying to calm himself when the door banged again. He remembered the rain and rushed into the hallway.

'Sorry Luke.' Malcolm slurred from somewhere behind.

He ignored him and opened the door. Jack Mayberry stood smiling, holding a bottle of Champagne. He entered and hugged him.

'Denise isn't coming. Too tired. You okay, you look a bit better.'

Lucas hugged him back and smiled at Jack's girl. Another new one he didn't recognise.

'This is Barbara.'

'Hi. Pleased to meet you.' She smiled an excited grin. Another groupie. Jack couldn't help himself. Lucas smiled back.

'Jack Mayberry!' Sadie shouted over the chatter and laughter and Rolling Stones.

Jack and Barbara went into the kitchen and Lucas got a tap on the shoulder. Lucas turned and grinned.

'Des! Mate!' He hugged him. 'Glad you came mate,' he said into his ear.

Des stepped back. 'Can't wait to hear the new stuff mate. Has Dizzy got any...?' he mimed a joint.

Lucas smiled. 'Have you ever met Dizzy?'

It was only now that Lucas realised that while he was talking to Des the front door had closed behind him. He turned.

'Hello, you.'

Lucas was almost struck dumb. It was Jack's other plus one. The one for him.

'Shelley, hi.'

For just that split second, the problems and writer's block and Mal's drunken idiocy all faded and he was propelled back five years into a time when there were no problems. No problems even though the band was playing to packed out pubs instead of arenas. No problems even though he was living not in his own paid-for house but a shitty two room flat and no hot water with Des. No problems even though the band had nowhere to practice instead of the best studios in

THE WILDE DIARIES

town. A simpler time. When Shelley was all he needed. Before his mind could move on to the end of that golden time where Shelley was tired of his drinking, she thankfully replied.

'How are you?'

'I'm okay.' It was only half a lie.

Lucas suddenly had a good feeling about the night. Then he smelled the Busker.

***

As the moment to introduce the new songs neared, Lucas did everything to put as many people as he could between him and Mal, and chatted with Shelley, Jack and Barbara. Jack had moved on from champagne, gone past beer, and was now on his fourth bourbon, he'd enjoy the songs tonight, but the chances of him remembering them tomorrow were diminishing by the minute. Sadie was talking the back legs off anyone who'd listen. Dizzy's pot intake was reaching watershed levels and if the reveal didn't come soon, he'd miss the whole thing. The party had finally moved from the kitchen and was now entirely in the recording room, people leaving only for toilet breaks and to top up drinks.

'Malcolm hasn't changed,' Shelley said.

Lucas felt embarrassed. He glanced at Malcolm and it was like looking back in time, at himself.

'I can't believe that used to be me.'

Shelley placed a hand gently in the small of his back and looked him in the eyes. A warmth passed through him.

'You're not like that now, I can see.'

Lucas was about to smile back. Their faces were close. Before he could lean in for a kiss, a familiar, foul smell rose.

He quickly turned his head away from Shelley and emptied his glass. 'Ready for another?'

'Er, yes. Please.'

He'd surprised and disappointed her. But she hadn't reacted to the smell. It was impossible she hadn't smelt it. He took her glass and headed into the kitchen.

'Get me one,' Mal slurred as he went past.

The kitchen was quiet and empty and cool. It was a relief to be alone. Only now, he didn't feel alone. There had been times when he'd looked up at the party and caught someone staring at him, like they knew his dirty little secret. Nobody knew. The smell was the Busker, fucking with him. A reminder of who was really in charge here.

He poured a large bourbon for himself and a smaller one for Shelley. As he added lemonade to her drink, he felt the gentle pressure of a bony hand on the back of his head, stroking his hair.

He screamed and dropped the lemonade bottle. It shattered on the floor.

'Lucas?'

He screamed again, turning to see Shelley. She covered her mouth to hide a guilty laugh.

Lucas laughed back.

'You scared the shit out of me.'

THE WILDE DIARIES

She moved around the table and crouched beside him, helping him pick up the broken bottle.

'Are you really okay?' Shelley asked.

Lucas straightened the back of his hair, 'Yeah, fine.'

'You seem on edge.'

He forced a smile. 'Bit nervous about how everyone will react to the new songs, that's all.'

'And when do we get to hear these new songs?' Johnny boomed from the doorway behind him.

'Yeah come on, Lucas!' Sadie shouted, not slurring a single syllable despite the full bottle of wine she'd put away.

'Your public awaits,' Shelley smiled. She kissed his cheek.

He turned and kissed her on the lips. Just briefly. It was all he dared.

He switched off the turntable, and carefully loaded the first tape from the cannisters by the reel to reel.

Before he played, Mal came out of nowhere, teary-eyed and put a hand on Lucas' shoulder. 'Mate,' he said, not slurring at all now, like a drunkards moment of clarity, 'I'm sorry I got wasted. I was just nervous. I didn't mean to be such a twat. I love you mate.'

Lucas was taken aback by the maturity and honesty from a guy he'd wanted to kill a few hours before. 'Thanks mate. I appreciate that. Now sit and listen to this,' he said with a wink.

Everyone sat around as the first chord sounded to *Greater Than Me*. The sound quality on the tapes wasn't the best, but the emotion and songwriting shone through, heavily outweighing the echoing acoustics. The party was rapt, everyone in the room it seemed holding their collective breath until it finished. When it did there was silence.

Jack spoke first.

'Rubbish.'

Lucas felt a massive weight lift from him as the room burst into laughter. It was a joke they shared, saved only for the absolute best in quality. Comedian Eric Morecambe had said an amazing musical performance on his television programme was 'Rubbish' and the band always said it now in honour of any great performance.

'Really, what did you think?'

Jack shook his head, eyes half closed, 'It's fucking amazing mate.'

The rest of the room piped up now with their own platitudes.

'You fuckers had me going, I thought you didn't like it.'

'Put the next one on!' Mal shouted.

He decided to play the third song next. The slower number *All the King's Horses*. This time he watched the women's reaction in the room. He knew this was a tearjerker, and the ladies all dabbed their faces throughout the song. When it finished he already knew this was a winner. He turned to get Johnny's opinion and saw that his eyes were watering.

'Fucking twat. Made me cry, you have.'

The room laughed again, this time the relieved laughter

THE WILDE DIARIES

that it wasn't only them the song had touched. The third song had everyone on their feet dancing and for the fourth he slipped his own composition into the mix to see if the theory that the others would elevate it held. It did.

'I liked that one best,' said Mal. 'I can't say why, I just do.'

Lucas smiled.

'Okay, ladies and gentlemen,' Lucas announced, the rain still pelting the window in the silence, 'now the moment I've been waiting for... I've saved what I think is the best for last.'

Theatrical *oohs* and *ahs* came from all sides and Lucas was now fully relaxed. The thought that his guests knew about his private moment with the Busker long forgotten, the notion that the night was about to take a dark turn nowhere in his mind at all.

'Ladies and gentlemen, I give you *Heaven Knows Best*.'

Enthusiastic applause burst and then died down as the first notes floated into the air. He glanced at Shelley not surprised to see she was already looking at him. Elation bloomed in him when he caught the gleam in her eye. He thought he'd seen glimpses of it before, but then the smell would arise, or an invisible hand would stroke the back of his head; such distractions were miles away. Now it was almost as if it was only the two of them in the room. She winked her secret wink and he knew then that the clock had turned back for her too. He winked back as the song entered its final phase and now he turned to see the faces of the others, all lost somewhere in the little world he'd created

MARC W SHAKO

The little world He'd *created.*

and then it was over. The room sighed collectively as if they'd returned from an epic journey and cheers and clapping erupted. Jack stood and hugged him and Des joined in. Dizzy looked over from the armchair he'd melted into and just shook his head, mind blown by the masterpiece he'd just heard.

'Johnny?'

The room fell silent and all eyes fell on Johnny. Johnny who'd been in the business for nearly two decades. Johnny who'd told anyone who'd listen that Hendrix and Clapton were going to become Gods before anyone had heard of them. Johnny looked at Lucas and smiled.

'I think we're going to be rich.'

The room exploded in cheers again and more hugs and congratulations were shared.

Shelley came over and draped her hands over his shoulders and looked into him with those smoky eyes of hers, eyes full of promise and desire. Without a word she kissed him, for just long enough for him to know that she wanted more than just friendship.

'I'm off for a drink, who wants one?' Mal shouted. All replies came in negative. While the songs were playing, nobody drank. A couple of Dizzy's joints did the rounds, of course.

Lucas looked over, 'Get us a whiskey, Mal.'

Mal looked back and smiled, nodded.

THE WILDE DIARIES

The next few minutes flew by in a whirl of congratulations and admiration, until Mal reappeared with his drink.

'Here you go mate.'

'Cheers.'

Lucas took the glass and took a gulp. Then the smell hit him again.

'Those songs are unbelievable mate.'

Jack stood beside him, talking, slurring, but after the first few words, the sentence faded into silence. Lucas stared into the glass Malcolm had handed to him. Suspended in the liquid was a thick white squirt of semen. Hanging there like some foul lava lamp.

'You fucking bastard!' Lucas screamed and leapt at Mal, throwing the glass aside.

At first everyone turned, thinking that the shout was good-natured horseplay, but it soon became clear it was not. The chuckles of interest turned into screams from the women as Lucas jumped on Mal and started punching. Mal fell back with Lucas on top of him. He'd put his hands up to block the punches but one in three got through and connected with his face. Lucas had landed four or five good blows before Johnny and Jack dragged him off. He was still swinging and shouting as they did.

'You fucking dirty bastard you twat you fucking couldn't help yourself could you?'

Mal had dragged himself upright against the wall, and

Sally crouched beside him. Mal was nonplussed at the attack, shocked by its suddenness and severity.

'What's wrong?' he said to Lucas. 'I don't know what I've done.'

'You know what you've fucking done.' Lucas shouted, almost revealing the dirty secret to the rest of the room himself. 'Get the fuck out and don't fucking come back. You're fucking finished. You too,' he shouted, pointing at Sally.

'Fuck off!' she shouted, helping Mal to his feet with Des at the other side.

Jack spoke softly into the silence. 'You can't let them go, Luke. Look at the weather. They've been drinking.'

The words fell away leaving only the patter of rain on the window.

'I don't know what I've done,' was all Mal could say.

'We wouldn't fucking stay here if our lives depended on it,' Sally screamed.

'At least let us get you a taxi,' Johnny offered.

'Let them go, John. They've been nothing but trouble since the fucking beginning. Dead fucking weight,' Lucas said.

Sally threw a venomous glare over her shoulder, but when Mal looked back, there was no anger in his eyes. He was simply heartbroken.

***

Shelley looked up at Lucas. 'It's just whiskey.'

THE WILDE DIARIES

Gooseflesh broke out in a wave up his arm and settled in a shudder between his shoulder blades. It was impossible. He moved closer to see for himself.

'What? It can't be.'

'That's all there is. Nothing else. What makes you think he'd put something like that in your drink anyway? That's a disgusting prank even for Malcolm.'

'It doesn't matter.'

Lucas was confused. But she was right. Just whiskey. The rest of the guests had ordered taxis and gone, saying they'd come back for the cars tomorrow, leaving him and Shelley to clear up, the atmosphere well and truly dead after the fight. Johnny of course had told him to sleep on it and they'd sort it out in the morning. Johnny didn't know that Mal had put jizz in his drink, and the idea of reconciling after that was unthinkable.

But he didn't jizz in your drink.

Now all he could see was Mal's teary eyes as he looked back over his shoulder on the way out of the door. Shelley was right. She'd known Mal long enough to know that he'd never play a trick like that.

***

A loud growl of thunder roused Lucas. The rain still pouring outside. He turned to his right to see Shelley naked in bed beside him, the flashes of lightning illuminating her perfect pale skin. His eyes wandered to the window, and he asked himself why they hadn't drawn the curtains. Then he noticed something on the table beneath the window. A letter. He stood, mind and body not under the influence of any substances he'd consumed during the party. It was a plain piece of paper, folded in half propped up against the lamp. He turned the lamp on and behind him, Shelley moaned. He turned to see if she was awake, but she just turned over and away from the light. He unfolded the letter to see that it was more than just a letter. It was a contract. His mind instantly went to the dream he'd had but couldn't remember. The dream that had led to the third of the Busker's songs.

As he scanned the document, two words stood out amongst the others.

Sacrifice.

Death.

The temperature plummeted and another flash of lightning exploded outside. His eyes were drawn to the lonely, crooked tree that sat between him and the horizon and in that incandescent lightning glow, he saw something else. In the tree.

It was Mandy.

Swinging by the neck.

Feet thrashing.

Even across all this distance her bulging eyes met his.

And then thunder erupted.

THE WILDE DIARIES

16th September 1977

Lucas opened his eyes.

It was morning. The rain outside had stopped, but the skies were still that dull, leaden grey. The table beneath the window had no letter, but the lamp was on. He turned to his side, but he was alone, the bedsheets disturbed and folded back. Shelley had stayed behind after the party. Shelley. His mind flashed to the dream. The contract. The words.

Sacrifice.

Death.

He bolted from the bed and over to the window. His eyes went straight to the tree.

Please don't be there. Please. Not Shelley. Not now. I need her.

His heart hammered in his chest and nausea swept through him. At the window, his eyes fell straight on the crooked tree. But there was nobody there. Just the gnarled old branches, its leaves beginning to drain of their greenness preparing for autumn.

But Shelley. She was here. Where is she?

He felt sick at the thought of losing her again. He'd only just got her back. If she'd been with him the last few months, he'd have got through the writer's block and the insomnia no problem. She was the missing piece of his private life. She offered everything that was missing, just as Johnny had the professional side covered.

'Shell?' his voice echoed. There was no reply, but he heard a murmuring. 'Shell?' He stalked slowly out into the hallway. It was empty.

But the murmuring was still there. Louder. Then it stopped.

He saw that all of the other rooms were empty. Nobody had stayed over. The fight with Mal was real. Mal who had done nothing wrong. He'd have a coffee, gather his thoughts, and call him. Right away. Apologise. After the public show he'd made and another beating handed out, he wasn't sure Mal would accept the apology. But it should be offered all the same.

He approached the top of the stairs and stopped. A gentle sound floated upstairs. Crying. Sobbing. He froze and drew a deep breath, before grabbing the handrail. One foot, slowly, tentatively sought out the first step. Then the other the step below. He edged downstairs silently, listening to the gentle sobbing. It was only when he reached the landing midway that he saw her. Sitting at the bottom of the stairs, wearing his shirt.

It was Shelley. The phone receiver was beside her.

'Shell? You okay?'

She turned to face him. Her eyes were streaming.

He hurried to her and held her. 'What's wrong? What's happened?'

She drew a staggered breath and between the sobs he managed to make out five words.

'Malcolm and Sally. They're dead.'

THE WILDE DIARIES

***

The clearing was perfectly still. No breeze whispering through the trees, no friendly chirp of birdsong, just a heavy, all-encompassing silence. He lowered the needle on the gramophone before moving to the dining chair sitting a few feet away. With that first chord came a joyous explosion of sound.

The sun burst through the clouds and filtered through the trees, warming his body just as the music warmed his soul. The electric version of *Greater Than Me* was pumped full of energy and uplifting just to be near. The bass guitar added a warmth and depth that was lacking from the incredible acoustic version, Dizzy's drums powering the whole thing along. Jack's guitar gave the song a lift without stealing the show, a perfect accompaniment to what was already in place. The sad lyrics were startling to hear alongside what was, for the most part, an upbeat rhythm, and then, when all emotions had been touched, when you hoped there might be one more verse, the final chord faded out.

Lucas was delighted at how the song had finished as he watched the needle reach the end of the record. He had to hear it again. Once was nowhere near enough. He motioned to stand, to stop the record and restart it again from the beginning, but he couldn't move. It was as though his body was cement. The wind kicked up and rustled the leaves and the sunlight was blocked out. He felt a chill overtake him as the record slowed, slowed to a stop. Then, the wind up mechanism slowly whirled, as if turned by an invisible hand. He knew that something was going wrong, but he was frozen, unable to stop it. The record started to rotate again. Slowly at first until it was at regular playing speed. But something was wrong.

sdrawkcab s'tI

A chill rushed over him and he spoke aloud.

'It's backwards.'

He'd heard the backmasking effect before in music to recognise the growing decay and then attack of a note or drum hit rather than the opposite. But something here was badly wrong. The effect was a relentless, outlandish, onslaught of madness. This coupled with the gibberish of what were painfully beautiful lyrics when played in the intended direction. On it went. A swirling dissonance of melodies, uncrashing cymbals and nonsensical noises. And then something... else.

Faint at first. Many voices. Not just his own, nor even the backing vocals. Voices that screamed out in agonising cries. The wind blew harder now draining the sound from that hideous backwards insanity. A cold, unforgiving wind. It died and the record volume rose. Then, as if the backwards voices weren't enough, what sounded like the growling and snarling of wild animals mixed in with the growing cacophony. Not in the original recording, but there all the same, as if it were imprinted on the very soul of the song. Then the sound of the voices rose to match that of the awful music. What can only

THE WILDE DIARIES

be described as the sound of suffering. Both human and animal. All of this mixed into the chaos as if superimposed. It had no place there. Suddenly, the Busker's words came to him. Not here, but from a dream. A forgotten nightmare. The dream that preceded the third of his songs. Then, at once, the extra voices came into some horrific, audible focus as if being tuned on a radio by invisible, bony fingers. Again he went cold. Both animal and human voices coalesced, converged, into one voice. Neither human nor animal, yet surely *His* voice. Unnatural and broken in its cadence, but as clear as if he were whispering into his ear.

The voice was choked, and at once his thoughts turned to Mandy. Sweet Mandy who'd taken her own life by hanging. The image of her feet kicking out for the ground in frantic regret as if she'd changed her mind at the last.

The message finished and the Busker's laugh echoed through the trees. Lucas knew now that in his dreams, when the Busker was in the same room, that room felt smaller, cramped, claustrophobic. That same feeling hit here, out in the open, and with it came that foul, evil stench. His eyes widened and beyond the gramophone he saw Mandy, in the tree. Hanging. Swinging wildly in the gale, her body convulsing as her feet jerked reaching out for ground they'd never touch. The gramophone burst into flames, but the music continued, distorting further with the record player's demise, until he felt a cold, bony hand rest upon his shoulder.

***

MARC W SHAKO
17th September 1977

When Lucas woke up, he was already sitting up in bed, sheets wringing with sweat. Another nightmare. Another dream he couldn't remember, yet whatever it was, it was the most terrifying thing he'd ever experienced, he was certain. He turned to see Shelley and was met only with a note on her pillow. She'd got up early and gone to town to "pick up some bits", probably disgusted at the lack of food in the house. Despite not remembering the dream, he wanted her here beside him. That cold fear he'd felt still gripped him. But it was more than that. He didn't just want her, he needed her, just as surely as he needed Johnny. The two of them were what held him together: her personally, him professionally.

Up until this past week, losing Shelley had been the hardest thing he'd had to deal with. Half the songs from the second album were about her; from the subtle *It's Not the Same*, to the obvious *Losing You*. Shelley was the only one who stood up to him. All the fights about the music that he had (usually with Jack, occasionally with Dizzy) he tended to win. Not that he wanted his own way, but his feel for the songs was usually right. It wasn't ego, it was all about the music. With Johnny they had the occasional butting of heads over gigs, or tour dates. He got his way there too. This was more his ego than anything, but Johnny was a master at pushing back just enough to challenge him, but not enough to annoy him. Shelley was different. She told him when he was acting the arsehole, or when he'd had too much to drink (or smoke). She

THE WILDE DIARIES

told him what he needed to hear; told him things that other people may have been afraid to. And just like his musical arguments weren't ego, this wasn't her being a bitch, it came from a place of genuine care - something missing since his mum left him and his dad when he was a child to be with who his father referred to as "her fancy man". But the thing that counted for more than any of it was that she loved him. She wasn't in it for the money like Jack said Malcolm and Sally were (she'd already left him once after all), and it wasn't the fame. They were together until just after Soothsayer hit the big time.

He dressed and went downstairs for breakfast, still shivering in the icy aftermath of his nightmare. On the kitchen table was a note next to the last of the cornflakes and milk saying that she'd left this for him. He measured just enough milk out to leave enough for a cup of tea (a builder's brew, his dad would have said), and poured the rest over the cereal before ambling into the recording room to eat.

The reel to reel looked somehow different. He couldn't pinpoint it, but something had changed. The cannister with *Greater Than Me* sat beside it. Maybe Shelley had been listening. He put his cereal down and loaded the tape into the player, but for reasons he couldn't explain, he loaded it in backwards.

'Why?' he asked himself aloud.

The dream.

There was the notion that he shouldn't do this, faint and

distant in his mind the same way instinct made him jump when he saw a spider. But against his will and the warnings he pressed play.

The moment he heard the decaying note fade in, the dream rushed at him like a strong wind, faint with the lingering smell of death. The song. The message.

'No. It can't be.'

The words of the message weren't clear, but it was to do with Mandy. And her hanging. And though this recording was just him and the acoustic, it felt like he was cloaked in the mist of déjà vu. Parts of this demo were in his dream. The snarl of a word here, the crawling drag of a note there.

But that doesn't mean anything. It could be a coincidence. Or a trick of the mind.

Yes, the mind is a powerful thing. Perhaps his subconscious told him how it would sound backwards. Then, the room suddenly felt smaller as an all too familiar sound started to grow. Voices. Many voices. All screaming, as if scorched by the savage fires of hell. Screeching and wailing, human voices and the pained howls of creatures he didn't want to imagine. It only went on for a second. A second that stretched out before him in minutes, then, just as in his dream, the voices started to unite, coming together in a gruesome confluence until he heard it. The message. In a voice neither human nor animal, yet surely *His* voice. The Busker. Unnatural and broken in its cadence, but as clear as if he were whispering right into his ear.

THE WILDE DIARIES

'Swinging feet. Feel the squeeze. Tighter. Hard to breathe.'

***

Lucas screamed and backed away from the player. It was impossible. Was he going mad? Was this how it started? Surely he was mistaken. He leapt at the player to stop the madness, his sweaty hands fumbling at the controls. He rewound the tape, and it had the strange quality of sounding like it was being played on fast/forward. He hit stop, then play, praying that it was his imagination. Praying that the strange sounds he'd heard weren't real. Praying that perhaps he *was* going mad. That would be better. That would be better than what he'd just heard being real.

The song played in reverse, growing decay followed by sharp attack, the garbled lyrics with that odd snarling cadence.

But that's all it was! Nothing else. The room felt lighter, and the backwards song still gave him the creeps, but that's all. No strange voices. No sounds of suffering. He threw his head back and laughed aloud, the room filling with relief.

But then, faintly, came something else.

A second voice. And a third. Not singing. Screaming.

'No!' Lucas screamed himself.

The lightness left the room chased away by that familiar foreboding. A cool chill took over and, just as before, at the same point, those voices started to converge.

Lucas hit stop halfway through the message and leapt

back from the player. It couldn't be. He'd recorded the song before he knew Mandy would take her own life, let alone the method she'd use. He couldn't possibly have known.

But the Busker could.

'No. No fucking way.'

His head shook from side to side like he was trying to shake the truth from it, but in the end, that's what it was. The truth.

He paced the room in the cloying silence, finding it at once soothing and unbearable. His hands trembled in fear and cold sweat enveloped him and just at the point where he felt this couldn't be any worse, somewhere from the ether of that room, an idea struck him.

'Oh Jesus Christ no.'

He felt sick to his stomach, the nausea climbing up his throat forcing him to swallow hard, the pain in his bruised throat flaring. He started to cry faintly as he staggered across to the player.

'No. No. No,' was all he could repeat. Barely audible, like a prayer.

He reached the player and took down the tape and dropped it into the empty cannister with a clatter. His lungs filled themselves that same way they did before he stepped out onstage before a show. He reached down and slid the bottom drawer open and stared. Stared like it wasn't four silver cannisters looking back at him, but four black, hand-sized spiders. He drew in another deep breath and reached in,

THE WILDE DIARIES

picking up the cannister marked with a number 2.

Now he sat in silence, staring. There were no prayers. No mantras. Just two whirling spools making him feel sick.

The whirring of the mechanism.

The heavy oppression of the atmosphere.

The backwards sounds of a guitar.

The reversed gibberish of his own voice.

The rising thud of his own heart pumping in his ears.

The shrinking of flesh into goosebumps.

The sound of voices other than his own.

The shrieking madness of suffering.

The nightmare convergence of sound into one voice.

His voice.

The message.

The message:

"See the danger. See your fate. See the end. Much too late. Too late."

Malcolm and Sally. The accident. It must be. At once, he was in those chaotic final moments of their car crash, viewing from the back seat as Malcolm and Sally sped through the rain-soaked night away from the house. The corner that seemed to appear from nowhere up ahead. Advanced warning of a danger unavoidable. The chilling screams from Malcolm and Sally matched by the brakes and tyres on tarmac. The car left the road and plunged down the wooded embankment and for a moment it looked like they might avoid the trees. It looked like the thinner branches would slow their fall and save them. And then those branches parted to reveal the thick trunk of a tree. He saw this like it was a projection on a screen. The impact with the tree not affecting him. But Malcolm... his head snapped forward bursting red as it hit the windscreen, smashing the glass into a spider-web. Sally left her seat. With no seatbelt to save her, she flew through the shattered glass and out, into the tree with a sickening thud that folded her head back against the onrush of her body.

Lucas leaned over the side of his armchair and vomited, relieved not to see the thick black ooze of the Busker's seed. His heart was gripped by fear. But not at the message he'd just heard. That was connected with the past. Mandy was dead. Malcolm and Sally were already gone. Nothing could save them now. But there were two more tapes in the drawer with songs from the Busker. No-one else had died. That he knew of.

***

Tape number three sat in the player. Loaded in reverse. Lucas clutched the half empty bottle of Bell's he'd drunk to calm his nerves. He paced the room, muttering to himself about what he'd done. They were dead. It didn't matter about the Busker, the songs were his. The songs were in his voice. The Busker couldn't be arrested, he lived in his mind. He didn't want to hear what else was to come.

But maybe...

Maybe if he heard it now, before it happened, he could

THE WILDE DIARIES

stop it.

He leapt at the player and hit play. He waited. The energy in the room now felt like a violent storm was about to break out.

He didn't have to wait long before he heard the message. Before he heard any of it he knew in a round-about sort of way what it was going to say. Nonetheless he waited through the gibbering insanity until the suffering came and converged into one message. This time, through the stuttering snarling cadence, he recognised something in the Busker's voice. Glee.

"One lives. One dies. Time to choose. Whatever you do, you lose."

There was time. Time to save one person. And one person only. It was between the two people that meant the most to him. One an anchor in his personal life, the other, his professional life. The Busker was going to kill Shelley or Johnny.

He had to get to them first.

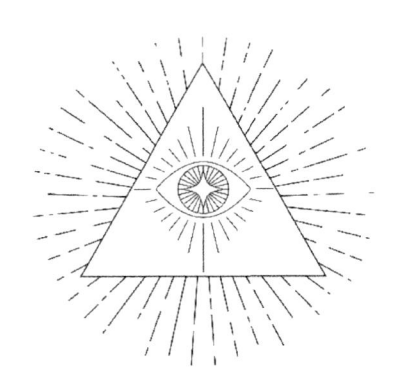

THE FALL OF ZACH FOX

15th October 2015

That was it. That was where the last diary ended. As much as I was a fan of Lucas Wilde's music, I had no idea what became of Shelley or Johnny, and I was doubtful as to how much an internet search would reveal. Johnny and Shelley weren't famous enough in their own right to have entries written in Wikipedia. Although, there was something else much more pressing.

    I was back in my room at The Ship. The night outside was fading into dawn and even though I'd read in the diaries about people from dreams appearing in real life, and the man from the dreams not actually being a man but having hooves where his feet should be, I believed it. All of it. I'd put my scepticism aside and had weird events verified by other sources. Or seen physical evidence to prove what was in the pages of The Wilde Diaries. But for some reason, reading that the songs had backwards messages in them was a stretch too far. The amount of planning one would have to put into such an idea was monumental. I didn't see the point. I couldn't work out why someone would go to such trouble. This was going to be one of those seeing-is-believing (or in this case, hearing-is-believing) moments. And that is where my scepticism waned.

What if it *was* there? What would that mean?

The idea of such a thing made me go cold. If the messages really were there, I wasn't sure I *wanted* to hear them. The way it was described in the diaries, I was certain I didn't. And I couldn't think of a single reason Lucas would make such a thing up. It would be easily verified. I had the tapes.

'Not yet.' I muttered to myself as I stood and went to the bathroom.

There was too much going on. Too much weird, too. I needed a little normality. Needed to ground myself in something real before I went off looking into bizarre claims made by a dead writer. I would complete my business transaction with Zach Fox first and then investigate further.

As I stood under the hot stream of the shower, one thing did strike me: just as Zach and Lucas surely felt the same thing, the moment I was under the water, shampoo running down my face, unable to open my eyes - in that moment, when I was at my most vulnerable, naked and blind and half deafened by the white noise hiss of running water - I felt him. *Him*.

Standing there, watching, with me unable to do a single

THE WILDE DIARIES

thing about it. I gasped for air and flushed the soap from my face, half choking under the water. In the blurriness of my eyes, a shape formed in the doorway. Tall. Thin. Black. I screamed and fell back, awaiting my fate. In that corner, blinded, coughing, exposed, I awaited what surely came. Eventually the water rinsed the soap from my eyes and when I looked, I was alone. As much as this irrational fear came at me from nowhere, along with it came the knowledge that this would be the way of things, something to happen every now and then, when I least expected.

Back in the room, the kettle bubbled. The idea came to drink coffee rather than tea. To stay awake. What if, when I slept, he came to me? I decided to check my Twitter messages, just to see if there was anything from Zach.

My inbox was empty. But Zach Fox was trending...

My mind raced. Had he exposed his lie himself? Was he dead? Something had happened, clearly. Most of the scenarios my mind conjured ended with me receiving nothing from my little blackmail scheme. Fighting against any reluctance, I clicked one of the links.

There was a video. And when I saw the opening scenes, my heart sank.

***

The first shot of the video is from outside his hotel. Grey skies. Rain.

The panic is palpable. A barricade set up by the police

holds back screaming teenage girls. The street is filled with people and cars. Police cars. No sirens. Lights flashing, reflected in the slick wetness on the street. But mostly screaming girls. But these screams aren't the overjoyed delirium seen during Beatlemania. This is sheer terror.

Uniformed officers and firefighters rush to and fro in the cordoned off street. A man in a suit peers skyward with a bullhorn. The camera pans, following the man in the suit's gaze, upward. The events leading to this point unfold in seconds.

Zach Fox left the house and went straight back to his hotel from our meeting. I'd given him no time to check out of his room, and judging by how tired he looked, he'd probably just gone back to sleep as soon as he'd returned. Then, something else. Something unknown. Whatever that unknown was, it had left Zach Fox standing on the ledge outside his room on the sixth floor.

Anything bad happened to him, it happened to me.

I turned on the television news and the banner scrolling across the bottom of the screen confirmed my fears. Developing news with a suicide hotline phone number for anyone with intentions similar to Zach's. I had my laptop open on the bureau in front of me, a live feed that someone was sharing from the scene. Another angle zoomed up to the dizzying heights of the sixth floor where Zach Fox was shouting to the streets below. Only he wasn't shouting to the gathered fans. He was shouting to me.

THE WILDE DIARIES

His face was contorted into a mask of pure fear as he screamed, 'Listen. You'll see for yourself. I tried to warn you. I tried.'

And suddenly the fear fell away from his face. Suddenly, Zach Fox was perfectly calm. At peace. Serene. Like he was asleep. His apparent calm eased the throng of young fans, who temporarily held their screams. And at that moment, when the noise faded to nothing, the grip he'd held on the stone architecture behind him released.

***

The television news cut away as he leaned forward. My eyes were drawn to that social media live feed. It was sickening. A part of me hoped he'd recover and grab hold of safety. But he didn't. He leaned until he was horizontal and then reached back. But it was too late. As he fell, my life flashed before my eyes.

There would be no blackmail. No money. No life of ease. And because of that, whatever fragile hopes remained of a future with Edie were dead too, just as sure as Zach Fox was. Whoever was filming watched all the way down. He fell silently, without a scream.

Then, my heart bloomed in hope.

Two fans squirmed out from behind the police barricade and rushed towards him. To catch him. To save him. They couldn't have been more than fifteen years old. They tried to catch him, amid the chaos and the screaming, and the sirens, and I hoped above all hope they'd succeed. I didn't care if they broke his fall. His life was worth more than theirs.

Zach's fall seemed to last forever. My stomach lurched and sank as he hit one of the girls. There was a chance... But as soon as it appeared, it was gone. Above all of the noise rose the sickening sound of Zach's skull popping on contact with the hard concrete. The girl took most of the weight and she may have saved him. As it was, she didn't. The impact with her did nothing but propel his head into the floor that much harder. In the end, his head exploded. *All the King's Horses...*

Later I would hear she was fighting for her life in the same hospital where Zach was pronounced dead. The weight of Zach falling broke her back. The outlook was grim, doctors "doing everything they could". The other girl just missed him. Instead, she ended up covered in the blood and brains of her hero.

Zach was dead, so was my blackmail scheme. I was penniless, and if the police made any connection between myself and Zach, I'd be in trouble. Even though Seth's suicide was nothing to do with me, two suicides in a week would be difficult to write off as coincidence.

My phone rang.

My heart leapt and I was expecting the police. Detective Ellison inviting me for a conversation about the recently deceased Mr Fox. It was not.

'Edie.'

'Have you seen the news?' Her voice echoed. A

THE WILDE DIARIES

clandestine call made from a hotel bathroom.

'Yes.'

'I'm sorry.'

That was it. That was all she said. That's all she needed to say.

Sorry that Zach is dead.

Sorry that my money making scheme was as dead as Zach was.

Sorry that because of that, her decision was made.

To stay with David.

And with that, the line went dead.

Fury raged deep inside me. Fool me twice. Edith's decision to go back with David shouldn't have come as a surprise. I don't know what hurt more: that I thought I actually had a chance with her, or that she left me for the second time to get together with him. Now things were different. I had learned one thing from the previous time. Before, I had tried to move on with my life and start afresh. The best revenge is living well. Fuck that. The best revenge is good old-fashioned, served-cold vengeance.

That is what was coming to the golden couple. They had made a fool of me for the last time. I didn't know how, but I was going to store this rage and use it as fuel. My fists balled into tight knots of anger. I knew what she was thinking. *He won't do anything. He didn't before, he won't now.* Even if I told David about the affair it was her word against mine. She'd laugh it off.

MARC W SHAKO

First time around I'd been wounded. It hurt more than anything I could imagine. It was true love, for me at least. She'd apologised. It was her, not me. What a fucking joke. She didn't care. She was following the money. David's promotion. David's riches. She'd have no problem spending them. Fuck David. And fuck her. Never meant to hurt me? What did she think would happen? She thinks I'll slink away, tail between my legs, oh-well-maybe-next-time attitude. Fuck that. I'll think of something.

The phone rang again. I snatched it up.

'What?'

'Mr Brewer?'

'Yes?'

'It's Detective Ellison.'

***

I stood frozen in my room at The Ship, phone glued to my ear. It felt like the silence would be eternal, like Detective Paul Ellison would never speak. Like he was waiting for me to blurt out the whole truth and implicate myself in everything. Even though I'd had nothing to do with Seth's suicide, now I was starting to doubt myself; thinking that I was misremembering and that the police had found something. There was something in the evidence. Planted by *Him*.

'Mr Brewer, there's been an update in the investigation into your friend...'

Here it comes...

THE WILDE DIARIES

'We found gunpowder residue on your friend's hand and the ballistics report, well, long story short, the evidence backs up your story. We've decided to close the case.'

Relief snatched the tension from my joints and I sank onto the bed. Innocence confirmed. Zach Fox was a different story, but at least I was blameless when it came to Seth. A silver lining. And the transfer of property. The house would be mine.

'Thank you for the update.'

The phone went silent and I lay back onto the bed. That was it. I was in the clear. Zach was dead, Edie was back with David and now the police were finished, I was pretty sure that David would be happy to go back home until the funeral.

I was left with the tapes, a house, and Seth's novelised notes that went along with the diaries. The best I could do was to work out how to make money from the tapes. I could sell the house. I would go back to the house for one last look around, make sure I hadn't left anything. Something I was not looking forward to. The house I would sell, on the cheap as it was by now accustomed to, and I'd ask Edie to take anything she wanted from inside.

I glanced at the box. I would destroy that too, just as Zach Fox had. From the angle I was looking, light bled through the gap, through that ragged tear and onto the sheet of paper inside. It was one of Seth's sketches. But it wasn't the sketch of Him. It was the room in the attic. The room in the attic with the door boarded up, crudely painted with a warning.

Part of me wanted to get the hell out of town as quickly as I could and forget that this whole episode had even happened. Lock the memory away in a room in my mind and paint a *WARNING! KEEP OUT!* message of my own. But that wouldn't happen. The house had other ideas. As afraid as I was to return to the house, I wanted to know what was in that room as badly as I'd wanted to know what was in the box Seth had given to me a week ago.

My reservation here at the hotel still had a couple of days on it.

As much as Zach Fox dying and Edie and David reconciling felt like the end, there was a little bit further to go. I would have to go back to the house.

***

I drove out to the house as soon as I'd finished breakfast. The café was quiet and I was, for the most part, alone. I sat with my back to the window and the rain splashed streets and I stayed long after I finished eating, partly trying to absorb the events of the morning, and partly building up the nerve to go back to the house for one last time. The day was grey and dark, the fading hours of remaining daylight already prompting me to leave. I didn't know how much time I'd need at the house. The last thing I wanted was to be there after sunset.

The house loomed on the horizon, beckoning, drawing me closer. The place was alive, I was sure of it. Alive and

THE WILDE DIARIES

drawing energy from the living to keep itself going. As I drew closer to the house I couldn't help but feel despondent at Zach's suicide. I should have felt bad at grieving more at Zach's passing than Seth's, but I didn't. I was numb. There would be no happy ending for me. No wealth. No retirement. No days spent free from the cloud of financial worry. No days spent playing golf. I didn't even play golf, but wasn't that what the rich did to pass the time?

'Fuck it.'

My mind went back to the diaries. To Lucas and The Busker (it seemed wrong by now not to spell his name with capital letters and I wondered when that had started) and what Lucas had been through to get the songs. I thought about it and wondered how much I'd be willing to go through to get the same.

I wondered exactly what Zach had to endure to get where he was, aside from the worry that someone like me would come along and expose his fraud. That washed out, haunted look on his face as he recalled the wild parties that intensified as his fame grew now haunted me. Had that recollection pushed him over the edge? What exactly had gone on at those parties? I got the sense it was more than he'd been willing to share with his blackmailer. That aside, the worry that someone would expose him was a cloud that would have followed him every single day of his life: Is this the day the world finds out my truth?

And he said the parties weren't just musicians. Actors.

Politicians. What horrors had they perpetrated to get where they were? Was it the same for them? My mind wandered to what I'd be willing to sacrifice to reach their level. What was the line I would not cross? Before I came to an answer, I had arrived at the house.

***

Inside the house, rather than heading straight upstairs, I went to the room where Lucas and company had held the séance all those years ago. I still had the habit of taking the box with me everywhere and set it on top of the drawers. I stood before that chest of drawers, staring into the black space between its feet.

What if it was still there?

The Ouija board?

You could contact *Him*.

What then? Maybe get an answer to my question about the line that represented the edge where my moral compass could not reach...

I dropped to my knees and reached under, desperately hoping to feel the cold wood of the Ouija board, hoping that each time my hand patted around in the dark would be the last. That my hand would land upon the board and that would be that. But there was nothing.

Back to work, old boy.

I could still sell the place and expose Zach. He had an estate. A legacy. Someone would cough up to keep his secret.

THE WILDE DIARIES

But that was for the future, for now, my next stop was the attic.

***

The staircase leading up to the attic stood before me. At once too narrow and too steep, challenging all comers, the uneven stairs asking the question: Do you *really* want to come up here?

I did not.

I went anyway.

With each step the light faded and I ascended further into darkness, fearing what lay within the shadows, yet fighting not to run into them, driven onward by the sense that the Devil himself was behind me.

In the inky dark, the white lettering fought to be seen.

WARNING! KEEP OUT!

I stared at the planks nailed across the door, waiting for the bloody, skinless undead arm to reach out and grab me. Grabbing the rough wooden board I yanked and the nails screamed as they gave way. The planks clattered to the floor and I tried the handle. The door was locked. Whoever wanted to keep people out had been serious.

I barged the door and felt a little give. Enough to encourage me to try again. On the fourth attempt the door flew open and faint light escaped into the hallway.

I immediately regretted opening it. It slammed against the wall and my mouth fell open. I had made a grave error in coming here. Yet here I was.

Old newspapers had been plastered across the window, filtering the grey daylight from the other side trying to seep through. It was in that faded light I spotted a naked bulb with a pull-string. I grabbed it and gently tugged. Bright light exploded onto the walls revealing the unsettling truth. As soon as the darkness was vanquished and my eyes fell upon those walls, I contemplated something that hurt me to admit. Perhaps there was nothing to the diaries. Nothing at all. Perhaps all of the strange stories within were just that - stories. Perhaps everything else that had occurred was nothing more than coincidence. I took in the madness plastered on those walls and had to consider a terrible possibility - my dead friend Seth had gone mad.

***

I stared at the walls in an attempt to fathom what Seth had been trying to accomplish with this bizarre redecoration. Each wall was covered from floor to ceiling with headshots of famous celebrities. Dozens upon dozens of pictures of actors, musicians, politicians. The wall opposite the door had musicians and actors, all people considered 'A' list, sometimes more than one photograph of the same person, but they all shared one common factor. In each photo the subject was covering one eye. Crude writing painted over the entirety of the collage. "Hair over eye", or "Hand over eye", or "Eye obfuscated by shadow".

THE WILDE DIARIES

I turned to the next wall, a square of light shining from the window behind the pictures plastered over it. More actors and musicians, some of them prominent on the first wall, this time each one making the 'okay' sign used by divers. In the middle of the wall were four identical pictures of Zach Fox, more prominent than the rest because again, these were daubed in paint.

The first picture, the circle of finger and thumb was painted over, along with the little finger. The second photo was identical, but this time the ring finger was painted over. And in the third, the middle finger. Each one forming a number six. The fourth picture he had marked each circle and finger a different primary colour. Six. Six. Six. Over the faces of the movie stars and singers were painted the words,

THE NUMBER OF THE BEAST

The painting wasn't clean and smooth as I'd expect from Seth's hand. It was haphazard as if painted in a panic.

The wall opposite was incomplete. It too had been plastered with pictures, mostly of the same famous faces, but Seth had started in the top left corner and not made it all the way down. On this wall were two kinds of pictures. In the first type, their hands formed a triangle, usually held in front of the face, revealing an eye in the void between their hands, and in the second, the stars held a finger to their lips, suggesting there was a secret to be kept. *A secret like the one that prompted*

Zach to kill himself.

The whole room looked like the den of a madman. Like the room of a man capable of taking his own life. And there was more to come. I turned to face the fourth and final wall.

The words were painted strong and bold. Not the hand of someone losing his mind, but of someone strong and sure in his sanity. I read the words over and over.

1. ALL-SEEING EYE?
2. DEVIL WORSHIP?
3. PYRAMID?
4. WHAT IS THE SECRET?
5. DO THEY KNOW <u>HIM</u>?

I had no idea what the first and third points were referencing. The second point Seth was making was obvious, to him. The all-okay sign the stars were making was nothing to do with being fine, and something altogether more sinister. What shocked me was how Seth believed that these people were honouring Satan. But the thing on the list that really unsettled me was point number five.

<u>Him</u>.

It could have been talking about any number of people. A record producer. A label owner. A guitar maker. It could have been any of those and more. But it wasn't.

As I stared at that wall, a wall bordered with pictures of dead musicians, one thing was abundantly clear. Seth was

THE WILDE DIARIES

talking about The Busker.

***

I reached up for the string and tugged; the bright, naked bulb blinked out throwing the room into that grey gloom. The stairs down to the first floor creaked as I hastily descended. There were still a few hours of daylight left, but I wanted to get out of here. Any thoughts or ideas left my mind as I reached the landing in the U-shaped stairs to the ground floor hallway. Sitting in front of the door, almost like it had been posted, was a blue rectangle.

A diary.

I stopped dead. Nobody knew I was here.

'Hello? Anybody there?'

Nothing.

Not even the tick of the grandfather clock. I hadn't been winding it, and hadn't really thought about it, it had kept such good time. I reached down and picked up the diary. There was no number on this, but as it was the same style as the others, I could only presume it was number five. When I opened the hard front cover, folded A4 sheets fell to the floor.

On them were notes from Seth.

I left, there and then. I wanted to read right away, but the thought of being in that place for another minute sickened me to my stomach. I sped back to The Ship, Lucas Wilde's final diary in the passenger seat beside me. Inside were the answers, finally, to what became of Shelley and Johnny. And what transpired in the final few days in the life of Lucas Wilde. Before I read though, I had to read Seth's notes. Just like I had to know what was in that box, and in that room, I had to know what my friend had written with whatever was left of his sanity.

***

My visit to the attic room left me troubled. It was like I'd wandered into the paranoid nightmare of a maniac. I left with more questions than I had answers. And yet... As crazy as it all seemed, wasn't there a ring of truth to it? Weren't there too many examples of symbolism on display for it to be dismissed as coincidence? With the exception of the four pictures of Zach, there were no duplicates, yet the photographs numbered in the hundreds. Seth had alluded to stories of sacrificing others to propel careers, and Zach said his friend had died on the eve of his tour, a non-musical news story that would introduce his name to ones who might not have heard it otherwise. But to what end?

Seth had his own ideas.

Seth's Notes

What is the point of symbolism? To convey a message.

Here, the idea is to convey it not necessarily in secret, but certainly not overtly. Hidden in plain sight. The symbolism

THE WILDE DIARIES

on display in the pictures Zach had amassed upstairs is overt, but it's only noticeable once you are looking for it. Perhaps they are all drawing attention to the fact that they are all part of the same group, with The Busker as the common link. The pyramid symbology ties in somehow to the all-seeing eye of the group identified as 'The Illuminati'.

Are these the gatekeepers to the entertainment industry? The powers that be, pulling the strings from behind the scenes, deciding who makes it and who doesn't?

It certainly doesn't make sense that artists, people who strive for an individual identity and who hold originality up as a paragon would so blatantly copy one another. So why the control? The cult of celebrity. It's almost religion these days. The faces in the pictures Zach had amassed in the loft are those worshipped by the youth of today. Internet social media accounts with following in the millions. Such influence cannot be left unchecked in modern society. There is another piece to this puzzle that I feel I am missing. I hope you can succeed where I have failed and uncover it.

I'm sorry to you Joel. Reading this must come as a shock. I'm sure it sounds like the ramblings of a madman, but since I started researching this I've had my mind opened to the most outlandish of possibilities.

Were I in your position, I would have read about the backwards messages in the songs and washed my hands of this whole affair, declaring it nonsense and turning my back on it, happy for it never again to cross my mind.

MARC W SHAKO

I would have done the very same myself, if I hadn't seen *Him*.

It was not a grandiose event. It was very plain. That only served somehow to make it worse. At this point I had found two of the diaries and heard two songs, *Greater Than Me* and *All the King's Horses*. I was at The White Hart in town for a quiet drink. There was hardly a soul in the place. An old man feeding pork scratchings to his white and brown cocker spaniel, a businessman absorbed in the financial papers, and a bored young barmaid, eyes glued to her mobile phone. As always these days the television was on in the background, playing BBC News with the sound turned down to a murmur and subtitles trailing across the bottom of the screen.

It happened like you'd expect things to unfold in a dream. The old man got up to leave and put on a hat. A wide-brimmed fedora. That was the moment I knew something was going to happen. He left without saying a word and didn't even look at me, but my eyes were drawn to him as he passed by the windows outside. Nobody else reacted, as you'd expect. Then the volume rose on the television. Those of us left in the bar turned to look at it. There was a news story about the death of the High Street. The businessman complained about the volume, but the barmaid was already trying to turn it down. The remote control, like the rest of us in there, was powerless. The reporter was interviewing locals of some town or other in a street full of boarded up windows, of course there weren't many people to interview, and the reporter

THE WILDE DIARIES

mentioned this himself. There was an old lady who lamented the death of the High Street and said she was forced to go longer distances to buy groceries, and then the screen cut and there he was. The Busker. I just knew it was him at once.

The barmaid was still fumbling with the remote, and the businessman, while not stating it aloud, was visibly upset by the volume of the television. The reporter asked the Busker if he found it difficult to make money, seeing as everything was all happening in a shopping centre.

The Busker said, 'It's never easy getting your message out,' then looked at the camera and said, 'but I'll find a way.'

I know it's hard to imagine but I am one hundred percent convinced it was him. That wicked smile under the brim of his hat. Under his long coat, he was wearing a *Soothsayer* T-shirt.

I'm not even sure you'll see this, but I think you're supposed to. I thought I had all the diaries: an incomplete, unsatisfying story. I researched everywhere I could to find out what had happened to Johnny and Shelley, to no avail. Then, as I was about to leave the house one day, the final fifth diary was sitting by the front door. I was supposed to see it and I think you were too. I'll put it with the others, but I get the feeling by the time the urge to open the box has become too overwhelming, this final piece of the puzzle will somehow be missing. If you're supposed to get this message, then you will.

I've put some sketches in a notepad and some notes on a pen drive. Please, Joel, take my notes. And this final diary.

Read them. Just promise me you won't do it at the house.

***

The attic room madness wasn't Seth's work. It was Zach's. I was happy I'd read the note from the comfort and safety of my room at The Ship. Now I was ready to read the final diary.

THE WILDE DIARIES

LUCAS WILDE'S DIARY #5

17th September 1977

Lucas left the final song playing to itself and bolted into the hallway and snatched up the phone receiver. The last message could only refer to either Johnny or Shelley. He didn't know where Shelley was, but he could call Johnny. The line was dead. He jabbed at the buttons in the cradle in a bid to get an outside line, but there was nothing. He grabbed the wire that fed into the phone line, but rather than getting a tug of resistance from the phone socket, the line floated lightly in his hand, light gleaming from the bare wire at the end. It had been yanked clean from the wall. Did he do that?

He snatched his car keys and burst outside, not stopping to close the door behind him. Nothing in there mattered. Not now. The key slid into the lock on the third attempt, a task made all the more difficult by a mixture of nerves, panic and booze. He sped through the country roads and plotted how quickly he could get to Johnny. The roads were quiet for the time of day and—

Why Johnny and not Shelley?

His train of thought slid to a screeching halt. He knew where he'd find Johnny. Johnny would be at his office. He always was. Trying to find Shelley would waste valuable time.

Shelley's note said she'd be shopping for food in town. It's not Greater Manchester. It's a finite space.

He shook the thought from his head and raced on, twisting the wheel to draw the car back into the centre of the lane.

'Fine, I'll stop in town,' he said aloud. 'I'll use the phone there to call Johnny's office. If I see Shelley I'll take her with me. If Johnny's okay I'll look for Shelley.'

But trying to appease his internal thoughts was pointless, no matter how he tried to justify it. A decision had been made. He'd decided to put his professional life ahead of his private life. However many ways he tried to frame it, he'd chosen money over love.

The town was unusually busy when he entered. More cars than he expected and a lot of chatter as the Saturday crowds wandered between shops. He jammed the breaks, coming to a sliding stop next to the bright red phone box, drawing eyes and muttering from passers-by. He leapt from the car, again not bothering to close the door, thrusting his

THE WILDE DIARIES

hands into his pockets for change as he went. The phone box had the stale smell of air trapped inside for hours. He lifted the receiver and piled coin after coin inside as the phone rang to itself in Johnny's office. He span round to face the street to see if his eyes might happen upon Shelley. Then the ringing stopped.

'Hello?'

A soothing wave of relief coursed through him as he heard Johnny's voice.

'Oh, Johnny, thank Christ.'

'Who is it?'

'It's me Lucas. Are you okay?'

No sooner had the words left his mouth than he set eyes on Shelley walking up the side street that led to the grocer's. Between the passers-by he saw as she carried a bulging bag of groceries in one hand, struggling with both hands to hold her handbag open. She walked slowly, eyes fixed firmly in the dark recesses of the handbag as she stepped absent-mindedly into the road.

His heart leapt. Johnny was answering his question, but the words had faded into a meaningless mumble as the car sped up the side street. At the same time Shelley was scouring the corners of her bag, so the driver was doing the same to his glove compartment. Lucas realised that the street she was on was empty apart from her. Nobody else around to warn her of her impending doom. He dropped the receiver and pushed against the phone, propelling him against the door and out into the street, the whole time unable to draw his eyes away from Shelley. Her long dark hair was obscuring her face, gentle breeze blowing her emerald green dress tight against her body.

'Shelley!' he screamed, unsure that from here she'd be able to hear him against the background noise.

At that moment the driver looked up. Lucas watched his face drop into a mask of horror as Shelley stepped in front of him.

'Shelley!' He screamed louder this time, and she looked up.

Attention drawn from the confines of her bag, she finally noticed the sky blue machine death heading towards her. She took a half-step back, dropping her bags. The driver swerved, hitting the breaks and the horn at once, drawing all eyes to the scene. But he was going too fast. He wasn't able to stop. Lucas' heart dropped and his stomach somersaulted as a frozen grip clutched his body. The sounds of the street faded and Shelley disappeared behind a crowd of onlookers. He stumbled into the road, unsure of what awaited.

***

The crowd enveloped the scene obscuring any view Lucas might have. The blast of a car horn brought reality crashing back. He'd staggered into the road, and when he looked around, a car had stopped inches from disaster. He came to his senses, waved an apology and darted across the road to the

THE WILDE DIARIES

crowds and Shelley. He forced his way to the front and saw the green of Shelley's dress. She was sitting upright, leaning against the back wheel of the passenger side of the car.

'Shelley?'

She looked up.

'Lucas.'

He fell to his knees beside her.

'It's okay. I'm okay. He missed me.'

The driver got out and stood over them, his face an ashen white of alabaster. 'Is everyone okay?'

Shelley stood and dusted herself down. 'You missed me. I'm not sure how.'

'I'm so sorry.'

'I wasn't looking where I was going either,' she said.

Lucas scooped up her handbag and grabbed her hand, 'Are you okay to walk?'

She nodded.

He led her across the road and into his car, closing the door behind her as shocked onlookers followed them with their eyes. Lucas rounded the bonnet and re-entered the phone box, grabbing the receiver.

'Johnny, are you there?'

But the line was dead. He hung up and got in the car.

'What's going on.'

'It's Johnny. He's in trouble.'

Lucas checked his mirrors and sped out of the car park.

'How did you know to come and find me? You saved me.'

Lucas laughed internally at the thought of him saving Shelley. She was the one saving him, and anyone who knew the two of them knew it as a matter of fact. He never answered.

'What's going on with Johnny?' she asked, the Busker's words trailing through his mind:

Time to choose. Whatever you do, you lose.

You lose.

You lose.

He was struck with a creeping horror that this was actually part of the plan and reached for his seat belt. He told Shelley to do the same.

***

All the way to Johnny's office, Lucas couldn't shake the feeling that the Busker was toying with him. That the latest riddle was actually meant for him. That there was to be another accident, like the one which had claimed Malcolm and Sally, and that Shelley would die in this car, and he would be killed too. But he had to try. If Johnny's life was at risk, he would do everything he could to save him. His life was worthless without Johnny anyway.

Johnny's office was two rooms on the first floor of a storage warehouse on the outskirts of town. It was cheap rent to begin with, and, as time went by, it became home and the original idea of moving somewhere more fitting for a music manager became unthinkable. The roads leading there were

THE WILDE DIARIES

empty, and it wasn't long before they were safely parked outside, the only company, a dark blue van with brown rust spots parked a few hundred yards along the road.

'Wait here,' he told Shelley as he got out.

Shelley got out too.

'What are you doing?' he asked.

Her face was pasty and for the first time she looked vulnerable and Lucas found it was a look which didn't fit her. It made her unattractive.

A small voice came from her. 'I don't want to be on my own.'

'Come on then,' he snapped, failing to conceal his contempt.

The door had a buzzer, the kind that always reminded Lucas of the apartment blocks in New York City, and he jabbed, not expecting a reply. But one came. Not a person, but the door buzzed, the lock clicked and he and Shelley stepped inside.

Peering to the back of the warehouse past the stacked cityscape of beige boxes he saw the light was on in the reception. It was odd that Johnny had Margaret working on a Saturday, but there she was, curled brown hair and matronly glasses, peering back at them to see who it was. Lucas walked closer and Margaret came to the door at the top of the stairs.

'He's not here. You've just missed him.'

'Where did he go?' Lucas snapped.

She looked over the glasses at him, showing her

displeasure at his tone. 'He went home, Lucas, why?'

'Did he say anything?'

'He said that he was going home,' she replied a look of confusion on her face.

Lucas grabbed Shelley's hand.

'But...' Margaret said from behind them.

Lucas turned.

'He did look... strange. Said he had to nip home for something and to call him there in half an hour if he hadn't come back.'

Shit.

He grabbed Shelley by the shoulders and stared at her intently. He had to act now, he didn't what to have to explain himself, there was no time. 'Stay here. I'll go and check on him.'

'I want to come with you,' that soft neediness in her voice again.

'Stay here with Margaret. I'll be back soon. Margaret,' he shouted looking up at her. 'Call him now. Make sure he's okay.'

'He said to call him in half an—'

'Just fucking call him now!' he yelled.

Shelley shrunk back and Margaret stared at him. He glared back at her until she went into the office. He ran outside without saying another word. He would be at Johnny's house in twenty minutes.

***

THE WILDE DIARIES

Johnny's place was in a pleasant, three storey terrace in the town. Red brick, tree-lined, quiet. By the time Lucas arrived, Johnny's car was missing. He jumped out and raced up the four stone steps that were worn to a dip in the middle and up to the green front door. The doorbell barked an ugly buzzing ring inside. He stepped back and shouted up at the windows.

'Johnny. Open the door! It's Lucas!'

He jabbed at the doorbell again and grabbed the cold brass of the door knocker, rapping heavily.

'Johnny! Come to the door or I'll kick the fucking thing down.'

He jabbed again at the doorbell, then there was a voice behind him.

'What the hell's going on?'

He turned. It was Johnny.

He ran to him and hugged him. 'Oh you're all right.' He let go and stepped back, 'Are you all right?'

Johnny chuckled and patted him on the back until Lucas let go. 'I'm fine, silly bollocks, are *you* all right?'

Lucas breathed a deep sigh, 'I am now I've seen you. Margaret said you looked funny.'

'I forgot my pills that's all. Had to come back for them, now I've left my bloody glasses, when did you see Margaret?'

'About twenty minutes ago.'

'And she let you in?'

'Yeah. Why?'

He shook his head, 'I told her not to open the door to

anyone.'

Lucas was confused. Margaret had opened the door to him without even checking to see who it was. 'What do you mean?'

'Oh it's probably nothing, but there's been a couple of robberies lately. The papers reckon they're armed. Sawn-off shotguns, they've got.'

Lucas shivered at the memory of the blue van parked along from the warehouse.

Time to choose. Whatever you do, you lose.

'What's up?' Johnny asked.

'Probably nothing.'

'What?'

He frowned. 'I just saw a blue van parked near the office when I was coming here.'

'Shit. Fucking hell.'

'What's wrong?'

'The safe. I left the fucking safe open.'

'What's in it?'

'Fucking everything. My money, contracts, the fucking lot.'

They both ran to their cars and Lucas led the way.

By the time they got back to the warehouse, the blue van was gone. In its place, outside the door to the warehouse, sat an ambulance. It was silent, blue lights atop flashing.

Lucas slid to a stop, with Johnny close behind. Lucas sprinted to the warehouse door, dismayed to find it propped

THE WILDE DIARIES

open. Images of the two women soaked in blood ran through his mind turning his stomach. He entered, and between the piles of boxes, at the bottom of the stairs, saw the ambulance-men loading Margaret onto a gurney.

'Shelley?!' he screamed.

Shelley stepped out from behind the boxes, looking concerned.

'Shelley!'

She turned. The aura of vulnerability still cast an ugly glow around her. It should have roused some protective urge within him, but the effect was the opposite. He found it repellent. This wasn't the woman he'd fallen in love with. Her strength and confidence was what had drawn him to her in the first place. In that moment, Lucas knew he was no longer attracted to her.

You lose.

'She fell,' Shelley said.

'Those bastard stairs,' Margaret shouted as the paramedics wheeled her past.

Lucas' eyes were drawn to the grapefruit sized swelling of her ankle.

'I've told him to get them fixed. Look at the state of it,' she said throwing a hand at the swelling. 'I'll bloody kill him. Where is he?'

Margaret was still whinging about the stairs as Lucas turned to point to Johnny.

But Johnny wasn't there.

MARC W SHAKO

***

Lucas found Johnny slumped outside near his car. He hadn't made it as far as the warehouse.

The ambulance men worked on Johnny for twenty minutes. In one hand, Johnny was clutching his heart pills. The excitement at the race back to the warehouse had done it. Lucas racing inside when they got back left Johnny's gasped cries for help unheard.

You lose.

Shelley cried, her head on Lucas's shoulder as they watched powerlessly, praying the ambulance men could work a miracle. They could not.

Johnny was dead.

***

Lucas dropped Shelley off and told her he needed some time alone. She looked hurt at him leaving her now, but he didn't give a shit. Now, he wanted to drink, without having to listen to her nagging and whining.

He didn't know where to go from here. Maybe the band could get a new manager, get the new material out. But it felt like momentum had been lost. In the couple of weeks since the séance, the band had fallen apart. It had begun long before, when his creative juices had dried up, but now that Johnny was gone, it almost felt like they were starting from scratch. Starting at the bottom of the mountain. So, he did what he always did when the going got tough.

THE WILDE DIARIES

He opened a bottle.

It was already dark by the time he got home. It was almost midnight when he passed out drunk. It was hard to say how long after that the dream started.

This one had no fancy location. No Royal Albert Hall. Not even a forest. It was at the house. In the attic. In the room where he'd signed the contract. Sitting opposite sides of the small desk, with the reel to reel player between them. Lucas felt nothing. No fear. No disgust. No anger. He was empty. A husk of a man. Beaten. Broken. Bereft.

'Have you heard it yet?'

Lucas didn't reply, but he knew exactly what he meant.

'The last song.'

He shook his head.

'Oh, you gotta. It's the best one yet. Consider it a gift.'

'A gift?'

'Happy Birthday, Lucas,' the Busker said with a smile. Then he hit play.

18th September 1977

Lucas awoke on the morning of his 27th birthday and ambled downstairs. In the cupboard under the stairs he found a plain brown box. He couldn't recall what had been in it. It didn't matter. He took it to the recording room, opened the bottom drawer and put the cannisters inside. For reasons he could not say, he grabbed five notebooks that he would have used to write songs and took those upstairs too. He grabbed the reel to reel player and took it upstairs, not pausing on the first floor, instead going straight up to the attic.

In the narrow hallway, he walked to the door that, years later, Zach Fox would board up in a moment of panic. He placed the box down and stared at the door. It wasn't often you had the luxury of knowing that the door you're about to open, the room you're about to enter, will be your last, but that was what he felt now. He opened it. In the middle of the room was the small desk, above it a naked bulb with a string beside it. He snapped the string and the dim bulb glowed, barely cutting through the deep black. He took the first of the notebooks and wrote the story of what had happened to him until it was full. In the end, all five notebooks were needed. Then he set up the reel to reel and took tape number four from its cannister.

He loaded it into the tape player, backwards, and pressed play.

THE WILDE DIARIES

THE END

15th October 2015

That was it. I leafed through the rest of the book, but it was blank. The diary stopped after only a handful of pages. I still had Seth's notes on the pen drive and reached for them, hoping to find some sort of analysis within, but before I could put the drive in my laptop, my phone rang. Not my mobile, the room phone in The Ship. I quickly hid the last diary and pen drive in the drawer of the nightstand and got up, feeling like I was in the cold grip of some nightmare aftermath: the pages of the last diary scaring me beyond words. It was only now, in the short silence between the ringing of the phone, that it dawned on me that in my haste to leave and read the last diary and Seth's notes I had left the box at the house.

I picked up the phone. It was John, the landlord.

MARC W SHAKO

'Mr Brewer...'

The police are here. They discovered something on Zach Fox's laptop. Messages from you. About blackmail. They think you're connected to his suicide.

'I'm afraid I've got some bad news. The fire brigade are at your friend's house...'

John's words faded and I ran to the window stretching the phone cord out across the room. There, on the horizon, aflame like a ritual sacrifice, the house. A fire engine at either side spraying water into the windows of the first floor.

The tapes. The diaries. I'd left everything there. All I had now was the last diary, just a few pages long. Without the other diaries it just sounded like a horror story. There was nothing in it to suggest it was once Lucas Wilde's. It could have come from anywhere.

I slammed the phone down and rushed to the car. It was futile, but I felt I had to go. Try to retrieve whatever was left of the house. The house.

Whatever my previous thoughts about Zach's death and Edie reconciling with David being the end, they were wrong. From here, there was no way back. This truly was the end.

***

Fire had gutted the house. I tried to go in, but the firefighters on the scene had held me back. Going in, they said, was suicide. Perhaps that's what I'd wanted. It was there gazing into the hypnotic flames it dawned on me there was nothing

THE WILDE DIARIES

left for me to do but to go home. Back to my normal life. Back to reality. As alone and as broke as I'd started. No Edie. No fortune. The editor at a small, local newspaper, writing about ring-roads and supermarket openings. Tonight, I didn't feel like driving. Physically and emotionally exhausted, I'd stay at The Ship and leave in the morning. Tonight, I could use a drink.

***

I sat in the bar at The Ship, in John's awkward presence. He'd passed on his kind words about the fire. That was all I had now. Kind words. As much as it felt like things couldn't get worse, now I was waiting for another phone call.

A call from the police looking into Zach Fox's tragic death. A half decent copper would put the pieces together at some point. Connect my blackmail plot with his suicide. Ellison was certainly up to the task. There was even a part of me convinced that was what He wanted. Now I'd become Zach. My dirty little secret circling above me like a hungry vulture. From here on out, every time the phone rang, I'd be fearing the inevitable - my misdemeanours catching up with me, just as Zach's had caught up with him.

The more I drank the more that final diary and the idea of the backwards messages in the songs played on my mind. I hadn't heard them for myself. Lucas had, that much was certain. Whether Zach and Seth had was another question.

Lucas had killed himself. The last thing he mentioned in

his diaries was listening to the fourth song - *Heaven Knows Best*. After that, there was nothing. Had he heard it and then killed himself? Is that what Zach had done? Seth was listening to something, before he took his life. I had presumed it was *Greater Than Me*, the first song, but the more I thought about it the less that idea rang true. It couldn't have been. Edie was listening to that at the house. Whatever Seth was listening to was taken away by the police on that first night. Which meant that there was still one of Lucas Wilde's tapes. One tape with a partial diary and I had a story.

I drained my glass.

'Same again, Mr Brewer?'

'No. Get me a taxi.'

John nodded. He turned for the phone and then turned back.

'Where to?'

'The police station.'

***

The wide eyes of a shocked desk sergeant greeted me as I burst into the police station. The nauseating stench of bleach hung in the air, coupled with the gentle buzz of the overhead strip light. But for that sound there was an awful silence which was broken by the bubbling of the water cooler.

'I need my tape.'

The officer stared, ballpoint hovering over the paperwork he was filling like he was a reluctant signee.

THE WILDE DIARIES

'Are you listening to me? Do you speak English? My tape. I need my tape.'

He sighed and jabbed his pen into the lid, setting it down on the half-filled forms.

'Can I help you?'

'Are you taking the piss? My tape. Where is my tape?'

'Control your language, please sir. Which tape are you looking for?'

I fought to control my rising rage, beads of sweat forming on my brow.

'Last week. My friend killed himself. Seth Haywood? You took some things from the house. As evidence. One of the things you took was a reel to reel tape. I own that house and everything in it. I never got my tape back. Where is it?'

The desk sergeant stared at me, this intruder to the quiet at a small town police station. 'Sir, keep your voice down.'

'Fuck this.'

I moved around to the counter and lifted the hatch. 'Where is he? Where's Ellison? He'll know.'

The desk sergeant slammed down on the hatch and knocked it from my hand, eyes hardened in an icy glare. 'Sir it's late. The detective isn't here.'

I glared back. If I didn't get that tape it was all over.

'Get him on the phone,' I urged. Then, before the sergeant could reject my request I reached for my mobile phone, 'Fuck it. I'll call him myself.'

I fished his business card from my pocket and dialled,

the desk sergeant watched on as we spoke.

It shouldn't have surprised me that Detective Ellison had no recollection of the tape. He asked me to pass the phone to the sergeant who would be happy to get a full inventory of what was removed from the house.

'Yes, sir.' The sergeant said, handing me back my phone.

'Thank you.'

The detective just ended the call. I waited while the desk sergeant huffed away, begrudging the extra work I'd brought. I paced the pale green linoleum for fifteen boring minutes, glancing at anti drink-driving and lost pet posters. My legs were weak but sitting would have driven me to distraction. At the moment I thought I might actually go mad, he returned.

'Here's the inventory.'

He handed the list of everything that had been taken from the house, and as I read, I watched in my mind's eye from the front seat of my car as officers trailed past with those items: the gun, the reel to reel player. Loaded onto the blood-smattered reel to reel tape player, was the tape I was looking for. The tape of *Heaven Knows Best*.

Every item that had been removed was noted to the last detail. Everything except the tape.

I knew why it wasn't there. That's what *He* wanted. I was supposed to fly off the handle. Get myself arrested and speed up the part where my involvement in the death of Zach Fox was revealed. I gently placed the list down before the desk sergeant, turned, and left. It was over.

THE WILDE DIARIES
9ᵗʰ November 2015

The first time I considered taking my own life was weeks later, when I was back at home. The detectives working Zach Fox's death caught up with me. We had a phone conversation. They told me I was a 'person of interest' and not to go anywhere without letting them know first. I knew then it was just a matter of time before the relevant dots were connected. That was shortly after I discovered that Seth's finances were badly out of order. He was broke. Waiting for royalty cheques to arrive so he could eat. The insurance company had been left with no option but to cancel his policy on the house. I'd inherited a pile of ashes.

Since I'd returned, I'd tried my best to carry on with life as if the previous few weeks hadn't happened at all. Not too difficult a task; I barely had contact with Seth when he was alive, same with Edie. I tried not to think about Lucas Wilde, Zach Fox, even The Busker.

The last one wasn't so easy. He was still there, whenever there was an unusual sound in the house, or a strange shadow. He was still there: the presence behind me when I was washing dishes; the way the shadows in the bedroom organised themselves into human form; standing in the doorway to the bathroom when I was at my most vulnerable, unable to see him, rinsing shampoo from my face.

But now I was considering my own mortality, one question did arise. It was a question that had occurred to me every day since I'd got back, but one I'd tried to forget. Were there really messages in the songs? In the case of the songs written by Lucas, I'd never know. Nobody would. The songs were gone. Up in smoke. But I wondered if the same messages would be in the songs written by Zach. It was, after all, the same words. And surely if you reversed words, they would sound the same backwards no matter who was saying them.

I found a computer program which modified audio tracks. You could do pretty much anything. Change the volume, the key, fade in, fade out, reduce white noise. And of course reverse.

So that's what I did.

I looked down at the CD case. I noticed my hands were shaking. It was as if every fibre of my being did not want this to happen, yet I felt compelled by an outside force. I took a breath and opened it. I removed the CD and headed cautiously for the laptop. I remember clearly having to steel myself to put it in the disc drive. I opened the music program as the disc whirred into action. I opened another program which asked me if I would like to rip the CD into MP3 music files. I clicked 'Yes'. Uneasiness washed over me, and I grabbed the collar of my shirt, trying to shut out the chill in the air. The CD spun faster now as if trying to escape the laptop altogether. My stomach tightened and I shivered. One by one, the laptop transposed the songs into their new format. A few moments later the screen proudly displayed the message 'Done!' The music program asked me to select the file I wanted to open. I felt invisible eyes burning into me as

THE WILDE DIARIES

the cursor slowly slid into position over the file.

Greater Than Me.

Click: "Importing MP3 file..."

In seconds the song was before me. Represented in bright blue pixels as a mountain range of jagged peaks and valleys of brilliant noise and deathly silence. I barely remember the next sequence of button presses and clicks, but before I knew it another message appeared which triggered another wave of nausea, this one stronger than the last: "Reversing highlighted section..."

A series of small squares hung in a pop-up box as a timer. One by one, a few seconds at a time, they disappeared. I'm not sure why, but as each disappeared I felt a growing sense of... Fear? Despair? I wanted this, but all the same I tried everything to stop the process. Clicking on every part of the screen. I had to stop it. With just three squares remaining, the screen froze. I clicked desperately. Nothing. The cursor a dead weight. Motionless. Moments later it leapt into life and shot across the screen. The relief was so strong that I hadn't noticed the squares were gone. In fact the whole pop-up was missing. I repeatedly left-clicked again. Then: "Reverse complete!"

I sat frozen as the cursor had moments before. The mountain range of sound now facing in the opposite direction. It felt as if time had stopped, even though the dusk outside had been replaced by pitch darkness. The laptop was now the only source of light. The only on-screen option was to click 'OK'. The excitement of before now seemed light years away. I dragged the cursor to the 'OK' on screen and acquiesced. If there was a pair of eyes on me before, I was certain there was now a sinister grin. I moved the cursor over to the play button and paused for breath.

That's when my mobile phone rang.

***

I jumped and gasped, my heart racing. I glanced down at the ringing mobile glowing in the darkness.

"Edie Calling..."

The feelings of fear and trepidation evaporated, quickly overtaken by anger. I was still enraged by her decision to stay with David. She must have known she could never be at peace with him - constantly living in fear of the idea he could cheat on her at any time. Every night he worked late. Every late phone call...

But still, deep down, I wanted her. I loved her.

'Hello?'

For a moment, there was nothing. Silence. Was it David fucking with me? Had she kept my number in her phone under another name? Then a noise. A sniffle. It was Edie, and she was crying.

A million thoughts rushed through my mind, none of them good. Had he cheated on her? Perhaps he'd been cheating on her and left her for someone else. Or better still. Something had happened to him. He travelled a lot for work.

THE WILDE DIARIES

An accident perhaps.

'Joel, I'm pregnant.'

All of my thoughts left my head at once. I felt sick. A baby meant that she and David were moving on to the next level. Another level away from me. It was truly over. Why would she call to tell me this? It was cruel.

Then it hit me. Pregnant. She told me that she had been trying for over a year to have a baby with David, and now, all of a sudden, a few weeks after we sleep together it's happened.

'Are you sure?'

She was crying still, 'Yes. I'm never late. Not by a single day. I've just taken two tests.' There was a moment's silence then, 'I'm scared Joel.'

Suddenly the song I was about to listen to took on new significance. It was no longer to satisfy the curiosity of a man on a collision course with his own mortality. Now, if there was something there, it was proof. Proof of plagiarism. A message on the first song meant a message on the fourth. That message had already led to the deaths of Lucas and Seth. The fourth song would be proof that it wasn't because of me that Zach had killed himself. Blackmail, yes. *Attempted* blackmail. Accessory to suicide. No.

I'd be in the clear with the law. Without legal problems hanging over me, I could sell the story to the newspapers. Write a book. Then there would be a film. I'd have enough money to take care of us. The three of us. I'd be able to raise our baby. She could leave the worry of David and the lingering doubt of his infidelity behind.

'I'll do the right thing. We'll get through this. It'll be okay. Everything will be fine.'

'No.'

I was stunned.

'What?'

'No.' Her tone was cold. Dead. Empty.

'What do you mean, "No"?'

'It's David's baby.'

'But you know that's a lie—'

'I'm telling you about the baby because I didn't want you to hear it from somebody else. But this baby is David's. He'll be the father. He'll raise it as his own.'

'Edie, wait—'

But she'd already gone. I sat alone, bathed in the glow of my laptop screen.

11th November 2015

It was another two days before I listened to the song. I spent the following hours after the call with Edie drunk and in tears. Then I slept, awoke, and repeated the process. By the time I awoke on the second day, it was already dark. My laptop was still glowing in my study. I sat before it, glass of bourbon in one shaking hand, and pressed play.

The words from Lucas Wilde's diary came flooding back

THE WILDE DIARIES

as the nightmarish sound unfolded.

Relentless, outlandish, unnerving, frightening. Coupled with the gibberish of what were painfully beautiful lyrics when played in the intended direction. The endless swirling dissonance of melodies, uncrashing cymbals and nonsensical vocal lines. And then, as surely as in Lucas Wilde's original recording, something else...

Faint at first.

Growls and snarls mixed in with the growing cacophony. Here as surely it was in the original. As if it were imprinted on the very soul of the song. Then the sound of suffering, just as Lucas described. Human and animal. Sounds from the pit of Hell itself. All of this mixed into the chaos as if superimposed. It had no place there. It was absent when the song was played in its natural direction. Then, at the very moment it felt the horror had peaked, the animal voices and sounds of hellish pain and anguish came into a horrific, audible focus - exactly as if being tuned on a radio by invisible, bony fingers.

Again I went cold.

Then came the message.

The same message from the original.

"Swinging feet. Feel it squeeze. Tighter. Hard to breathe."

It was true. True, chilling and sickening. But...

As horrific an experience it was, I wanted to hear the others. I had to. Just as I had to know what was in the box. And in that attic room.

All of the messages were there, in *Greater Than Me*, in

MARC W SHAKO

Once Upon a Time, and in *All the King's Horses,* until the moment came to hear song number four. *Heaven Knows Best.*

This was the last thing that Lucas Wilde heard. It was almost certainly the last thing that Seth had listened to. Deep down, in the same place I knew that the child Edie was carrying was mine, I knew it was the last thing that Zach Fox played, before his date with that wet Bristol street.

And so, there in the darkness, bathed in the glow of the light from my laptop screen, just as I had with *Greater Than Me,* I reversed the track, and pressed play.

***

It was in that slow-motion way a nightmare unfolds that I first saw it. Saw *Him.* As the horror spewed forth from the speakers, in a half-lit corner of the room, a shadow grew. I watched frozen as, in my peripheral vision, the shadow of a tall man in a wide-brimmed hat and long coat grew until it loomed over me. Finally, it moved.

'Hello, Joel.'

I couldn't speak.

'Don't worry. I'm not going to ask you to do anything of a sexual nature. That is what you were worried about, isn't it?'

Finally, my throat opened up and I could speak.

'I don't know.'

The Busker moved, in that horrible, stilted gait, around the computer and stood beside me, all too close for me to be comfortable. The stench of rotting flesh that Lucas told of

THE WILDE DIARIES

hung faintly around him.

'Are you the devil?' I asked.

He threw his head back and laughed, a dry, rasping laugh. The croaking snicker of a forty-a-day smoker.

'Not I. But I've got friends in high places.'

'Am I going to die now?'

His face became serious. There was no transition from the laughter, like a jump cut in a movie.

'That's up to you, Joel. I have an offer for you. A deal.'

'Is this the same deal you offered Lucas? Zach? Did you offer this to Seth?'

The Busker slowly shook his head and tutted. 'Anger is a bad emotion to carry with you, Joel. I'm going to help you. Help you get rid of your anger.'

'Tell me. Was Seth right? What does it all mean? The symbolism?'

'Your friend Seth was a smart man. He was right about most things...'

'You control everyone?'

'Not everyone. I don't need everyone. And not everyone needs my help, Joel.'

Musical heroes who had died before their time passed by me in a parade. Janis, Jimi, Cobain...

'So you kill them?'

'I have no use for them. They are powerful people. Imagine somebody being that popular, having that much sway, and nobody being able to control them. Somebody like that might have a message of their own. One that doesn't align with ours...'

Those cloven feet clumped around the desk.

'...Some of them. Not all of them, of course. Sometimes a coincidence is just that. People die. But the others? They carry with them a lot of energy.'

Joel's mind went back to Lucas Wilde's first diary. The concert. The energy of the crowd feeding the band, the band doing likewise. Positive energy. But if someone beloved died...

The Busker nodded. 'I think you're starting to get it, Joel.'

'Energy?'

'Energy and control.'

Joel frowned. 'Control?'

The Busker smiled. His teeth no longer the straight set of perfect white, but the rotten yellow mess from the later diaries. 'Did you know Pythagoras was a musician? He found a formula that could sooth or anger people, just with his music... Well, I say 'found'... other times it's a different type of control. Narrative control. Distraction. It's powerful what a death can do.'

'And the symbolism?'

'A movement. A growing army of my soldiers. They know themselves what to look for. They know who they can trust.'

'To what end?'

'Smoke and mirrors. Misdirection. That's part of it, at least. If some are getting too close to the truth. That's the

THE WILDE DIARIES

smaller part. The bigger end game... It's the year two thousand and fifteen, Joel. The time is near. Soon I won't need to tell you. You'll be able to see it for yourself,' he said, calmly passing on the gospel of his truth down to me, the newest member of his flock. 'So the offer...'

I nodded.

The Busker paused and a chill crawled up my neck. 'The offer is this: your life, or someone in your place.'

'What?'

'A sacrifice.'

I couldn't believe the next words from my mouth.

'What's in it for me?'

The Busker believed, all right. He smiled. 'There it is. The big question. The one that your good friend wouldn't entertain.'

'You didn't want Seth. You never did. You've been trying to get to me.'

'Eventually, someone always agrees.'

'And if they don't they die?'

The Busker smiled again, dry cracked lips parting to reveal his decaying, misshaped teeth. 'Joel, I'm making you a very generous offer.'

I was frozen. Petrified by the presence before me. But the anger at Seth's life being taken was subsiding by the second. The Busker was silent, waiting for me to speak, and when I finally did, the same question came. 'So? What's in it for me?'

'Your heart's desires.'

Another life in place of my own. A life for a life. I choose someone to die in my place and all the riches in the world are mine. The decision seemed easy enough. There was one man who had everything I wanted. My life. My woman. In a few months' time, he would have my son. David had everything I wanted. I could replace him. With him out of the way—

The Busker tutted and waved a bony finger hypnotically from side to side.

'That won't do now, Joel, will it?'

'I don't understand...'

'Sure you do. How much of a sacrifice is it if you choose someone you care little for?'

Cared little for. That was an understatement. It dawned on me then that my life was full of people I cared little for. I was very fond of Seth. He was an odd character, but a good man. His refusal of this monster's deal proved as much. He was the closest thing I had to family. When it boiled down to it, my lonely life meant the people I cared for numbered only two. Edie, and her - *my* - unborn child.

The Busker said, 'In exchange for a life of wealth previously unimaginable. All you have to do is sign.'

He placed a parchment before me and grabbed my hand. We were still in my study but the desk we were standing before was not mine. It was in the attic of the house. The cold steel of a blade sliced across my palm and warm blood dripped into a pot. He gently dipped the sharp point of a large

THE WILDE DIARIES

white feather into the pot and smiled at me.

'Choose.'

***

The moment I finished signing my name, images bombarded my mind. Images so awful that even though they lasted a mere fraction of a second, I was left shaken and nauseated. I immediately understood what exactly Zach meant when he spoke about wild parties. The levels of depravity and vile exploitation taking place ensured the silence of anyone in attendance. The powerful drug that became Zach's strongest addiction and its source were suddenly clear to me, extracted from the living in the moment of death. Revealing this truth would mean more than embarrassment. It would mean jail, and the cruellest of treatment from the other inmates, the kind of treatment they reserved for the foulest criminals.

I was awoken. It was the phone, a call from The Ship. From John. I'm guessing they don't have much business in the way of hotel guests, because almost a month after my stay, someone had found a pen drive in the drawer of the nightstand in my room. Seth's document. See, when I said earlier that some things might not quite make sense, but to bear with me, this is what I meant. Seth's document was written after all of the diaries were read. That's how I knew what Lucas Wilde's dreams were, even when he didn't. They all came to him later. Just before he - someone - took his life.

I took Seth's novelised version of events in his document

and turned them into a novel. A horrorbook. The Wilde Diaries. It even made the New York Times Bestseller list. Of course, I had to change the names. There is a real rock star, but no "Lucas Wilde". Zach Fox is a made up name too. You could probably put the clues together though, if you were so inclined, to find out who they really were. And just as there's no *Lucas* or *Zach*, so there's no *Seth*. Not really. He was a real enough man, but I had to change all of the names. Song titles. People. Even my own. Obviously. You'll see my real name on the cover of the book, if you see the bestseller list.

My little horrorbook got me a five book deal with a top publisher. Very lucrative. Success seems to land in my lap these days. Funny how things work out. I fulfilled my contract my rewriting old ideas. Because I was known, the books sold themselves.

Any regrets?

I regret that "Seth" had to die for me to get where I am. But there again, he could be here himself, if he'd made the right decision.

As for my sacrifice...

I do still think about her sometimes. David took the loss very badly. He's not doing so well these days. Even left the magazine, the last I heard. They kept his position for him as long as they could, but he never got over what happened. A heavily pregnant woman falling over the mezzanine in their house like that. Terrible accident. Her and the baby, well, they never stood a chance.

THE WILDE DIARIES

I should tell you, I got a phone call from the detective looking into *Zach*'s death recently too. He was told to drop his investigation. Friends in high places. There was nothing he could do, he just had to accept it. He did sound upset.

One thing that does strike me as odd. The same people who question this, who say it's impossible that such a secret could be kept, seem oblivious to the fact that the same incredulity has helped us keep our secret for as long as we have.

Just a thought...

The End...

...Actually, not quite. There is just one more thing. 'Zach Fox'.

His album? It's real. If you're any kind of music fan, with a decent sized collection, chances are you've already got his album. After all, it's in one in six homes in the UK. You'll find it, if you put the clues together. You'll find the album, the songs, and if you look in the right places, the messages.

Pretty spooky. Worth a listen though. Just be careful with number four...

You've made it this far, congratulations! Thanks for reading! Almost done…

Reviews are gold for authors!
If you liked *The Wilde Diaries*, please rate and review at Amazon.com, it would be a huge help and would mean a lot to me!

Just one more thing…

To stay abreast of the latest developments with future book releases, why not join my mailing list? You'll even get your hands on a FREE digital copy of my gripping short story 'Infinity'!

For more information, I can be found at the following:

My website: www.marcwshako.com

My Facebook page:
https://www.facebook.com/marcwshako/

Follow me on Twitter at…
https://twitter.com/MarcWShako

THE DEATH OF LASZLO BREYER

A **JACK TALBOT** THRILLER

A FULL MOON, AN EMPTY GRAVE,
A SERIAL KILLER HUNGRY FOR REVENGE...

"Pure spine-chilling brilliance from start to end!"

"One of those books that you pick up and cannot put down."

Former detective Jack Talbot stands accused. The grave of Laszlo Breyer, his dead wife's killer, has been robbed.

His former colleague would love nothing more than to pin the crime on Jack. And his alibi of being too drunk to remember is helping nobody.

Then a dead body turns up, with the dead killer's MO. Torn to pieces as if by a wild animal. All on the night of a full moon.

If Jack's not the killer, then he's surely on the copycat's hitlist. And he'll need all his cunning and determination as he treads the fine line between suspect and detective to catch the killer… before the next full moon.

"One of the most … gripping stories I've ever read." Isabel Fuentes Guerra, author of *The Island of the Dolls*.

THE DEATH OF LASZLO BREYER

Available now at Amazon

"QUANTUM LEAP MEETS 9/11."

GHOSTS OF SEPTEMBER

WELCOME TO THE STRANGE WORLD OF MARC W. SHAKO

Ray Madison is trapped in a nightmare.

Slave to the grip of alcoholism, Ray is stuck in the past, reliving the same week over and over - the week where his life fell apart. But all that is about to change...

Ray goes to bed on a normal Wednesday evening, but the next morning what awaits him is far from routine. Thrown back in time with no explanation, horrified Ray discovers the date: September 6th, 2001.

Faced with the worst week of his life all over again and scrambling for answers, with only the mysterious stranger Charlie for help, Ray is trapped in a race against time, with terror fast approaching.

The clock is ticking...

GHOSTS OF SEPTEMBER

is out now!

For more information visit:
http://www.marcwshako.com/ghostsofseptember.html

ABOUT THE AUTHOR

MARC W. SHAKO is a horror/thriller novelist, screenwriter, and aficionado of all things paranormal, from Yorkshire, England. When not reading or writing about the undead, hauntings, modern-day wolf-men and UFOs, Marc can be found watching football, playing the guitar with various degrees of success, or engrossed in his latest addiction – binge-listening to podcasts.

www.marcwshako.com

Printed in Great Britain
by Amazon